R.I.P.

CHARITY B.

ISBN: 978-0-9993575-8-3

Editor: Kim BookJunkie
Formatting: Champagne Book Design
Cover Design: Simply Defined Art

Author's Note

As an independent author, your ratings and especially reviews mean more to me than you realize. If you enjoy the book, please consider lending your support by leaving your thoughts in a review.

This story is in no way an accurate representation of any real life disorders. Please do not take it as such.

Trigger Warning
This book contains many triggers. If you are not comfortable reading about taboo subject matter, gore, explicit/graphic situations and disturbing content, this book may not be for you.

Dedication

To the nine other amazing authors in the Thou Shall Not Anthology: Michelle Brown, Murphy Wallace, Ally Vance, Faith Ryan, Natalie Bennett, C.M. Radcliff, C.L. Matthews, M.R. Leahy, H.B. Jasick, and Faith Ryan… This story wouldn't exist without you, and I am beyond honored to have had my name next to yours.

R. I. P.

Part One

Rest In Peace

Undertaker

Azalea

25 years old

"Are you sure you'll be okay? I really don't mind staying home. The kids will be awake soon, and I know you haven't been..." Micah's light blue eyes scan the morgue, searching for the perfect words that don't exist. "Feeling well lately."

You're a worthless piece of shit.

Everything's going to be okay.

He hates you!

Not 'feeling well.' That's a pleasant way to put it. Since becoming pregnant with my youngest child, Adriel, I've changed—become someone new. At first, things felt clearer. Brighter. As if someone had turned the earth's light on. But now, I'm drowning.

My eyes see things no one else's can, like the brown, gooey glob creatures with sharp teeth and skeletal legs that follow me. Only I can hear the voices that scream, whisper and sing, peeling apart my brain piece by piece. My reality is not the same as those around me.

I'm barely able to wake up in the morning let alone take care of my kids. Even mustering up the energy to have sex with my husband is impossible. I'm twenty-five years old, and I act like an old woman. Work, sleep and holding my little boy are the only things I look forward to.

Waste of life.

Shhhh.

'You make me happy when skies are gray.'

PATHETIC CUNT!

Worst are the thoughts I have about my newborn daughter. Just last night, while she watched me from her swing, I washed the filet knife from dinner. As the soap ran down the blade, all I could hear was: *Stab her. Things will be so much more peaceful without her. KILL HER!* The voices were so loud, I screamed at the top of my lungs to get them to stop.

I've never felt anything like this with my son, Malakai. With him, all I've ever experienced is love and the overwhelming desire to protect him.

"I'll be fine," I respond, though I'm not sure how long ago he asked.

Disinfectant burns my nose as I brush the blond hair away from the glassy eyes of the cadaver. The black holes that sometimes appear to me spread across his face, growing larger, deepening into his flesh.

I point to the baby monitor. It looks odd, crawling with huge, one-eyed maggots when everything around it sparkles clean. I often wonder how Micah would react if he could see the things I do.

"I'll hear them when they wake up. Besides, I don't think Mr. Olson here will mind if I take a break to tend to them. That's why I wanted you to bring the T.V. and their playpen down to the hall this morning—so they can watch cartoons while I work."

He does mostly everything around the house, so I attempt to control my irritation at his failure to do what I asked. Then I question if I'm remembering correctly and glance toward the hall to see if the playpen is there. As his raven hair falls across his narrowed eyebrows, he gives me that terrified look I'm so tired of seeing. He needs a haircut.

"You never asked me that, Azalea. The only thing we discussed this morning was how you wanted me to make your eggs."

You're a fucking stupid bitch.

He loves you so much.

AHHHHHHH!

He's under a lot of pressure right now, and I despise myself for adding to it. Being a pastor has been his dream since we were in high school. He's always been full of faith, desiring to spend his days honoring God. Now it's finally happened.

The Baptist church hired him three months ago when the prior preacher passed. His plans are grand, and his passion is one of the things that made me fall in love with him.

Ignoring the brown, gooey, glob-like creature crawling across his head, gnashing its teeth, I adjust my goggles. At least I'm able to pull myself together enough to do my work. This may be a small town, but being the only mortuary keeps us above water.

"I'm sorry, I must have just thought I mentioned it. It's all right. Go on, have a good day. I'll get it. You have a church to run." I smile up at him with all the authenticity I can muster.

He sighs, hugging me against his tall frame. I hate my desire to pull away.

"I love you," he whispers. At the same moment, Adriel cries over the monitor. "I'll grab the T.V. and bring the kids down."

Nodding, I follow him up the stairs for the playpen before setting it up in the hall outside the prep room. The maggots that seem to follow me everywhere crawl across my feet, blinking up at me with their bulging, cyclops eyes.

In the nursery, Micah coos at Adriel in his arms. Black, slimy webbing grows from the ceiling, moving as if it's breathing. The maggots crawl across it and my skin beads with sweat as the voices scream: *They're going to hurt him!* Then murmur: *It's not real. None of it's real.*

"They can't touch him," I whisper.

Malakai's standing in his crib, holding his hands up, waiting for attention of his own. My palm rubs against my chest. They can't hurt him. I pick him up, his tiny arms around my neck my only source of joy.

You don't deserve him.

Sweet, precious boy.

"I'll bring him down. You can bring Adriel," I tell Micah as I back out of the kids' room.

One day shy of a year apart, my children couldn't be any more different. Where Kai was always a happy baby, Adriel does nothing besides cry. More than once, the bodiless voices have told me to hook her up to the embalming machine just to make her be quiet.

I situate Malakai in the playpen and kiss his jet-black hair as I softly sing, "*You are my sunshine, my only sunshine. You make me happy when skies are gray.*"

Micah carries down Adriel, lying her down next to her brother. Malakai is such a sweet boy. He clearly loves his sister the way he cuddles with her like she's his stuffed giraffe.

Continuing with preparing Mr. Olson's body, I clean the dead flesh with disinfectant solution while Micah retrieves the tiny T.V. from the kitchen.

Adriel wails, and I rub my temples raw at the screeching sound. I can't concentrate like this!

Make her shut up!

She's your little girl.

I almost sob with gratitude when Micah returns with not only the

but the diaper bag filled with a bottle for Adriel and snacks for Kai. Guilt weighs on my heart as I watch my husband risk being late to his new job to help me with the children that I should be able to take care of myself.

With food and *Blue's Clues* to occupy them, they quiet down. Micah makes his way back to me at the embalming table. "Maybe we should see about a nanny?"

It's fine, everything's fine.

You're nothing.

Worthless cunt.

He's sincere in his suggestion, only making me feel worse. Money is tight as it is, and hiring a nanny would be solely for my incompetence.

"We don't need a nanny. Paying Bennett is bad enough."

"Bennett's a necessity and a blessing. You should appreciate him more."

He's right. My brother is the only family I have since my father died. Not to mention, I've never been interested in the business side of things. I prefer the dead over the loved ones they leave behind. Bennett takes care of the families and finances. All I have to do is prepare the bodies and tend to my children, yet I can't even handle that.

"I do appreciate him. I couldn't do this without him. It's just…we're strapped. I wish I could do more."

We dropped every last penny we had into this place when we took it over from my father. Even though Courtenay

Family Funeral Home is a small operation, it takes a lot of money to run.

He wraps his strong arms around my waist and bends down to kiss my neck. "Pray about it, Azalea. God has the answers. I don't." I do pray, but what am I supposed to do when the voices are louder than any answers I may receive? He lifts my chin and gives me a smile, trying so hard to hide his worry. "The only thing I know for sure is I love you. You and our babies. I would do anything for the three of you."

"I know you would. Now go, you're going to be late."

Glancing at the playpen one last time, he backs toward the stairs. "Call if you need anything."

YOU ARE SHIT!

You are beautiful and lovely.

Shhhhh.

I sigh. His uneasiness at leaving me alone grates on my nerves when I should be seeing it as sweet.

"Of course."

***

I stand over Mr. Olson inspecting my work. He looks pretty good. There wasn't much deflation with his eyes, and he had naturally full lips. I push up the right side of his mouth just a hair so he appears more peaceful. The poor soul. He was barely into his thirties.

With ear-bleeding music from the kids' television show in the background, I wheel Mr. Olson into the embalming room, leaving the door open in case Malakai cries for me.

My hands are perfectly steady when I work. Only when I work. A small incision above the clavicle and another one to open the artery is all that's needed to insert the tube. I take the surgical blade to make my last cut at his jugular. The embalming machine whirs when I turn it on, drowning out the *bings* and *boings* of the cartoons.

Watching the pale blood scurry down the drain, I tug at my gloves and lean over the cadaver to massage and adjust the body.

"Why didn't they stop me?"

The raspy voice is different from the ones in my mind, startling me and making me jump away from the table. My heart ricochets around my chest cavity, becoming worse once confirming I'm alone. I stumble over the boot covers on my feet to check on the kids when a cold hand grabs my wrist over my polyethylene gown. I'm able to scream for barely a second before it gets caught in my throat. Mr. Olson's eyes are open despite my putting in eye caps to ensure they don't do that. The cloudy irises stare at me, causing nausea to swirl in my belly.

"Nobody stopped me."

Terror forces immobility onto my limbs as I shake my head. I'm completely crazy. I wired his jaw shut. How is he speaking? What am I talking about? He's fucking dead!

Smell the flowers, blow out the candles.

My breathing slows, though his pressure on my arm gives new meaning to the term 'death grip.' With a shaky breath trembling through my lips I whisper, "Stop you from doing what?"

"They trusted me. I was their teacher."

His lips stay still, yet I can hear him as clear as I hear myself when I ask, "Who?"

"The boys!" he screams. "For years I scared them into letting me touch them. None of them told. Nobody ever stopped me. I would have kept doing it if death hadn't intervened."

Tears burn my eyes as I try to pull my arm from his grasp. All I can imagine is his hands touching Malakai. "Why are you telling me this?"

"Because you need to stop them. You need to stop them before they do any more damage."

I shake my head again. What the fuck is happening to me? "Who? Stop them how?"

"The sinners and evil doers of this world. The same way I was stopped. Death is the only answer. Who better than an undertaker? A henchwoman of the grim reaper?" He finally releases my wrist, his hands resting across his stomach just as I had arranged them moments earlier. "Evil leaves a residue, a feeling you can sense in your gut. Most people ignore it, unaware of what they're experiencing. Don't ignore it, Azalea."

My nostrils flair with my rapid breaths. His eyes close, and he lays as still as...well, a corpse. The words he spoke burst apart in my brain as I nudge him.

"Mr. Olson?"

Lifting my face guard, I walk into the prep room and out to the hall, watching my children who are oblivious to the evil around them.

Rigor Mortis

Malakai

14 years old

I swear I'm gonna jump over the desk and choke this bitch with her ugly-ass green scarf if she says, '*do you understand?*' one more fucking time.

"I just don't get it. The fighting, the cheating and now a weapon?" Principal Richards holds up the blade I pocketed from the Wiggle Mart. "This is very serious, Malakai. Do you understand?"

With flaring nostrils, I grip the wooden armrest of her office chair and glare at her. "It's not like I stabbed anyone."

Her beady eyes widen only for a second before she narrows her gaze at me. "I had no choice but to call Pastor Micah. He's on his way."

Sweat wets my hairline, my heart picks up pace, and I slouch in the chair. I'm completely screwed. He warned me not to mess up again. I cross my arms to look out the streaky, snow-covered window.

My dad's the pastor at First Bethel Baptist and how lucky for me, the only church in town besides the Catholic one on

Main Street. Around half the teachers are members of the congregation, giving them some weird sense that I'm somehow their responsibility.

I scowl at Principal Richards while we sit in mostly silence—besides her dramatic sighing every five seconds like she's expecting an apology. Yeah, right. She'll hyperventilate before that happens. Her frazzled, red hair sticks out around her head, and her pencil *tap, tap, taps* against the desk, driving me crazy.

Leaning back in her seat, she takes off her wiry glasses. "Technically it's against school policy to ask you this, but since I know your parents on a personal level, I feel it's all right." The chair squeaks beneath her weight before she makes eye contact with me. "What's your relationship with God like?"

I snort and shake my head. That's not hers or anyone else's business. "Probably about the same as your relationship with your diet."

Her red lipstick-smeared mouth falls open, and I kind of feel bad, but she asked for it. A knock at the door has us both looking up to watch my dad walk into her office. As soon as my eyes meet his, I want to disappear. He doesn't acknowledge me when he holds his hand out to Principal Richards.

"Hello, Janet. I'm sorry—I have no words. I don't know what's gotten into Malakai this past year. His mother and I are at a loss."

She waves him off. "It's a tough age. Don't be so hard on yourself." I shove my hands under my arms to keep from grabbing my knife when she holds it up to show him. I hate people touching my stuff. "This, however, cannot happen again. I have to keep the other children safe. He's suspended for three days, and if he's caught with any type of weapon again, expulsion may be the next course of action."

"I understand completely. This *won't* happen again." I feel his gaze burning against my temple before he digs his fingers into my shoulder. "Do you have something you want to say to Mrs. Richards?"

My eyes meet her brown ones when I hold out my hand. "Can I have my knife back?"

The second my smart-ass response leaves my lips, my father grips my shirt, yanking me to my feet.

"Why don't you try that again, boy."

I sigh in defeat and say, "I'm sorry, Mrs. Richards."

She nods before I'm shoved out of her office by my father. He towers over me as we walk down the hall in silence. Once we reach the glass double doors, he pulls on his leather gloves and fastens his black scarf.

"This was your last chance, Malakai. Things are about to change drastically." He pushes open the door, and a flurry of snow blows across my face the moment I step outside. I follow him to our station wagon, seeing my sister, Adriel, already in the front seat. Turning to me he snaps, "Riding in a warm car is a privilege—not a right. We'll discuss this at home."

He climbs into the already running car and slams the door. The fumes from the tailpipe puff up in clouds as he backs out of the parking space. Frigid air slices my bones like a blade, causing me to hug my coat tighter. I sigh and head toward the playground to start my mile walk home.

The town of Lettleton is unspectacular in every sense of the word. Even in the summer there's a gray cast over the town, as if the atmosphere knows how lame it is. I hate it here. I have six years until I can take my sweet Adriel and get the fuck out of this shit town. I'll earn millions from my photographs and finally make my father proud. I won't be a disappointment forever.

The truth is, I don't really know why I do the things I do except it's what I wanted to do at the time. I don't have any friends besides my sister, and I guess I just get bored.

Every time the frozen wind blows, it makes breathing impossible. I can't feel my nose or ears, and my coat pockets do little to warm my fingers. I wasn't planning on walking through two feet of snow today, so my shoes and socks are soaked all the way through.

When the *Courtenay Family Funeral Home* sign in front of my house reaches my line of vision, it gives me an extra boost, and my feet move faster.

I know I didn't beat my father home, but the station wagon isn't in the driveway, meaning it must already be in the garage. I really want to see Adriel before having to deal with my parents or my Uncle Bennett.

Pushing the trash can against the house where the roof is lowest, I stack a few boxes of empty embalming fluid bottles on top to hoist myself up. My feet are soft against the snowy shingles as I walk to her bedroom window. I push on the glass, groaning when I find it locked.

She's sitting on the floor playing with her dolls. Her long, pin-straight, raven hair curtains her face as she concentrates on whatever's in her hand. I tap on the window, and she stands before my fist lifts from the glass.

She was expecting me.

"Thanks," I tell her, climbing inside.

"You were bad again today," she says in her high-pitched voice. It's almost childlike, and I wonder if it will ever soften.

Her pink dress circles around her as she sits back down on the floor with her toys. Kneeling beside her, I watch her wrap a baby blue ribbon around her doll, binding it to a handful of sticks. It must be her newest creation because I've never seen it before. The shaved head is from a Barbie, though it's much too small for the plush body it's stitched to with cockeyed thread. One of the arms is missing, and the lips have been melted into a pink blob. The other toys, also enhanced by Adriel's touch, are scattered in a ring like they're waiting for something.

"Whatcha doin'?"

She doesn't stop her task of setting the bound doll in the center of the others. "She's a witch." I hear a *snap* as she grins, taking a freshly lit match to her doll. "So, she needs to burn."

Her soft giggle makes me smile, and I love watching her eyes light up as the fabric of the doll's body catches fire. She's had an obsession with the Salem witch trials ever since she learned of them in class.

I push to my feet, peeking my head out of her door before I hurry to the bathroom for a water-filled cup and a wet rag. When I return to her room, I find the 'witch' consumed in flames.

The stench of melting plastic fills my nostrils as I pour water on the fire and toss the wet rag over the charred doll corpse.

Shit. She singed her carpet.

"If Mom and Dad find this, tell them it was my idea to burn the doll, okay?"

She tilts her head, her black bangs falling to the side of her forehead as she blinks her sparkling silver eyes. "It wasn't your idea though."

She hasn't seemed to grow up much these past few years. She's exactly three hundred and sixty-four days younger than me, but sometimes I feel years ahead of her. She should have outgrown the dolls, and her vocabulary hasn't really matured either. Regardless, her grades are fine, so she's still only a year beneath me. Her social life, however, is worse than mine.

I brush her black, silky hair over her shoulder. "I'm already in trouble. Why should you be too?"

"Both of you," my father's voice booms up the stairs, "get down here."

Jumping to my feet, I grab her hand as she picks up a My Little Pony with a chopped off tail and a plastic monkey head hot glued in place of its own.

Dad waits at the landing, staring at us as we make our way to meet him. "Adriel, please set the table. Malakai, go downstairs and get your mom."

I should have known family dinner would be first. Before we deal with anything, we always eat.

"Okay, Daddy," Adriel complies, squeezing my hand before she lets go.

"Yes, sir."

As I walk down the hall, I pass the framed needlepoint Ten Commandments hanging next to our family photo. *Thou Shall Not Dishonor Thy Father and Thy Mother* is written larger than the rest because my parents say it's the most important one. Follow that, and all the others will fall in to place.

By the time I get to the bottom of the stairs leading to the morgue, I'm glad I'm still wearing my coat. It's fucking freezing down here.

When I reach the preparation room, I find my mother hunched over, massaging a body as she whispers in urgency. It's nothing new, the talking to herself. Some people find it odd, but she's done it for as long as I can remember.

I walk around and look at the man on the embalming table. An older male, probably died of natural causes. She has yet to set his features, so his vacant eyes stare up at me.

Jumping in surprise, she looks up with confusion. "Malakai?"

I've gotten used to this too. She needs to confirm it's me. "Dad says it's time to eat."

Continuing to break the rigor mortis, she softly smiles. "I'll be up in a few minutes, sweetheart."

With slow steps, I climb back up the stairs and slip into the bathroom, locking the door behind me. Beneath the sink, behind the bottles of toilet and glass cleaner, is one of my knives. My breathing slows just holding it in my hand. Tossing my coat on the floor, I roll up my sleeves and press the blade next to the scars on the inside of my arm. I slice sideways, careful to not go too deep so there's minimal blood and I don't do anything fatal. As soon as my skin splits, relief loosens my muscles, and I sigh, watching the red bloom from the wound.

I make four more cuts before cleaning and drying my wrist. After rolling my sleeve down, I walk to the kitchen to find ham and potatoes already on the table. Adriel's sitting with her hands in her lap, her creation lying beside her plate. I take my place next to her, shifting in my seat at how quiet the room is. The *clanging* of serving spoons against the dishes is the only sound until my Uncle Bennett pokes his head in the kitchen.

"Good night, family. I'll see you tomorrow."

We all turn to tell him goodbye, and I almost ask him to stay for dinner to delay whatever punishment is coming.

My mother arrives minutes later, still smelling of formaldehyde, and sits next to my father.

"Hello. How was everyone's day?"

Dad's face falls, but he composes himself quickly. I wish I had a fraction of his self-control.

"Malakai's behavior has become intolerable." He scoops potatoes on her plate, barely drizzling gravy over the top. "So tonight, he and Adriel are joining us."

She freezes, her hands shaking next to her plate. "What did you say?"

He passes the rolls to Adriel. "We've been discussing this for months."

It's making my hair stand on end trying to imagine what they're talking about. My mother's already pale face lightens as she rocks in her chair. "They're too young. They can't—"

His fist slams against the table. "That's enough, Azalea!" He continues through clenched teeth. "You started this. Malakai needs to learn where these sinful decisions are leading him, and I will not give Adriel the chance to go down the same path. Now, we're finished discussing it until after dinner." I take the plate of ham from the table, even though my appetite has suddenly vanished. My father adds, "Adriel, baby girl, will you say grace?"

Nodding her unfailing obedience, she presses her palms together. "Dear Jesus, thank you for this food and for Malakai, Mommy, Daddy and Uncle Bennett. Please help Malakai be more obedient," I barely peek open an eye to look at her, but hers remain firmly closed, "and please make Ashley Radcliff pay for lifting up my skirt at school today." I open my eyes all the way and stare at her. Her eyebrows are scrunched with her furious prayer. "Amen."

I swallow before looking to my parents. My mother takes a bite of potatoes, seemingly oblivious to what her daughter just said, while my father stares at my sister. "She lifted up your dress? In front of people?"

Adriel stabs her fork into the ham and saws her knife across the meat. "Yes. She said I was flat chested and that maybe I was a boy, so she checked."

My father's fury burns through the room like a heatwave as Adriel stuffs a bite of ham into her mouth. "That is unacceptable."

"It's okay, Daddy. I'm not a little kid like everyone acts like I am. I can take care of myself."

His mouth raises into the smile he only gives to her. "That's my girl."

The rest of dinner continues without any more discussion of school. They drone on about renovations to the church and the supplies my mother needs to restock. When our plates are empty, the energy in the room shifts, causing a weight in the atmosphere and a chill in the temperature.

My father throws his napkin on the table and glances between me and Adriel. "Both of you, go upstairs and change into something you don't mind getting rid of. Then meet us in the car."

Adriel picks up her creation which she informed us during dinner was named 'Ponkey' and laces her fingers with mine to walk up the steps to our rooms. After I throw on a pair of grass-stained, hole-covered jeans with a threadbare thermal shirt, I meet her back in the hallway.

She's still carrying Ponkey, wearing a faded, purple dress that's much too small. Her tights have holes in them, and her black MaryJane's are scuffed. She looks so pretty. We throw on our coats before she follows me into the garage where our parents wait for us in the car.

"Where are we going?" I ask as I climb into the back of the station wagon. Adriel scoots in behind me, and I buckle my seat belt.

"To the church," my father responds while reversing in the driveway.

Why the hell are we going to the church at 6 p.m. on a

Tuesday night? Adriel's humming is the only sound during the five-minute drive to First Bethel. It's dark, and the parking lot is bare when we park at the front entrance.

Grabbing Adriel's hand, I tug her behind me and follow our parents inside, sighing in relief when the heat of the church lobby touches my face. I hold her hand tighter as we make our way down the hall. I don't understand what's going on. What's all the secrecy about?

The doors to the basement are made of heavy metal, creaking when my dad pushes them open. What the fuck are we doing? There's nothing down here besides storage and holiday decorations.

We aren't even halfway down the stairs before I hear a grating sound. I look at Adriel, who seems unaffected by our parents' strange behavior, still humming to herself. As I step onto the landing, I hold my breath to absorb my surroundings.

Saran wrap covers the floor, the boxes, and a large man bound to a folding table. His attempted fighting causes the metal legs to scratch against the floor through torn holes in the plastic. While he can't speak, his eyes are wide with rage and his yelling is muffled. Dad walks across the room, grabbing two aluminum chairs before scraping their legs across the cement floor and setting them next to the table.

"Take off your coats and sit." Adriel obeys without hesitation, but I can't stop staring at the man struggling in front of me. "Malakai." My father's stern voice tugs me into the seat next to my sister. Shrugging off my coat, I look up at my mother who's nearly gone catatonic, standing there like she's on pause.

"Who is he?" I ask.

My father rolls over an old AV cart also protected by cellophane. "When you were both very young, your mother received an ability that I believe was given to her by God. Though, I think it would be better if she explained it. Azalea?"

"Hmm?" My mother looks at us as if she's just realizing we're here.

Dad presses his lips together, trying to hide his frustration. "Tell them how we got here."

I glance at Adriel smiling and waving to the man on the table like he's a friend from her class. Mom's steps are slow while she wrings her hands, eventually kneeling in front of us.

"I..." Her head shakes which seems to elucidate her. "I do much more than prepare the dead." She holds my hand, simultaneously giving me the desire to yank away and squeeze back. "They speak to me."

My mom isn't the type to joke, and still, I find myself laughing. "What?"

Her grip becomes tight as her eyebrows narrow. "It isn't funny, Malakai. These people have done atrocious things." She lets go of my hand to jump up and jam a finger into the man's stomach, making him groan. "This is Roger Brown. Do you know what he was charged with before he got off on a technicality?" I shake my head, though I don't think my answer was needed. "Breaking into the homes of elderly, helpless women to rob and rape them. He even killed a couple of them." My stomach goes sour watching the man's fear-filled eyes bulge with his stifled screams. "Do you think we should allow him to continue these things?"

Adriel pipes up next to me. "Nuh-uh." She waves Ponkey around singing, "*If you're bad, you must kneel and pray. For your sins, God will make you pay.*"

Sometimes it feels like I'm the only sane one in this family. "No, but isn't this just as bad?"

"Would you feel that way if it were your mother or sister

who was attacked? Or you?" my father asks. I didn't notice how busy he's been since my mother started talking. The AV cart is now adorned in what looks like a mix of power tools and my mother's utensils from the morgue.

My heart pounds, swirling around the nausea in my stomach. Of all the things I could imagine my parents keeping from me, this would never have made the list.

"Do you kill them?"

Mom's face softens. "Of course we kill them, sweetheart. It's the only way to guarantee they won't keep hurting people."

"Silly," Adriel giggles.

My cheeks burn with embarrassment when tears roll down my face. While I may have thought about killing people when they pissed me off, this is way too real for me to handle. My father walks over to me, kneeling like my mother did.

"It warms my heart to see you distressed over taking a life, but what we're doing saves lives, Kai. People like him don't ever change, they just get better at hiding while leaving a path of destruction in their wake." He stands and takes my mother's hand. "His last victim was eighty-five years old. He raped her so badly she had internal damage that could have killed her if he hadn't beaten her to death with her cane first."

He pulls my mother to the stairs, and I jump up after them. "Where are you going?!"

"You need to see the evil for yourself," he says. "I know you will both make the right choice."

They're leaving us here?! To do what?

I force my fingers through my hair as they climb the steps. The door closes behind them before the *click* of the lock stabs my ears. I'm sweating and freezing at the same time when I hear a diluted yell.

I spin around to see Adriel's tongue sticking out in

concentration while she cuts at the man on the table. Ponkey sits on Mr. Brown's heaving chest as she holds the knife like a crayon, writing on his skin. When I get closer, I see she's drawing stick figures that I assume to be our family.

Swallowing, I place my hand over hers. "You're okay with this?"

She slices out a bow for her stick person's hair when she says, "Mommy and Daddy told us to. Obeying them is the most important commandment." Looking up at me with a smile that could light up a midnight sky, she drawls out, "Remember?"

Cremains

Adriel

13 years old

Malakai is the best brother in the whole wide world. I've always thought his sensitivity was beautiful and curious. He acts tough, but I can see the sadness that's hiding in his eyes. I wish he would be more obedient though because Daddy's right; if he keeps doing things like fighting and cheating, eventually it will turn into things that will make him evil like the bad man in front of us.

Mommy and Daddy love us. Only, Daddy loves me more, and Mommy loves Kai more. That's just the way it is. They want what's best for us, and they know what's best because God picked them to teach us to be good.

I had no idea they were doing something this holy though. They're kind of like reverse missionaries. I don't understand how Malakai can't see that. All he's seeing is murder.

Daddy may have been preparing me for this because after we say our prayers and he tucks me in to read me the scriptures, he talks a lot about being born with sinful desires and using them for good. *Violence is natural,* he told me, *but we must use it to honor God*. This is what he was talking about. It makes perfect sense to me.

I place the knife on the AV cart and stand on my toes to kiss Malakai on the cheek. "It's okay, you don't have to do anything. I'll do it." His nostrils flare as he rips the plastic covering Mr. Brown's mouth. I gasp. "What are you doing?"

"I want to hear it from him." Why? He'll probably lie anyway. He places a hand on either side of Mr. Brown's head, leaning toward his face. "Did you do what my mom says you did?"

He hawks a loogie on Malakai's cheek. "You're all fucking psychotic!"

"Did you do it?!" Kai screams.

"Fuck you!"

Malakai wipes his face as I glare at the man. Nobody talks to my brother that way. I reach in between the cellophane for his fingers as *The Hand Song* bing-bongs in my brain.

"*Here's the church*," Grabbing his pointer finger, I snap it sideways while singing, "*Here's the steeple*." His wails are strangled when Kai's wide-eyed gaze whips toward me. I move on to the middle finger. "*Open the doors...*" Mr. Brown's screams are like an applause telling me how good I'm doing. "*And bless all the...*" Next is his ring finger. I don't know if I can break his thumb, so I finish with the pinky. "*people*." He gasps and whimpers as his limp hand shakes. "My brother asked you a question. Did you hurt those ladies?"

Scrunching his face, he spits in fury, "I gave those bitches one last good dicking. Their pussies hadn't seen a cock in years." Mommy and Daddy were definitely right. What a yucky man. Pulling the plastic down, I undo his jeans. "You want some, little girl?" he groans as he thrusts against my palm.

Malakai glares at the action and back hands him. I smile at my big brother. It was only a matter of time before he understood. Mr. Brown sucks in a breath when I take the squishy organ out of his underwear. It lays limp in my hand as I reach over to grab the biggest knife off the cart.

"Hey, Kai, remember how Daddy used to cut up our hot dogs? This kind of looks like a hot dog, doesn't it?"

Mr. Brown screams, "Fuck, no!" shaking his head. I pull out the stretchy skin as Malakai shoves a wad of Saran wrap in his mouth. While I don't complain, I wish he wouldn't have done that. I want to hear how loud the bad man can get.

The first piece I cut off is the mushroom looking top. Even though the skin is rubbery, the knife slides through easily enough. Thankfully, the plastic wrap barely mutes his sounds of agony as blood spurts across my dress in pretty red splotches. It gushes when I squeeze the stumpy end, working on the next piece. It looks so silly that I laugh. He won't get to use this again. By the time I get to the last section and his penis looks like sliced franks, I hear Malakai retching behind me. I'm not sure why this is getting to him so bad. It's only a little blood. Well, a lot of blood, but we grew up around blood and death.

Mr. Brown's passed out so I kneel next to my brother. "Remember to breathe. Smell the flowers and blow out the candles."

"He's a human being, Adriel. How can you cut him apart like that?"

Why can't he understand? I sigh and touch his cheek, leaving bloody fingerprints. "Because of his sins. You heard him, he would do the same thing to me given half a chance." Still holding the knife, I wrap my arms around him and smear crimson across his shirt. "Obeying Mommy and Daddy means trusting them." He still doesn't say anything, so I look up at him. "Are you mad at me?"

His shoulders slump as he leans over, pressing our heads together. "No, I'm just scared and confused. We could get into a lot of trouble for this. All of us."

I pray for him to have more faith all the time. It's always been hard for him. "Mommy and Daddy won't let that happen."

He tilts his head toward Mr. Brown. "Will you finish it? I want this to be done." I nod, kissing him before I stand up and return to the cart.

My finger taps at my chin as I contemplate what to use. Daddy left us lots of choices. I hope we get to do this again because there are oodles of things I want to play with.

Daddy can fix anything, and I'm so happy he taught me about tools or else I wouldn't know where to begin. Mommy's implements will be too easy. Kai might want this to be over, but I want to have fun. I brush my fingers across them before stopping on a sanding wheel. Once I plug the tool into the outlet, I climb on top of Mr. Brown to have a better angle.

Drumming my finger on his forehead, I sing, "*It's early in the morning, so get out of bed, it's time to wake up, you little sleepyhead!*" His eyes flutter open, and I smile at him. "It was nice to meet you, Mr. Brown." I turn on the grinder, and it whirs to life, the sanding wheel spinning at full speed. I press it against his temple, and the skin instantly shreds, bleeding and shooting onto me. My heart goes *boom, boom, boom,* and my stomach flips like I'm on a rollercoaster. He screams, thrashing beneath my bottom. After a couple seconds, he passes out again, and I huff with a pout. I can't keep waking him up or we'll be here all night.

Before long, I reach the bone of the skull, but that's a lot harder to get through. When I finally see the brain, the sanding wheel touches the slimy, pink organ and fluids gush everywhere, surprising me so much I laugh.

There. All done.

The tool *clangs* against the cart as I lay it down. Climbing off Mr. Brown, I sit next to Malakai. His head is in his hands when I whisper, "I'm finished."

He nods, wiping a tear from his cheek. "How long do you think it'll be before they come back?"

I shrug and point to the body bag folded on top of one of the boxes. "Will you help me put him in there?"

His shoulders relax. I think now that Mr. Brown is nothing more than a dead man, he's less tense. "Sure."

I was right. By the time we get the bag around the body, he seems almost back to himself. "Do you think they'll make us do this with them every time?"

Zipping up the bag, I stop right before covering the face. I want to look at his death for one more moment. "I hope so."

His eyebrows twitch before he puts his arm around me, and we huddle together in the corner. "What was it like? To kill?"

My cheek snuggles into his chest, his body warming me like a wool blanket. I suddenly feel very sleepy. Closing my eyes, I yawn. "Fun."

The last thing I hear before my dreams is Malakai singing to me. "*...Please don't take my sunshine away.*"

I wake up to Daddy carrying me outside. They brought the first call van. He places me in the seat in back and kisses my head. "I'm proud of you, baby girl."

"And Malakai, too?"

He smiles, brushing his hand over my hair. "And Malakai, too."

The back opens up before Mommy and Malakai push the gurney carrying Mr. Brown inside, almost right next to me. I grin at Kai over my shoulder. It makes me so happy when he smiles back. I still feel like I upset him even though he promises he isn't mad at me.

Daddy says to sit on Malakai's lap since there are only three seats. My heart flutters when Kai grabs my hand. Curling up against him, I rest my head on his shoulder.

The drive home is short, and soon we're parking in the back of the house by the morgue entrance. We all get out and walk to the back of the van.

"Okay," Daddy opens the doors and says, "on the count of three, pull out the gurney."

"Are we counting just one, two? Or one sugarplum fairy, two sugarplum fairy?"

Daddy smiles at me. "Just one, two. Ready?"

At 'three' we all pull. When the body is all the way out, Mommy pushes the cot inside, and we follow her through the morgue. As we cross the preparation room, I take in a breath at the heat of the crematorium. The furnace is already on, and the cardboard box the corpse will burn in sits half assembled on a dressing table.

The dead are oodles heavier than the living. Normally, Mommy uses the lift machine to move the bodies, but with four of us, it's not hard to carry him from the gurney to the cardboard box.

Malakai takes my hand, and we follow our parents who are pushing him onto the furnace lift. "Can I press the button?" I ask.

Daddy nods. "Go ahead, baby girl."

Letting go of Malakai's hand, I skip over to the button and push my finger against it. My tummy tickles watching the cardboard box move into the flames. I love when it first catches fire.

I'm so grown up. I killed the evil man all by myself. I won't tell Mommy and Daddy that though. Unless they ask. I don't want Malakai to get in more trouble. I also don't like to lie.

The door to the cremation chamber closes, and Mommy sits in a chair. Daddy walks over to me and places a hand on my back. "Come here. I want to talk to you and your brother."

Once I'm next to Malakai, I take his hand. We follow Daddy out of the crematorium and into the preparation room. I hop up on one of the dressing tables sitting crisscross applesauce while Malakai scoots next to me.

Daddy's hands are in his pockets as he paces in front of us. "I need to apologize, specifically to you, Malakai. While I don't regret having you do this tonight, I am sorry about how I handled it. I was angry. There's so much evil in these...people. The idea of that becoming either of you is maddening. But I should have prepared you better." He walks over to my brother and moves the hair from his forehead. "I love you both so much. You need to know, I don't have all the answers. All I can do is what I feel our heavenly father wants me to do."

"You think God wants us to kill people?" Malakai scoffs, "Wow. You should be Iowa pastor of the year."

Daddy's eyes narrow before he takes in a big breath and sighs. "I think He wants to use us as His instruments on Earth. A type of divine intervention." He backs away and pulls a cigarette pack out of his pocket. He only smokes when he's stressed. "Believe me, this wasn't easy for me at first either. I mean, talking to dead people? That's a stretch even for your mother." He hits the pack against the top of his palm. "You both did extremely well tonight. I promise this gets easier. Someday you'll understand how important the work we do is."

He turns to go outside, and I jump off the table, tugging on Malakai's hand. "Come on, he's gonna start curling soon. I want to see it before they make us go to bed."

Malakai's laugh makes me warm while he follows me back to the crematorium. A body the size of Mr. Brown will take more than two hours to become cremains, giving us plenty of time, but the first thirty minutes are the best.

Mommy is reading a book when I run up to the window on the furnace door. Mr. Brown's hands are balled into fists, and he's sitting partway up so he looks like he's doing crunches. I think I see the top part of his skull coming off. When some bodily fluid squirts against the window, I clap. That's my favorite.

"You really get a kick out of this shit, don't you?" Malakai whispers as he stands next to me to watch.

I shrug. "Dead bodies do neat things."

"It's getting late. You two should head upstairs and get ready for bed," Mommy says. "And leave your clothes in the hallway so your father can get rid of them."

I don't pout even though I want to. I was hoping she would let us stay up to watch her sweep him out. Sometimes, part of the skull will stay intact, and it will crumble right before my eyes. I've always wanted to crush it with my bare hands to feel the powder beneath my fingers.

As I walk upstairs with Malakai he asks, "Did you really have fun tonight?"

I tap my chin as I think about his question. It makes me feel good to obey Mommy and Daddy, and Jesus wanted me to do it, too, which also makes me feel nice. It was more exciting than the last day of school. My heart beat in my chest just like when Malakai picks me up and spins me real fast.

"Yes, I did." I stand on my tippy toes and kiss his cheek before skipping to the bathroom to shower. Smiling at him over my shoulder I sing, "*Nighty-night, sleep tight, say your prayers in case you die tonight!*"

Body Bag

Micah

43 years old

A thick drag of smoke escapes between my lips. I loathe that I still succumb to this disgusting habit. I need to clean the church and make sure the van is free of anything that could prove Roger Brown was here. The body still has a couple hours before we can dump his ashes in the river. I drop the cigarette and crush it beneath my shoe, debating even saying goodbye to my wife.

I love her, God, I love her, but she doesn't make it easy. This isn't the life I had planned when I married her. She became a different person after Adriel was conceived. I thought she'd get better over time when in fact, she got worse.

There have been times that I've questioned if maybe we should see a doctor, but the very thought goes against what we believe. God makes us the way we are for a reason. Taking medication to alter that is like saying He's wrong. Lately though, I've wondered if it would help her return to the woman I married. The one who would smile at me and let me touch her. The one who loved me.

I take the van keys from my pocket. I need to switch them out for the station wagon keys anyway. In the crematorium, I find Azalea staring into space, seeing a world I can't imagine.

"Are the kids in bed?" I ask.

"Hmm?" Shaking her head, she waves her hand. "Oh yes, they just went up."

I kiss her temple and walk toward the door. "I'm going to go clean up the church. I'll be back soon."

"All right," she barely whispers.

From the amount of blood on the kids' clothes, I'd be willing to bet Adriel did most of the actual killing tonight. There's a darkness in my little girl, just like her mother. She's also innocent and good. Always obedient and respectful. Malakai though, his rebellion is what really scares me. He reminds me a lot of my brother. I feel like a horrible father for not preparing him better. Regardless, it needed to be done. He has to understand where his choices can lead him.

Pulling on latex gloves, I set to soaking up as much blood as I can with the towels. Every time I do this, I think of my own family and the darkness that I come from. It's impossible not to wonder what my parents and brother would say about all this.

Tearing the plastic off of every exposed surface, I shove it all into black, industrial-sized trash bags. The sight brings about memories of mine and Azalea's first sinner.

The cadavers don't always tell her who's guilty, sometimes she goes off the 'residue' as she calls it. She first felt it while we were at the park with the kids. A man was talking to children yet appeared to have none of his own. I conceded to follow him with her for a week until we finally saw it. He stole a little girl right off the street. I couldn't believe it. Azalea was right.

After that, everything happened so fast. Once the opportunity presented itself, she hit him with a crowbar, and I smothered him with a chloroform-soaked rag. I didn't know where else to take him besides the church basement, where he eventually confessed to selling the children overseas as sex slaves. The only thing that got me through the night was the idea of that happening to Adriel or Malakai. What horrors they would go through if that had ever been their fate. It still didn't stop my vomiting though. Azalea was more controlled and lucid than I had seen her in a long time as she chopped him up one body part at a time. She didn't simply kill him, she drowned him in agony through his very last breath. I was both in awe and horrified.

The more sinners we found and the more atrocious stories I heard, the easier it became until, eventually, it was a pleasure to end the lives of those who had caused so much suffering. I felt a peace that what we were doing was not only right, but what God had planned for us all along.

Involving the kids was a discussion that came up last year, and I was surprised at Azalea's aversion to it. We both know we're doing holy work, so why wouldn't she want that for our children?

Ultimately, it feels like a weight has been lifted now that they are included. We finally have something that might bring us closer as a family.

I walk into the kitchen, pulling out my phone to check the time. Twenty past midnight. It took me longer than it should have. Regardless, the church is clean, the van has been gone over, Roger Brown's ashes are floating down the Des Moines River, and the trash bags of cellophane have been disposed of in three separate dumpsters outside of town. I'll burn the clothes and towels in the fireplace tomorrow morning.

Azalea isn't in our bedroom, so she must still be downstairs. When I reach the prep room, my heart falls. A body bag lays on top of a dressing table, the top puffing out every few seconds with her breath. I hate that she does this. It comforts her, but it makes me uneasy, and I'm scared the kids will catch her sometime.

"Are you coming to bed?"

Her voice is muffled inside the body bag when she responds. "Yes, I'll be up in a few moments." I drop my head and look at the ceiling before turning back the way I came.

She keeps her word. A few, short minutes after I shower and lie down, I hear the *creak, creak* of the stairs and the *whooshing* of water rushing through the pipes.

Dim light from the hall shines across the bedroom when the door opens. She slips between the sheets, and I scoot behind her, smelling her clean hair as my hand glides up her hip. I can feel the curve of her waist beneath the flimsy fabric of her nightgown. It's been so long since I've felt her, since she's touched me. Kissing her neck, I lift the material up her leg.

"Not tonight, Micah. I'm tired."

I tense as the rage at her lack of affection bubbles up my throat and through my lips. "It's not any night, Azalea." I sit up and grab her shoulder, pushing her on her back. I do everything for her within my capability, yet she still can't love me enough to act as my wife. Frankly, I've had enough. Half of our life has to be hidden, and now our children carry that burden as well. All for her and her abilities. "This has gone on for too long." I push up her nightie and force open her legs.

She shakes her head, covering her face. "Please, Micah, don't make me."

Her words evoke nothing besides more pain and anger. "I've been patient with you, Azalea, but I'm finished waiting." My cock throbs in my sweats as I push the waistband down to fist my pulsing erection. I fondle her dry pussy, the absence of arousal making me want to hurt her like she's hurt me. "You are my wife—it's time to act like it." There's no lubrication, making it almost painful to push inside. I don't want her waking the kids, so I cover her mouth as I finally get my full length into her body. It's been so long, I'm gonna come at any moment. Her cries are muted, so I remove my hand.

"Please, Micah, please stop," she sobs.

I'm her husband! All I'm doing is what every other husband on the planet gets to do to their wife. "I'm almost done. You're so tight."

She coughs and chokes on her tears, the shaking of her body causing my orgasm to shoot through me. I moan, "I'm coming, baby. Oh, God, I'm coming in that dry pussy."

Her hand covers her mouth, quieting her whimpers. As soon as I pull out, I wipe the excess come on her leg. She rolls over to her side, crying into her pillow. The guilt of what I've just done slams against my chest, and I place a hand on her shoulder.

"Daddy, is Mommy okay?"

My head jerks up to see Adriel in the moonlight, standing next to the bed holding her misshapen doll. My heart races in my chest at my daughter witnessing my loss of control.

"Y-yes, baby." My voice shakes as I lift my sweats and jump from the bed. "She's just a little sad right now."

I press my hand against Adriel's back to lead her to her room. She climbs onto her bed. "Daddy, were you fucking Mommy just now?"

My mouth goes dry, the fear of her repeating what she saw making me snap. "Watch your mouth, little girl. What Mommy and Daddy do is between us. It's rude to walk in our room like that."

She crawls under the sheets. "Okay, Daddy."

I nod to her and kiss her head. "That's my good girl."

The thought of going back to bed with my wife tonight is unbearable. I'd rather sleep in the morgue. Going to the closet, I pull out a couple of pillows and a comforter before making my way downstairs to the living room couch. I set my alarm early enough to ensure Bennett and the kids won't see me.

Removal

Azalea
38 years old

I don't move a muscle while I listen to the linen closet close and his steps descend the stairs. I'm so angry. I'm angry at him of course for crossing that line, but I'm really angry at myself for pushing him that far. He would have never dreamed of doing something like that ten years ago. Though I suppose everyone has their breaking point.

Go to him.

Fuck you! Fuck You!

I lie in my dark bedroom for what feels like hours before I push the sheets back. I need him. He's the only one in the whole world I truly love. My feet move slowly across the carpet as I pass Adriel's room. His door isn't closed all the way, so a light push is all it takes to open it.

He's in his bed when I lift the sheet and slide inside with him. My hand grazes across his chest, but he doesn't wake up until I reach into his pajama pants.

"Mom," he whispers in a shaky voice.

"Hi, baby." I kiss him, enjoying the fact that he doesn't

grope at me like his father does. He doesn't do anything at all because he wants me to take control. He's such a good boy.

There were times in the past when he acted as if he didn't want this, but I know he's just worried about his father finding out. He's told me many times that he loves me and what we do together. I don't know what I would do if I didn't have Malakai. I would have probably drunk a whole bottle of formaldehyde years ago. His touch is gentle and hesitant no matter how many times we do this.

"Are-are you okay?" he murmurs sleepily.

"I'm just sad." I kiss down his neck as my fingers roam across his body. "And you always make me feel better." I hear him swallow in the dark, and I whisper against his lips. "Be quiet, baby."

He loves you more than anyone.

Fucking sicko.

'The other night dear, as I lay sleeping. I dreamed I held you in my arms.'

The room feels like it's made of gelatin, the walls are wobbly, and everything is blurry and dark. Malakai's voice sounds like a shadow of itself when he says, "I will always love you, Mom. I wish we could run away together and it could just be us."

More than anything I want that. I hold him tight, feeling his body as I whisper the song I've always sung to him.

"You'll never know, dear, how much I love you. Please don't take my sunshine away."

Micah is thankfully already gone when I wake the next morning. He left bowls and cereal boxes on the kitchen table. I'm not hungry, but the kids might be.

Adriel leaves for the bus stop, taking the pollution in the

oxygen with her. The air is fresh and clean when it's only me and Malakai. I walk up to him, brush his shaggy hair from his gunmetal eyes, and kiss him. He keeps his hands at his sides as I wrap my arms around him, squeezing him tight.

"What would you like to do today? Maybe we could catch a matinee and grab some burgers after? Would you like that? Just you and me?"

"Uh...sure." He shrugs under my hug.

I hold his face in my hands and kiss his perfect mouth. "What you said last night, I want you to know I truly do want that too."

Beautiful, beautiful.

It's all your fault!

His mouth twitches as he raises an eyebrow. "What I said last night?"

"About leaving together."

He tilts his head, his brows narrowing in confusion when my brother Bennett walks into the kitchen.

"Good morning, family. Is there coffee?"

I gesture to the pot and lean against the counter. "Help yourself."

Ruffling Kai's already messy hair, he asks, "Why aren't you in school?"

"Suspended."

Bennett whistles. "Just like your uncle, aren't ya?"

"Don't encourage it," I murmur and rub my temples. I have a huge headache coming on.

He pours his coffee and says, "I just got a call from the nursing home in Madrid. They need a removal, and the family would like to speak with us, so I'm going to bring in Snow."

I groan. She's a necessary evil, but it's more money, and I've never been a fan of Snow Ryan.

"All right," I say. "I'll go prepare the van and meet you there. Text me the address."

"Right-o, sis."

"Come on, Malakai, grab your jacket. It'll be good practice for you to watch." He follows me down to the morgue. "I'm sorry about the movie. How long are you suspended for?"

"It's fine," he mumbles. "Three days."

I wrap my arms around his waist and give him a tight squeeze. "I promise, we'll go out before you have to go back." His nod is stiff as I kiss him. "Good boy."

Grabbing a cot, I pile the protective gear, body bag and cleaning supplies on top. "Put on a gown. We'll suit up the rest of the way when we get there." I follow my own orders, sliding the slick polyethylene up my arm.

Malakai stays quiet on the drive. I wonder what's eating at him, but we have a job to do, and he needs to know what's expected. He's rarely around the families of the deceased.

I explain about being quiet and respectful, not touching anything and getting the job done as quickly as possible. I pray Bennett beats us there.

We pull in front of the nursing home, immediately putting on our gloves. "Keep off the goggles and mask until we get to the room, in case we run into the family. It usually upsets them to see us looking like the C.D.C."

My cell phone rings in my pocket, and I groan at the school's number on the screen. Why are they calling me and not Micah?

"Hello?"

"Hello, Mrs. Courtenay? This is Ms. Lenora Leahy, the school counselor."

AHHHHHHH!

Tell this bitch to fuck off!

"Yes?" I snap. I don't have time for this.

"Well, I—I regret to inform you that we had a student pass away this afternoon. Ashley Radcliff."

"I'm terribly sorry to hear that, and I don't mean to sound insensitive, but I'm in the middle of working, so would you mind telling me what Ashley Radcliff has to do with my children?"

Malakai's eyes go wide, vaguely reminding me that Adriel mentioned the girl's name at dinner last night.

"Adriel and a few other girls were in the locker room when it happened. I feel it would be best if they were sent home for at least the day after witnessing something so horrific."

I want to laugh at her. Adriel probably adored every minute of it. She's in love with death. Micah would tell you it's because she's like me. She's absolutely *nothing* like me. I don't love death, I respect it.

"Picking her up right now isn't an option. She either needs to remain in school, or you need to call her father to pick her up."

"We already called your husband. He didn't answer."

"Look, I'm sorry. I must go. Send her on the bus after school. She'll be fine. I'm a mortician so she sees dead bodies all the time."

"O-of course, Mrs. Cour—"

"Thank you, Ms. Leahy. Goodbye."

I hang up when Malakai asks, "What happened?"

Stepping out of the car, I wave him off. "A girl in Adriel's class died today. Ashley Radcliff? Did you know her?"

He doesn't make a move to get out of the car, so I bend down to look at him. His hands are wringing in his lap as he stares out the front windshield.

I sigh before scooting back into the driver's seat. "Are you okay?"

He needs you.

It's your fault.

Shaking his head as if trying to comprehend my words, his black hair flops around. "How did she die?"

Looking at my phone to check the time, I take his hand. "I don't know, she didn't say." I've never been good at consoling. I never know what words will be best. "Do you want to stay in the car while I do this?"

With slumped shoulders, he wraps his fingers around the handle to open the door. "Nah, I'm fine."

We remove the gurney from the back, and I moan in gratitude when Bennett pulls up behind us. He agrees to get the family away from the exit path, and after a few moments, Malakai and I make our way inside. I'm tense with the likelihood of the deceased having something to tell me, but as much as it worries me to have Malakai see that, it may help him understand.

Bennett's text said the cadaver was in room fifty-four. Once we get in front of the door, I order Malakai to put on his head gear. The dead man's name is Allen Vance, and the lucky bastard went in his sleep. No pain, no fear…just bliss.

He's been dead for a few hours by the look and smell of him. "Remove the blanket, and place it in one of the plastic bags."

Malakai obeys, impressively hiding his disgust at the soiled sheets. I wipe down Mr. Vance, freeing him of feces before we place him in the body bag.

"Hello, Azalea." Mr. Vance lifts his head. One-eyed maggots crawl in and out of deep, black holes appearing in his skin and pour from his mouth as he speaks. I turn to look at Malakai who's oblivious to the reality before him. Being the only one who can see in a world of the blind is a lonely existence.

The walls crack with glowing fissures as brown blobs crawl from the gaps. I lick my lips and continue in my task.

"Hello, Mr. Vance."

I feel Malakai's eyes on me, but I'm looking into Allen Vance's milky ones. "What have you done?" His voice echoes every word, and I can't tell if he speaks with disappointment or anger.

"What do you mean?"

Maggots crawl to the tip of his fingers as he points to Kai. "Your job as his mother is to teach and protect him. You are doing neither."

Anger boils inside me at the judgmental cadaver. "You know nothing. I love him more than my next breath. I love him more than anything."

"That isn't love, and deep down, you know what you're doing with the boy is sick."

My skin beads with sweat as my heart rapidly pumps blood through my veins. Nobody will ever take him from me. We aren't doing anything wrong. What we're doing is pure. The fact that he would suggest that the one thing in my life that makes me happy is evil, brings my hand up to slap him. I hit him so hard, his head flies to the side in an unnatural angle, snapping back to stare at me with vacant eyes and a hateful grin.

I land three more blows before Malakai grabs me, his eyes wide in concern.

Formaldehyde

Malakai

14 years old

"Mom! Stop!" I grab her arm to pull her away. "What are you doing?!"

She falls onto the bed, weeping into her hands while murmuring, "He's wrong. He's wrong."

I don't know what to do. I'm partially stunned. She's talked to herself for as long as I can remember, but I've never witnessed her speaking to, much less getting into a disagreement with, a corpse. I swallow the stone in my throat because that was the freakiest thing I've seen in a long time. To me, of course, he's only a dead man, though it's painfully obvious that to her he's much more.

She's sad, so I naturally want to comfort her. I just don't want to give her a reason to come into my bedroom tonight. It's been happening for about a year. I've tried to stop her, tell her I don't want to, but it's like she doesn't hear me. When she touches me, I want to scream and vomit all over her, yet she's completely oblivious. What's worse is the part of it that feels good. There are times I find myself going along with it, simply to experience it.

I'm not dumb, I know it's a fucked-up dynamic. My father would be irate, and if anyone ever found out, she'd be in a ton of trouble. Obviously I want her to stop, I don't want this sticky overlay to stay on my skin, but I love her, and I don't think she really understands what she's doing.

The rest of the removal goes as smoothly as I guess it's supposed to. It's not long until we're back home, and I'm helping her wheel in Mr. Vance.

She begins writing his height and weight on a big white board on the wall when she points to her bag on the desk. "Why don't you get some money from my purse, and have Snow order a pizza?"

Food isn't really what I'm worried about. This morning was eventful enough, and I have a bad feeling about Ashley. Adriel was really angry with her, and with what we did last night, I'm nervous about the ideas that popped into my sister's dark, little head.

Two wadded up twenties are in my fist as I pass through the doors leading into the funeral home. Uncle Bennett won't be back for a while, and Snow isn't in the lobby. Just as I'm about to search for her in the display room, the arrangement room doors open, and she walks out with my dad.

They're both flushed, my father's top shirt button is crooked, and Snow's blue hair is a mess. My stomach rolls, stretching like silly putty. Meeting my father's eyes confirms he just fucked the funeral assistant.

I hold up the money. "Mom wants you to order pizza." Snow's pierced eyebrow arches as I shove the cash into her hand and snap, "I'm sure you guys worked up an appetite in there." She glances at my father before backing into the display room.

I spin around to leave, and my dad grabs my arm. "Malakai—"

Jerking free of his hold, I snap, "Don't worry, I won't tell Mom where your dick has been." His eyes narrow like he's actually going to have the audacity to try and defend his actions. When he opens his mouth to respond, I cut in first. "And just so you know, while you were in there putting your come in that freak, your daughter might have been killing a girl. You probably want to go pick her up from school."

His unnaturally confused expression would be entertaining if he wasn't just cheating on my mom. "What are you talking about?"

"Yesterday Adriel prayed that God would make Ashley pay, and today Ashley died. After last night, it doesn't seem all that unlikely, does it?"

It doesn't matter what he has to say. I don't want to be around him or my mother right now. Spinning on my heel, I turn to go upstairs to my room.

I lay in bed for at least half an hour before the sound of my door opening and closing burns my ears.

She's here.

"Hey, baby," she whispers as she lies behind me, her fingers finding their way beneath my shirt. "Your dad said you didn't want any pizza. Are you all right?" My skin shrinks around my bones, and I choke.

"I—I'm just not hungry."

She shifts in the bed and turns my face to kiss me. I swallow my sob when she removes my pants, kissing her way down my body as if what she's doing is loving.

Her eyes shift up to mine with a small smile. "I love you, too, sweetheart. I'm going to make you feel better, I promise."

Not a single word left my mouth, making me wonder what the hell she hears me saying in her head to make her keep fucking doing this. Closing my eyes, I cover my face. All it does is make the wet sounds louder in my ears. I wonder, if I scream, would she even hear me? My dad would though, so I keep quiet.

Her insensibility allows me to silently cry while my body fucking reacts to her violation. As arousal forces itself onto me, my thoughts take me somewhere safe. Somewhere peaceful.

"Do you ever wonder what it would feel like to have maggots eat your flesh?"

Adriel's beautiful, gray eyes widen with her grin, and I snort. "I can't say that I have."

She lifts 'Optimus Bunny Boo', a rabbit-legged Bratz doll wearing the head of one of my old Transformers. As she shifts around, her Hello Kitty panties flash at me, swelling up my throat. My face burns hot, and even though my stomach turns in embarrassment, I wish I had the courage to ask her to spread her legs wider so I can see…

My lungs open up, and her face is in my thoughts. My mother's kisses and body turn into my sister's, drowning me in fantasies of how she would look and feel connected to me this way. A moan falls from my lips as her whispered name slips into the air.

"Adriel."

Ashley doesn't get discussed at dinner, and neither does my father's failure to answer the school's phone call. They all go on, ignoring how fucked up this is getting, as if we're the goddamn Cleavers. Adriel talks of her school projects, and Mom leaves out her assault on the cadaver when she mentions the removal.

My father somehow comes up with a day full of events that he never could have done while spending the morning with Snow. I keep quiet, only responding when being asked a direct question, and leave a mostly full plate by the end of dinner.

I murmur a half-ass excuse about not feeling well and ask if I can skip church tonight. My father weirdly doesn't argue, and I get into bed without bothering to shower first.

My eyes flip open when my mattress dips, my heart stuttering at the sound of Adriel's whisper. "Kai? Are you awake?"

It's dark out, so church is over. I wrap my arms around her shoulders, pulling her against me, allowing her head to rest on my chest. "I am now. How was youth group?"

"It was fine." She nuzzles closer. We lay in silence, and I'm almost back asleep when she says, "I did something today…it's a secret." Her whisper gets louder with her eagerness as she shifts up into a sitting position, the fingers of her dark form spreading out in the moonlight. "You'll keep a secret, right?"

My veins vibrate beneath my skin, yet I keep my voice even when I respond. "Of course. You can tell me anything."

She giggles, barely containing her excitement as she bounces next to me. "I put some arterial fluid in Ashley's water bottle during her cheerleading practice! She was sick all through P.E. but wouldn't go home because she wanted to perform at the pep rally." With a shriek she adds, "I got to watch her die!" Clapping her hands, she abruptly stops when I don't join in with her glee. "Are you mad at me?" Her voice goes back to monotone, but there's a slight shake to it which is the closest she ever comes to crying.

I lift her chin. "I'm not mad. What she did to you made me furious. It's just… do you really believe she deserved to die for it?"

What I don't admit is that my mind is becoming numb. I understand by logical standards this is horrific, but with the events of the last couple of days, it doesn't bother me as much as it should.

She lies against me, squeezing tight and whispers, "Yes. She was a very mean girl." After a moment she asks, "Will you sing to me, Kai?"

Kissing her temple, my lips brush her skin. "*You are my sunshine, my only sunshine.*"

I look out the window to watch for Adriel. The bus should be dropping her off soon. She stayed home from school yesterday and we went sledding. While Mom and Dad were working, we cuddled up under a blanket with hot chocolate and watched T.V. as I played with her soft, black hair.

"Do you love me, Kai?"

Pulling my eyes from the cartoon she chose, I nudge her shoulder. "Why would you ask me that? Of course I do. I even love you more than Mom and Dad."

"You love me more than Mommy?"

I swallow, meeting her smoky eyes. Adriel is like a cat. She slinks around without anyone aware she's there. She always seems to know everything going on in this house, and it makes my eyes burn with tears and rage that she knows this.

"I don't like to do that stuff with her, you know. I just can't figure out how to stop it. I don't want to hurt her."

Scooting up to put her face directly in front of mine, she whispers flatly, "Thank you for not being mad at me about Ashley."

She leans forward, pressing our lips together. The beating beneath my chest is the only thing I can hear as she moves her mouth, soft and slow. She tastes like cocoa and peppermint. This isn't a normal kiss. I can't breathe. My skin pulsates over my bones with the urge to unbutton her dress and touch her chest. Moths fly around in my gut, and I don't understand why I want this.

Her.

Desperate to find a correct thought in this moment, I reach up and grip her face, deepening our kiss.

"Malakai," she whispers. Her voice saying my name strikes me with the reality of what I'm letting happen.

My breathing shudders against her lips. She's my little sister, she's supposed to be safe with me, yet here I am taking advantage of her just like Mom does with me.

I pull my mouth from hers and kiss the top of her head. I don't want her to think she did anything wrong. I've been wanting to talk to her about something that's sure to kill the mood anyway. "I caught Dad and Snow having sex in the arrangement room yesterday."

She doesn't say it, though her stiff body tells me this was not something she knew. "Why would Daddy do that?"

I wrap a tendril of her hair around my finger. "I don't know."

I've been on edge ever since. I constantly want to be close to her, that's nothing new, but now I keep thinking of kissing her like that again. Then my guilt sets in, and I force myself to stay away from her. It's an abomination in every sense of the word. Though my moral compass is on the fritz, it isn't completely broken.

On top of that, I'm scared about what will happen when they investigate Ashley's cause of death. When they realize she was poisoned by formaldehyde, the first person they're going to point to is the mortician's daughter who was ruthlessly picked on by the victim.

The final piece that's going to spring free and cause me to fall apart is that she's being so oddly quiet about Dad and Snow. Her not mentioning it makes me much more nervous than if she would express anger over it. She's always worshipped our father, and I wonder if this will alter that.

While she seems fine when she's around him, last night she was coloring her Barbie doll's blonde hair with a blue marker. I found her in her room dismembering it singing, *"Snow, Snow, don't you know? Don't you know? You did a bad thing, so it's time to go."*

The fact that she won't hesitate to kill her classmate eliminates any doubt about what she would do to our father's mistress.

Finally, the bus pulls up, and she steps out, turning away from the house and skipping to the alleyway between our yard and the Wallace's. I sprint down the stairs and across the dead lawn. The *creak* of the fence is loud when I open it to get to the alley. She's sitting on the ground, her long, black hair stark against her pastel, pink coat. I shove my hands in my pockets, scolding myself for not grabbing my own jacket.

As I get closer, I hear her talking to herself. It gives me a chill to think that she's like Mom. She's always playing make believe though.

The snow crunches under my shoes, so I know she hears me, yet she doesn't turn around or stop what she's doing. Once I'm near enough to look over her shoulder, I grimace before getting hit with a dizzy spell.

The body of a decapitated rabbit lays in the bloody snow next to its own head and the head of a squirrel. In her lap, she jabs a long stick into the neck hole of the headless squirrel. Once the stick is lodged far enough into the rodent's corpse, she picks up the rabbit head and rams it down onto the stick. She giggles, laying it on the ground with blood-soaked hands, switching it for the rabbit's body.

I kneel next to her. Her coat and dress are drenched, her face smeared in crimson. "What are you making?"

"Mr. Rabbit wanted to be a squirrel, and Mr. Squirrel wanted to be a rabbit, so I helped them." The rabbit's body *squelches* as she stabs the stick into its exposed neck.

"These are really neat, but they could make you sick. How long have they been dead?"

She's much more tender with the squirrel head, I'm guessing because of its size which suggests this isn't the first time she's 'helped' some poor creatures. I always wondered if she had something to do with the Wallace's missing dog even before Mr. Wallace came over accusing her. I almost choked at my father's response: *Adriel loves animals.*

Yeah, loves 'em to death.

"Since this morning before school." With the transformations complete, she picks up the rabbit-headed squirrel body off the ground. There's no visible decomposition, and thankfully since it's cold, the stench isn't that bad yet. She shakes it, making its tongue flop around. "Oh, thank you! This is what I always wanted!" She speaks in a screechy, high-pitched voice to talk for her new macabre friend. "I shall now be called, Mr. Squabbit!" Placing 'Mr. Squabbit' in her lap, she picks up the rabbit body with the head of a squirrel. "Oh, yes, Mr. Squabbit, I feel the same way! My name is now Mr. Rirrel!" She lets her new friends greet each other before having Mr. Rirrel add, "It's very nice to meet you, Mr. Malakai!"

Despite the morbidity of her playmates, her joy makes me

grin. "Well, hello, Mr. Rirrel and Mr. Squabbit. It's a pleasure to meet you." Glancing at her to see her smile I ask, "Is it all right if I take my sister inside to get cleaned up? She'll be back to play with you tomorrow."

She thinks for a second then makes Mr. Squabbit say, "Oh, yes. Mr. Rirrel and I have a tea party we need to go to anyway."

Laying the creatures against the tree she waves at them, taking my hand with her bloody one. "Did you have a good day at school?" I ask as I open the gate.

"It was okay."

"Did they say anything about Ashley?"

With a shrug she kicks the snow. "Since she did drugs, they think she took something laced."

My chest opens a little, making it easier to breathe. If they suspect drug use, hopefully they won't investigate any further. When we reach the house, I instruct her to take a shower and rinse the blood off her clothes while she's in there.

I walk into the kitchen where Snow is texting on her phone, twirling her blue ponytail between her tattooed fingers. There's nothing nice I have to say to her, so I keep my mouth shut on the way to the fridge to get a soda and a piece of leftover pizza. Dad told me this morning we'd be responsible for our own dinner tonight since he's having Bible study at the church.

"I want you to know," she says to my back, "what happened between Micah and me was a one-time thing. I swear. It won't happen again."

Rolling my eyes, I do nothing more than flip her off on my way to my room. I fall on my bed, eating the pizza as I slide on my headphones and reach beneath the mattress for a knife. Once I push up my sleeves, I swipe the blade across my skin. With a sigh, my nerves calm, bringing me back to something related to normal.

The light catches my camera sitting on my desk, and I get off the bed to wrap the strap around my neck. I push open my window, giving the lens a clear shot of the kids playing in the snow while Tommy Wallace and his father toss a ball to each other in the yard. They're all either blind to the darkness around them or they choose to ignore it. Either way, their existence is fiction. They hide behind the mundanity of everyday life and the responsibilities that come along with it.

The sun casts a golden glow on everything it touches, telling me that more time has passed than I'd thought. I check Adriel's empty room before heading back downstairs. She's not in the kitchen or the living room, so she must be in the basement with Mom. As soon as I turn down the hall leading to the morgue, I see her standing with Snow at the top of the stairs.

"I don't know why, she just wants to talk to you," Adriel says.

At the exact same moment, I open my mouth to speak, she shoves Snow with all her might. It's like those disgusting internet videos. I don't want to see what's on them, yet I can't stop watching.

I run up to Adriel as Snow hurdles down the stairs, thumping every time she hits a step. Her body lands at the bottom hard, hitting the wall before laying twisted and broken.

Adriel looks up at me, holding my hand as she smiles. "There. Now she won't touch Daddy ever again."

Toe Tag

Adriel
17 years old

I hate school so much. Having to be with these people for another year makes me afraid I'll go bonkers. Their constant teasing hasn't let up once since kindergarten. Daddy used to say I would find a friend eventually, but he doesn't say that anymore. My only friends are Malakai, my parents, and my creations. That's all I need.

I haven't killed outside of family night since Snow Ryan because I promised Daddy I wouldn't. It's the hardest promise I've ever had to keep. Ever. Especially because Bridgett Matthews is the worst. Since Ashley died, she's become the queen witch at Lettleton High. She spreads rumors that we eat the bodies at the morgue and have sex with the cadavers. It's stupid, yet all these morons believe it. I want nothing more than to turn her into a cyclops. It wouldn't be hard—I did it to Katy Reynolds' cat last year. I smile, imagining how fun it would be to scoop out her eyeballs and sew her eyelids together. I'd cut a hole in her forehead and glue one of her eyes inside. It would be even more fun if she were alive though. I've never done that.

Once I graduate, I'm going to take classes online, so I can work in the morgue with Mommy and Malakai. I hate that they're still fucking, even if it's become a lot less frequent. I despise seeing them together, yet whenever I know she's in there with him, I sneak out of bed to watch, sliding my fingers inside my slippery hole. He says he doesn't like to do those things with her, but I see how hard he thrusts into her when she moans for him, "*Yes, Malakai, make Momma come, baby*". It equally sickens me and makes me wet.

I've tried to get him to touch me like he does her, but last month, my bravery made him angry.

I love it when Kai lays in bed with me. He kisses me softly and slowly, touching me everywhere other than where I want him to. My desire to feel him is overwhelming. Reaching down, I softly rub his cock over his sweatpants.

His fingers squeeze my wrist as he seethes, "Adriel! What the fuck are you doing?" Even with the fury in his whisper, he grows in my hand.

"Please? I want to suck on it. I know you like that."

His eyes blaze with what I'm scared is repulsion as he shakes his head and pushes my hands off of him. "Don't ever do that again."

I almost beg him to come back when he gets off the bed and leaves without even saying good night.

My anxiety to get out of class is worse than normal because we get to kill a sinner tonight. Mr. Jasick. It's been months since our last family night. Daddy told us he was getting him yesterday. He'll keep him drugged long enough for us to get there, so he won't make too much noise during the day.

The final bell causes a chain reaction of books closing and

mouths talking. I shut my notebook, throw my backpack over my shoulder, and get out of there as fast as I can to find Kai. My MaryJane shoe hasn't even stepped into the hallway when I hear Bridgett's piggy-squealing voice.

"Hey psycho, you can answer this: Does a dead man's dick harden automatically, or do you have to do something creepy to get it up and ride it?"

The girls around her laugh, and I glare at them. They're such pathetic sheep. It obviously takes blood to make a dick hard, and blood doesn't pump in a cadaver. Death erections are rare. The only way angel lust could ever happen is if the dead were hanged or suspended in some way. I look at my homeroom teacher, and she's either deaf or uninterested in what Bridgett and her coven are saying.

Walking over to Bridgett, I whisper, "You better pray you don't die and get sent to us." I lean forward, brushing my gloss-less lips across the shell of her ear. "I will do things to your corpse that you can't fathom." I smile at her and wave, raising my voice to normal. "See you later." Her pale face makes my giggle hard to keep down.

Since we're not allowed to run, I walk as fast as I can to the senior hall. When I'm halfway to Kai's locker, I see him leaving class all by himself. My heart *pitter patters* at the way he brushes his raven hair out of his face. His worn, black shirt is old but fits him better than ever. I rush to him as he lifts his books into his locker, giving me access to hug his torso.

"Are you ready?"

He laughs, bringing an arm around me. "Oh yeah, let's get out of here."

Last year we got the old hearse as a birthday present to use as our car since Mommy and Daddy couldn't afford to buy us one. I love the hearse, but Malakai hates it. He says it makes us stick out. The truth is, we stick out more than he wants to realize, and what we drive won't change that.

We walk down the front steps when Stefan Marks says, "Hey, corpse fucker."

Kai spins around and smirks in that sexy way. "Corpse? That's a fucked-up thing to call your mom. Old people need love too."

Stefan puffs his chest out, ready for a fight. I glare at him, grabbing Malakai's arm to pull him away. "Come on, let's just go."

Someone yells, "Who's for dinner tonight?" as we walk across the parking lot, but we ignore it.

I hold his hand on the drive home, the pulsing between my thighs forcing me to look out the window, watching the leaves coming in for summer to get my mind off it. It gives me a rush to think about the summertime. Longer and warmer days, more time to make my creations, being away from the kids at school, and most importantly, having Malakai all to myself.

His hand travels to my thigh, and the fear that he'd get mad is the only thing keeping me from shoving it up my skirt.

By the time we get home, I'm so tingly that I run up the stairs before I see Daddy or Uncle Bennett.

Tossing my backpack on the floor, I leave the door open in case Malakai walks by. I want him to see. The bed squeaks when I flop onto it and lift my butt to pull off my panties, spreading my legs far apart. My fingers rub against my aching clitty, sliding easily into my dripping hole. I feverishly pump them in and out, closing my eyes to imagine Kai's tongue licking at my breasts, and his fingers inside me instead of my own. I've never had sex, so I conjure up what I think his hard cock would look like entering me.

My fingers aren't enough. I need more. I look around my room and see Beddy, my Barbie with a three-eyed teddy bear head. Grabbing her, I close her legs and carefully slip her feet inside. I shut my eyes to picture his body violating mine. Deeper and deeper I push the doll's legs until I can't go anymore. I remember watching Mommy bent over Kai's bed, his perfectly sculpted butt moving fast as he rammed her 'pussy', as she calls it, so hard her moans became cries. The fantasy of him doing that to me has me fucking myself harder.

"Kai," I whisper.

The door creaks, and my eyes flutter open, instantly finding Malakai's charcoal ones watching me from the door. I sit up to not break our gaze. Even though he isn't touching himself, his erection is clear beneath his jeans. I spread my legs wider, pushing my hips up to get my toy deeper. He groans, and I sigh with relief when he shuts the door and takes a hold of Beddy. Never touching me, he uses the doll to give me the pleasure he's too scared to. Thrusting my body onto the plastic legs, I rub myself, and I'm almost disappointed when my orgasm begins to build. My body is screaming for release. I want so badly to close my eyes and ride the explosion, but instead, I keep them on my brother.

I can't hold it back anymore. My come releases in shocking waves as I moan, "I love you, Malakai."

My body won't move. I can't believe that happened. As soon as my orgasm waned and my muscles relaxed, he slid out the doll. He tossed her on the bed and left my room without a single word.

I find myself laughing. I know he wants me, maybe as

much as I want him. His fighting is making me bonkers and turning me on all at once. Pushing myself off the bed, I go to the bathroom to clean between my legs with a wet wipe, bringing one back to clean off Beddy.

I sit at my desk and pull out my toe tag book. It's my most important possession. Even though morticians haven't used toe tags for a really long time, my mommy likes them. She uses normal wrist bands too, but those are sent home with the families—we can keep the toe tags. I've been sneaking my favorites since I first found Mommy's book. My collection is barely a fraction of hers which makes me love it even more since I choose each one special.

I brush my fingers over the names of the dead before flipping to the back where the newest tags are. My tummy tickles, making my grin stretch my face. Presents are not something we really do in this family. While I'll get something small for Christmas and birthdays, it's never anything extravagant. Then, two years ago, I was reading through the names and realized there were new ones! Malakai had taken them for me and has continued doing it ever since.

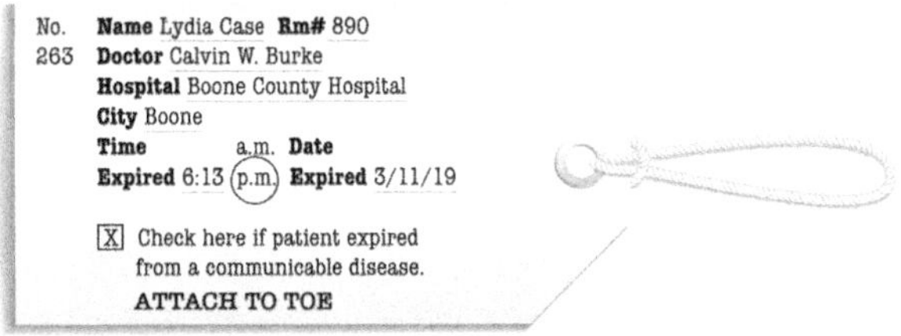
No. 263 **Name** Lydia Case **Rm#** 890
Doctor Calvin W. Burke
Hospital Boone County Hospital
City Boone
Time Expired 6:13 a.m. (p.m.) **Date Expired** 3/11/19
[X] Check here if patient expired from a communicable disease.
ATTACH TO TOE

I hold the tag close to my chest. He knew I would like it because she died from a horrible sickness. Between the toe tag and what happened earlier, my heart is flipping around like a fish suffocating without water.

Picking up Princess Sparkle, my baby doll with glittery horns and a fluffy pink teddy bear body, I hug her. Last year, Bridgett found my doll, Palinky, in my backpack. She never gave him back, and they still make fun of me for him, so I don't bring my creations to school anymore. I miss them all day.

I leave my room to meet Kai in the hall. He smiles as he takes my hand to walk downstairs. I don't want to bring up what happened with Beddy because then I might jinx it. Besides, he seems content with acting like nothing happened.

"Thank you for the toe tag."

His slate eyes glitter in the dim hall. "You're welcome. Mom said she died of *Hepatitis A*." He raises his eyebrows in mock horror, making me laugh.

We take our places at the table, and once our plates are full and we pray, Daddy clears his throat.

"Do you know what tonight is?"

I look up at him in surprise. He never speaks of family night at dinner, but I have no idea what else he could be talking about.

"Family night?" I ask.

Malakai shoves a spoonful of potatoes in his mouth, leaving some on his lip. I grin at him. He started running every morning a few years ago, and ever since, his appetite has become insatiable. It's so cute.

"Yes, baby girl. However, today is also the anniversary of when I became pastor at First Bethel. Associate pastor Westbrook and his wife surprised me today by inviting your mother and I out for dinner." His hand gestures to his plate. "That's why we're eating so light."

I clench my fists. No! He can't cancel family night! "What about Mr. Jasick?!" I try really hard to hide my frustration, but

I still hit the table a little bit. Daddy's eyes narrow as he leans forward, and I immediately sit up straighter. "Sorry, Daddy."

"Do you two think you can handle things alone, or do we need to figure out other arrangements?"

My eyes widen in excitement, and I clasp my hands. "We'll be fine, right, Kai?"

I look at my brother who seems to be more focused on his food than the conversation. "Uh, yeah, sure. We're good."

Mausoleum

Malakai

18 years old

Fuck. I can't get that image out of my head. I've never seen her pussy spread apart like that. And God, what she was doing with that doll… I came to memories of that image as soon as I was alone in my bedroom. More than anything I wish I could have touched and tasted her, but fucking her with the toy was beyond enough.

I keep thinking if I don't be alone with her, it will eventually be easier to control. So far, the opposite is happening, and it doesn't help that she's obviously taunting me. She walks around in these little dresses, bending over to show me her panties. She licks her bright pink lips in the most seductive way, just like she's doing now.

I flip on the blinker to turn into First Bethel, and once I've parked, I lead us in through the lobby. My father has Mr. Jasick already prepared, covered in plastic and incapacitated. He's still asleep from the drugs, so we go to the cart to choose which tool will decide his fate.

Adriel bats her eyelashes over her seductive irises and says, "You want to do the nail gun again?"

Her body language says she's begging me to kiss her, but I already let myself go way too far this afternoon. Eliminating sinners always makes her so aroused it's nearly unbearable. She sets her creation named Princess Sparkle on the AV cart and turns on the battery-operated drill, placing the drill bit into Mr. Jasick's thigh. Within seconds, he's screaming in muffled agony.

I bend down to rip off some cellophane and shove it in his mouth when she says, "Here. Use these." Reaching beneath her skirt, she tugs her rainbow panties down her thighs. She shoves them in my face, allowing me to smell her. My cock pushes against my zipper like it's reaching for her body. I swallow and pull apart the Saran wrap to shove her damp underwear between the wailing man's lips.

She climbs on top of him, grinding against his crotch, lifting her skirt so I can watch her pussy lips rubbing over his tan slacks, leaving a wet spot. She usually can't get sexual like this during family night because our parents are here. I bite my lip as hard as I can to stop myself from gripping my dick over my jeans.

Although there's a small part that's pissed she's touching him this way, her eyes haven't torn from mine for a moment, so I know the pimp is nothing more than a prop. She undoes his slacks and takes his floppy cock from his pants. Her little hand strokes him, her multicolored nails mesmerizing. It must feel as good as it looks because his dick grows beneath her fingers. As soon as he's hard enough to attempt a thrust, she holds out her hand.

"The drill please, Kai."

She takes it from me, and the moment before she puts the drill bit to his piss hole, he thrashes and grunts. His kicks and punches tear the plastic, throwing Adriel to the floor.

My mind isn't able to grasp what's happening quick enough to tell my body what to do, and my first reaction is to kneel next to her to see if she's okay.

Sitting up, she rubs her head. "Ouchie."

The plastic rips, and my heart pumps full speed at what could happen if he were to overpower us. He's a large man, but we've had men his size before, and this has never happened.

I spin around just as he breaks free. The moment I see him grab the drill is the same moment everything goes black.

"Get off me!" Those are Adriel's screams. "I'm gonna kill you, you big, smelly fuck!"

A man's laugh pounds in my head which feels big and swollen. Too heavy to lift off the concrete. *Crashes* fill the space between her screams. I have to get up.

First I need to open my eyes.

"Malakai! Wake up! PLEASE!"

Forcing my lids apart blinds me with light, and I grunt from the burning of my corneas. I reach up, feeling the back of my head, relieved by the small amount of blood that comes away on my fingers. Adjusting to my surroundings, my gaze finds Adriel.

She's on the floor, flailing beneath Mr. Jasick. He's pinned her down with his knees against her arms while she kicks her feet. Standing causes my body to sway, so I grab the table to catch my balance. Even with the room fuzzy, it's clear enough to see the cleaver on the AV tray.

Adriel screams as she fights. I've never seen her look so terrified before, and I fucking loathe it. My heart shatters, the pieces falling to my stomach. My beautiful little sister is innocent in so many ways, and if I don't force myself across this room, she'll be ripped away from me by this street trash.

Gripping the cleaver handle, I make sure my steps are slow and steady as I cross the basement. He squeezes his hands around her throat, and I lunge for the motherfucker, bringing the blade down hard into the side of his neck. It doesn't chop his head off, it doesn't even go halfway through, but it doesn't matter as his blood rains down on Adriel, bathing her in red. His body falls on top of her, and she groans.

"God! He's so fat!"

I push him off, exposing her spread legs and open pussy smeared in blood. "Are you okay?" I pant.

She nods, forcing my relief and endorphins to mix wildly. I grab her face and kiss her, tasting the nearly dead man's blood. She responds with eagerness, pulling at my shirt to bring me closer. We yank on each other's hair, our mouths desperate for something wrong. It's supposed to be anyway, but in this moment, it doesn't feel like a choice. She wraps her legs around my waist and pulls off my thermal shirt. Her fingers softly trace the fresh cuts on my wrist while her tongue explores my mouth.

I flip her on her back, resting her head against Mr. Jasick's abdomen. My lips refuse to leave her bloody body as I kiss and suck my way between her legs.

Touching her for the first time makes me frantic as I spread her apart and lick inside her little hole. She smashes against my face with her thrusts, my tongue searching eagerly for her clit. I suck it between my lips, finding it hard to stop my own rocking against the floor.

"Kai," she whimpers, "yes, I like that. Please, keep licking my clitty."

The way she moans that out drives me crazy, and I ram

two fingers inside of her. I look up at her fisting Mr. Jasick's shirt, looking so beautiful in her pleasure. Her legs shake as Mr. Jasick coughs up more blood. She tightens around my fingers, submerging them in her orgasm. With a soft moan, she sits up, smiling at me. I can't make myself stop fingering her.

"I want you to fuck me, Kai. Fuck me like you fuck Mommy."

Her words sober me. I hate my mother for still making me do that, and I hate myself for letting it continue to happen. Anger fills my chest at the fact that this could have been both of our first times. It would have been perfect for it to have been together. All my reservations about sleeping with her seem petty and small now. Had things gone a different way tonight, I could've lost her.

Adding a third finger pulls a squeal from her lips, and I push them in hard. "Not here. Not with him."

Her eyes blaze with a smirk. Jumping to her knees, she kisses me as she lifts off my fingers. "First you have to catch me!"

Quick as a flash she's on her feet, running up the stairs. I know exactly where she's going. Mom and Dad won't be back for a while, so I lock up the church to run toward the graveyard.

The wrought iron fence has been missing its door for a couple months, so I'm able to run right into the cemetery. Adriel pops out from behind an angel headstone and says, "Boo!" before giggling and skipping between the plots. We've always loved this place. For as long as I can remember, we've played here. Our favorite part? The mausoleum.

The *creak* of the door is loud in the still of the night when she disappears inside of the tiny stone building.

When I reach the handle, I freeze. I know what happens

in here will change both of our futures. My heart is still pumping from the struggle with Mr. Jasick, and my cock is still straining from the taste of her blood-covered pussy, making my mind up for me.

Moonlight streaks across the stone floor as I pull open the door, shining over her breathtaking, nude body.

My voice becomes misplaced at seeing her this way, so I do what every bone and vein in my body screams for me to do. It's never like this with Mom. Even when it feels incredible, it's never desire, much less an uncontrollable need.

The door slams shut behind me as I grab her face and kiss her, backing her against the crypts. Just as I'm about to reach down and undo my old jeans, her fingers fumble with my zipper. We both moan the moment her hand touches me. As she pushes my pants and underwear down enough for access, I pick her up.

"I love you so much, Adriel. Once we do this, we can't undo it."

A mischievous smile spreads across her lips as she whispers, "Good."

With those words, I fill her body with my own. And for the first time in my life, I feel a sense of peace.

Reaper

Micah
47 years old

The kids back away from the house in the hearse while I watch from our bedroom window. Azalea is still in the morgue, so I go to the kitchen to make some coffee, pleasantly surprised to find there's already a full pot. Pouring myself a cup, I settle on the couch to wait for her. The news is on, and I chuckle to myself thinking of what Adriel always says when I watch it.

"Come on, Daddy, not the news. I hate that show!"

When I got the invitation for dinner tonight, I was both trepidatious and hopeful. My marriage is in desperate need of repair. While I feel constant shame about my continued actions involving our sex life, I also feel somewhat justified. She hasn't willingly been with me since before Adriel was born. It infuriates me that she married me with a healthy libido only to change shortly after. I'm a man with desires given to me by God. I've tried to sleep with other women, but I don't want them—I want my wife. I love my wife. I think more than being angry, I'm heartbroken. Besides being in a mostly sexless marriage, it feels like I'm in a loveless one as well and have been for years.

We haven't had a night out in a long time, so while I'm hoping it will add some light to her face, she's also never been big on social situations, leaving me concerned tonight will have the opposite effect.

The newscasters sign off, telling me it's starting to get late. We need to leave soon.

I find her soaping up when I reach the prep room. "Hey, are you about ready? It's almost time to go."

She doesn't respond. I often wonder how much of what I say she actually hears. As she dries her hands, her burning gaze snaps toward me. "I've had enough, Micah."

Nausea hits me so hard I almost double over. What does that mean? I reach for her, and even as I plead, I know it's fruitless. "Azalea…"

"Don't fucking touch me!" She kneels down to the cabinet, and when she stands, she's pointing a gun in my face. "You won't ever touch me again."

My fear for our marriage quickly becomes fear for my life as I hold up my hands. "Come on, sweetie, we can talk about this."

"Oh, we're going to talk about it." She waves the gun behind me. "Go to the embalming room."

I keep my eyes peeled for something to incapacitate her while doing what she says because I, above all people, know how unstable she can become. Once we're inside the room, she closes the door behind her, never taking the gun off me.

How did we get here? There was a time we were so happy; the world was endless as long as we were together. Tears fill my eyes and pour down my cheeks at the fact that my soulmate, the one who would write me love notes and sneak them into my pocket, now hates me so much her only option is snuffing out my existence.

"Why, Azalea?"

She laughs in a maniacal way. "Asks the man who's been raping me for years." I'm about to apologize, try to explain things, when she adds, "You suffocated me, forced me into our son's bed, and made me no different than the sinners we eradicate."

It's incredible how quickly a single moment, a single sentence, can change every molecule of everything you've ever felt and snap it right down the middle. She hurt my son. Our son.

I lunge for her when I'm thrown backward with a *BANG*. My veins catch fire before the left side of my body screams in agony. Blood blossoms over my shoulder, dripping down my arm, surrounding a deep hole. She actually did it.

When I look up, it's down the barrel of a gun. "Get on the embalming table, and lie down."

I struggle to stand and do as she says, but I don't know why. I'm not leaving this place alive either way.

With a roll of duct tape, she confines my arms to my side, unknowingly adding pressure, relieving some of the pain from the bullet wound. After repeating the process with my legs, she does exactly what I was terrified of. More tears fall as I watch her fill a large syringe with embalming fluid.

"You're going to feel the same agony you've caused me to feel for years. The only difference is, you get the grace of the reaper." Finding a vein in my arm, she slides the needle beneath my skin. "There was a time when I loved you."

"What happened, Azalea? We were having problems before I..." I can't even bring myself to say it. I close my eyes as my heart lays heavy between my ribs. For the first time,

I truly understand what I did to her. I've rationalized it for years, refusing to admit to myself what a horrific thing I was doing to my wife.

And she did it to our son.

"How long have you been abusing Malakai?"

Her shoulders fall with her sigh as she pushes the fluid into my body. "I don't know what's real and what's not anymore. My answer might not even be true."

There was something I was going to say, a question I wanted to ask. None of it matters, when pain like I'm boiling from the inside out overtakes my every thought. I know I'm dying as my skin melts into the table.

Heaviness weighs on my stomach, and my eyes fly open to see what else she's doing to me.

"We are sinners and need to be stopped." She straddles me, and though she's not a large woman, the weight is excruciating. She's holding a small surgical knife with tears streaming down her face. "Goodbye, Micah. We'll see each other in Hell."

She holds the blade to her throat, swiping it across before my cry reaches my diaphragm. Blood pours from the wound in her neck like a red waterfall. She involuntarily chokes and coughs, grabbing the cut as if she can stop it from splitting. Her eyes meet mine, and I think in this moment, she realizes the atrocity of what she's done. To herself. To me. To our children.

To our beautiful family.

Her eyes shift to the ceiling before she falls against my chest, forcing me to wail from the agony of it. Blood seeps across my shirt, and even though it burns my eyes and may even make the pain worse, I cry. I cry for her, I cry for our marriage and our children. I cry for the life that could have been if we would have made different choices along the way.

With my dead wife across my chest, the torture is so unbearable, it feels as if I'm losing my mind. Anger, sorrow, fear, defeat, and every other morose emotion I've ever felt reaches a boiling point. Clenching my fists and tensing my body, I open my mouth to do the only thing I can.

I scream.

Part Two

Rot In Pieces

Graveyard

Adriel

17 years old

Moonlight strangles the dark, stretching across the tombstones like a haunted dream. This is my favorite place in the whole wide world. Death's murky essence bleeds the thickest in a cemetery. It has always comforted me to be so close to the other side. Most people are scared of dying, but I'm not. I'm excited to see what happens.

Mommy once told me I have a black soul. I don't think that's true though because I always try to be a good girl and obey. Besides, my favorite color is pink. For reasons I've never understood, she just plain doesn't like me. She won't even hug me.

The *pitter-patter, pitter-patter* between my ribs hasn't slowed since the basement. Malakai touched me. He tasted and licked me. Nothing has ever felt as good as his tongue did. The fantasies I'd had were nowhere close. I still can't believe he really did it.

In the black of the night, his hurried footsteps *scratch, scratch, scratch* against the gravel of the church parking lot.

I slip behind my favorite headstone. The granite feathered wings of the angel almost look like they could flutter at any moment.

Our Darling Daughter
Eliza Dupont
February 3, 1898
April 14, 1900
May you dance with the angels.

The silence of his footsteps tells me he has crossed into the graveyard. Crouching down to peak under one of the wings, I grin when I see he's almost at the tombstone. With my fingers spread out in front of me, I jump out to scare him.

"Boo!"

A tornado storms in my tummy when he smiles. I spin toward the mausoleum and take off in a run. The moment I'm inside, I hurry to tear off my dress. If I'm already naked, I'm hoping it will be harder for him to resist me.

Two faux candelabras, one in each corner, supply the only light inside the mausoleum. My bra barely hits the floor when the door opens, revealing Malakai's shadowed form standing in the entryway.

The moment he's in front of me, his fingers brush my cheek. Tingles flutter up my spine when he crashes his lips to mine. I wrap my arms around his neck, deepening our kiss as he walks us backward until my head hits the wall.

Desperation for this to continue eats my every thought. With frantic fingers, I undo the button on his jeans. My veins prickle with eagerness as I reach into his underwear, and the heat of his erection pulses against my palm. His quiet moans float into my ears, tugging on the tightness between my thighs.

how agonizing this is, I've never been closer to him. I refuse to give that up. His hand warms my cheek. "I'm sorry, it's never—Do you want me to stop?"

"No," I say, trying to move myself up and down to get used to it. "Just go slow, okay?"

Pressing his forehead to mine, he nods. Being held by him loosens my skin, my body rocking against him in response. His hands oddly feel larger than normal as they squeeze my waist to carry me away from the crypts. In front of my discarded clothes, he kneels, lying me on top of them. The chill of the concrete seeps through the fabric while I watch him frantically kick off his shoes and pants. Every ounce of cold evaporates the moment he climbs on top of me.

Kisses trail down my neck as his cock rubs against my exposed pussy. "I can't believe this is happening," he breathes.

Neither can I.

Looking down, he reaches between us to put the soft tip into my entrance. Hair falls into his blazing eyes when he lifts his head, giving me a grin that opens my legs wider. Slowly, I take him inch by inch. This time, the piercing sharpness softens to a dull ache.

I've never thought about other boys. I can't even remember ever thinking another guy was cute. To me, the concept of a 'crush' seems unnatural. How can you have feelings for someone you barely know? The girls in my class fall 'in love' within a couple months of dating. They wouldn't know what love was if it stabbed them through the chest. Me and Malakai? We were created in the same womb. Most people will never experience knowing someone as deeply as we know each other in their entire lifetime. I would plunge to my death without a thought if it would save him.

That is love.

"I only want to do this with you." I open my body further, consuming as much of him as I can. "You're my brother. I love you more than anyone in the whole wide world."

My words quicken his pace, and I wince, grasping at his shoulders. I need him to slow down. Just as I open my mouth to ask him, the sensation shifts. Suddenly it's…oh.

The heels of my feet scrape against the concrete. I wonder if his heart feels like it's glowing like mine does. My back arches as I trail my hands down his shoulder blades, his muscles moving beneath my fingers with each thrust. This is so much more intense than when I touch myself in the dark. Pressure builds between my thighs, forcing me to buck against him.

"You want to know a secret?"

His head dips before his warm mouth sucks on my nipple. My breathing comes out stuttered from the jolts of electricity thumping in my clitty.

"I love secrets." Soft strands tickle my fingers as I comb them through his hair with a moan.

Licking at my flesh, he kisses across my chest. "I think of you when I'm with Mom."

My heart spasms at his confession. It's shocking how much I wanted to hear those words. I smash my mouth to his, kissing him as deeply as I know how. If I had one wish, it would be for this moment to last the rest of my life. This mausoleum is where everything is perfect. We can't ever tell anyone. Not even Mommy and Daddy. Lying isn't something I like to do, but for Kai, it's worth it.

It's important that this is as perfect for him as it is for me. I've noticed that more often than not, he fucks Mommy from underneath her. I wonder if that's how he likes it.

"Can we switch places?"

His grin intensifies my ache. Fullness stretches me further as if he's growing larger inside me. "Hell yeah."

I squeal when he tucks his arms underneath mine to lift me up. Dread surrounds me like a shadow when he separates our bodies. The moment he's sitting upright, I scramble to straddle him.

Chest to chest, he grips the back of my neck and kisses me with urgency. His cock is wet and slippery to the touch. My tummy somersaults, pushing out a laugh against his lips.

The moment he fills me up, we gasp into each other's mouths. Gripping my waist, he moves my body up and down faster than I could do on my own. My skin prickles like locusts are flying around me. Not even my imagination could have predicted the way this feels.

"I don't want you to touch Mommy anymore." The words bounce from my lips before I know the thought has crossed my mind. It makes me want to scream thinking of him being with her now that he's been with me.

He shakes his head, sliding his hands to my bottom. Powerful fingers dig into my skin, pushing us closer. "I won't. I swear."

Our bodies writhe together in mutual euphoria. That promise, his body, his taste, this entire night…it all erupts through my veins as I come. Abandoning everything outside of this moment, I'm devoured by the blissful attack on my body. Quick little moans are the only sounds falling from my lips.

I love the lullaby of his fast breathing. With a groan, he rests his forehead against the crook of my neck.

"Fuck, you have to get off of me."

Heavy disappointment tugs my mouth into a frown. Resisting the urge to cross my arms I pout. "Why?" He shoves against my hips, attempting to separate us. No! I don't want this to be over yet. My legs tighten around his waist, and my arms hug his neck.

"Because I'm gonna fucking come!"

Holding his gaze, I whisper. "Do it inside me."

The idea of being able to walk around and still feel him in my body, even if it's only for a little bit, is the strongest desire I've felt in a long time. I move my hips faster to push him over.

"Seriously, Adriel. No! You have to—Oh, fuck! Oh, God!" He trembles beneath me. In the dim light I can see the odd mix of pleasure and horror on his face. Heat fills me up, and I involuntarily clench at the pulsing expanding deep between my legs. As soon as he's empty, the expression on his face pokes me with icy stabs. "Shit," he whispers, scrambling out from under me in a panic. "Shit, shit, shit."

Is he freaking out because we had sex or because he came inside me? Ripping his jeans up his legs, he tears his fingers through his hair.

"Are you mad at me?"

He scoffs, meeting my eyes. It scares me when I can't place what I see in him. "Get dressed. We need to call Mom and Dad."

His response sucks the air from my lungs. It's as if my blood evaporates, leaving nothing but desiccated veins. Our entire lives, every time I've asked that question, he's always answered, *no*.

The air is frigid as he brushes past me. I can't make myself move. Everything in me wants to chase after him and tell him I'm sorry. I just can't. Even when the mausoleum door slams behind me, my limbs remain paralyzed.

Orphaned

Malakai
18 years old

Fuck! Fuck, fuck!

I can't believe that seriously happened. Jesus Christ. As if sleeping with her wasn't bad enough, I had to go and come inside of her too. Why the hell wouldn't she listen? The thought of throwing her off was in the back of my mind, but it just felt so damn good. It happened so fast.

My stomach sours with nausea as I storm back into the church. I've known from the beginning that what we were doing was obscene, yet the moment I came, all the guilt and fear about what we've done multiplied tenfold.

In an attempt to slow my heart, I rationalize with myself. We're teenagers with hormones. Our adrenaline was high, and we made a mistake. An accident we can't take back…even if I wanted to.

Obviously, we can't be together like that again, and nobody can ever, *ever* find out about this. Not even when death feasts on our final breaths can we mutter a word of what we've done.

Mr. Jasick and the basement are a complete mess. Pulling up his pants, I fasten them before picking up Adriel's panties to stuff them in my pocket. Mom and Dad would probably ask about that.

Fuck. Mom. How the hell am I supposed to keep that promise when I've never been able to stop her in the past? The very thought of her or Dad finding out about tonight intensifies the panic already buzzing beneath my skin. What would they do? Mom would be furious for a different reason than my dad. I inhale deeply to settle the sickness threatening its way up.

Would she see this as betrayal?

Adriel's footsteps down the stairs are slow. The truth is, I'm not mad at her as much as I am myself. I made the choice to be with her. While, of course, I wish she would have listened to me and gotten off me, if I was truly determined to pull out, I could have.

She silently walks across the basement to pick up the body bag, lying it on the floor next to Mr. Jasick. With a sigh, I kneel beside her and take her hand. The hopeful expression illuminating her face stabs me between the ribs.

"I'm not mad at you, okay?" My fingers reach for hers before I realize it could make the already sucky situation worse. "It's me I'm upset with. Being with you like that is something I've wanted for years, but it's wrong. We can't ever do it again...or even talk about it."

Her forehead creases with her glare. "You wish it hadn't happened."

She says it as if it's fact, but the crazy thing is, if I had the power to go back and change it, the only thing I would do differently is come on the mausoleum floor instead of inside of her. Even knowing we can't be physically together again, never in a million years would I want to undo the fact that I was able to experience her.

I want so badly to kiss her, but this all has to stop. The knowledge that this will change things between us creates a barrier in my windpipe.

"That isn't true at all. It was incredible. It's just really fucked up. If it ever got out, our lives would be ruined."

Her words stay locked away as we tug Mr. Jasick's body into the bag. God, this really fucking blows. All I want to do is comfort her, touch her and tell her I love her. After tonight though, it would just make everything harder.

Shit, I need to call Dad. She focuses on her toy instead of me as I walk to my cell phone sitting on one of the boxes. The lock screen lights up when I swipe it open.

Uncle Bennett

Missed Call (6)

The last time I got a call from Uncle Bennett was on my birthday, so why the hell has he tried six times?

Since it's obviously urgent, I call him before Dad. Halfway through the second ring, his hysterical, nasally voice grills me. "Where the hell are you? I've called at least half a dozen times! What's the point in having a fucking phone?"

Uncle Bennett is one of the most laid-back guys I know. I don't think I've ever seen him inconvenienced much less angry. "Whoa, chill. We were just away from the phone."

"Is Adriel with you?"

"Yeah."

"You need to get home right now."

The way he says that freezes my skin solid. Something is definitely off. "Are Mom and Dad there?"

His gasp is lined with a sob. "Just get your sister and come home, okay?"

Adriel tilts her head in question, standing next to me as I put him on speaker. "We really need their help."

He breathes harder with a whispered, "Fuck!"

My skin instantly flips in temperature, the heat making my head feel like it's going to explode.

"What's going on, Uncle Bennett?"

The other end only offers silence. Finally, he sighs and says, "I didn't want to tell you this over the phone. You need to know that."

My knees weaken while I squeeze the cell to keep from dropping it. Somehow, I already know what he's going to say. Adriel's eyes widen the second she pieces together that something terrible has happened. Just as quickly, her face falls passive.

"I'm so sorry, kid. Your parents..." He groans in a painful way. "Azalea and Micah...they're gone. They've...They're dead."

The room stops. Even the dust particles in the air seem to freeze in place.

I should be overcome by grief. I should want to fall to my knees in mourning, but all my emotions feel dormant. Like when you react in an unlikely way in a dream. Everything's fuzzy and blurry.

I don't know how long I stand there, holding the phone, staring at the body bag that contains what is likely to be our last sinner. It's odd that after never particularly enjoying family night, it hits me that we won't ever have one again.

"Dead," Adriel whispers. The first twinge of heartache peeks out, threatening to destroy my resolve the second I look at her. She doesn't move or blink.

We, along with half this basement, are covered in blood, and there's a corpse that can't be here by morning. My heart punches my chest so fast I have to gulp in air to breathe. It's over. If you include Snow Ryan and Ashley Radcliff, Mr. Jasick was our twenty-first body. They'll lock us up for the rest of our lives.

"Kai? Are you there?"

With a *snap* in my brain, I suddenly know what needs to be done. My father has prepared me well for this. This isn't the end. It can't be. I have to protect her. "Have you called the police?"

"I'm about to."

I blow out a relieved breath. "Don't call yet."

"Kai—"

"Just listen, Uncle Bennett." Even with the knowledge that my mother always turns the cameras off on family nights, it's still a much larger risk than we can take. "You have to delete all the security footage."

"Wh-what?"

I'm out of time and options. Ignoring him before I can change my mind, I blurt, "After you do that, come to the church. Then we'll call the police." Adriel's eyes shifting to mine is the first move she's made in what feels like hours. "There's something you need to know."

It won't take Uncle Bennett long to get here. Not that there's anything I can do to make this scene less horrifying anyway. Adriel barely speaks a word and not a single one about our parents. Right now, I'm thankful for it. If we accept our reality, really believe it, I'm scared we won't be able to do what needs to be done.

Dad showed me how to clean up enough times that I

know how. However, half the shit I need is at the house. Razor wire wraps around my insides when I look at Adriel. She sits on the table, tugging on the fuzz of Princess Sparkle's bear body.

Taking her hand, I lead her upstairs. "Come on, he'll be here soon."

We wait in the lobby, watching out the double doors for Uncle Bennett's black Camaro. In the silence, Adriel's whisper echoes loudly in my ears. "What are we gonna do, Kai?"

Six words are about to make me crumble. I don't know how much longer I can keep the sorrow at bay. Her hair is smooth beneath my fingers as I cup the back of her head, pressing her body against my chest. "Stick together."

I'm so close to giving in to the tears.

Headlights flash through the glass of the doors, stopping right in front of us. Uncle Bennett gets out of his car, raking his hand through his hair. I've never seen him look like this. My mother once told me that he has more beauty products than she ever did. But now, his slumped posture and unkempt style makes him appear like someone else altogether.

As he opens the door, I take a step away from Adriel to give him a good look at our bloodied clothes. One, two, three seconds pass as he stares through us. Recognition flashes across his face like an 'on' button. His eyelids peel back from his bulging eyeballs, enlarging them to three times their size.

"What the hell?! Are you guys all right?" Beneath his disquieting stare, we allow him to check us for the injuries that aren't there. "What happened?"

Never in a million years did I plan to breathe a word of this aloud. Where do I even start? Turns out, I don't have to.

"There's a dead sinner in the basement," Adriel announces.

"Mommy and Daddy aren't here to help us with the body, so we need you."

An invisible eraser dissolves every one of his expressions. Only his eyes move between us. "What? Like a person?"

With a groan, I wipe my hands over my face. My sister's approach is rarely delicate. "An extremely bad person." His eyes beg me to say something that's not completely insane. "Mom..." I sigh. "We've been doing it for years. With Mom and Dad."

Tossing us a disbelieving scoff, he marches toward the basement. Fear fills my lungs at what his reaction to this will be. I grab Adriel's hand to pull her down the steps behind him.

He stands quiet and still for an eternity, staring over the body bag containing Mr. Jasick.

"What the fuck?!" We've been waiting in silence so long that I jump at his outburst. Adriel, on the other hand, just leers at him, not so much as startled.

"Are you going to help us, Uncle Bennett?" The tightness of her hand squeezing mine suggests she's as nervous for his response as I am.

He whips around, glaring between us. Just as I think telling him was a huge mistake, he walks over and places a hand on each of our cheeks.

"I'm not losing my entire family in one goddamn night."

D.O.A.

Adriel

17 years old

Malakai tries to tell the story of how we got here while I look around at our mess. Since Mr. Jasick got free, blood tracked in some places that weren't protected by the plastic.

"I knew Azalea had issues, but I never would have imagined it was this bad."

Princess Sparkle's fuzz lifts from her body as I clench it in my fist. I know he's helping us and that he's sad because Mommy's dead, but that doesn't stop the fury that's been boiling since we called him from erupting in me like a volcano.

"She didn't have *issues*!" I scream. Stomping over to him, I stand on my tip-toes to get close to his face. "She was special. Jesus gave her that gift."

He glances at my brother with scrunched eyebrows. "The last thing I want to do is disrespect her."

Malakai's warm hands rest on my shoulders to lead me toward the stairs, unknowingly calming me down. "Come on, let's go get cleaned up." Mid step, he turns back to our uncle. "You brought us spare clothes, right?"

With a nod, he digs into his pocket, tossing Malakai a set of keys. "In the trunk."

Princess Sparkles' horn keeps bumping the side of my leg on our way to the parking lot. Kai unlocks the black trunk to reveal the trash bag with our clothes, a jack, and jumper cables. He throws the bag over his shoulder on our way back inside, never letting go of my hand.

As soon as we're in the bathroom, he removes his shirt, his abs flexing as he pulls it over his head. The dried blood on my dress rubs against my chest when I take it off. The action gives me a flashback to the last time I undressed in front of him. As we clean each other off with soap and water in the sinks, I force myself to not touch him in the way I want to. My nipples harden beneath the paper towels when he dabs me dry.

Malakai kneels next to his crumpled jeans to pull my panties out of the pocket. His dark eyes look up at me as he clears his throat. "I didn't want M—" a sob tries to escape, "anyone to ask about them."

My sadness about Mommy and Daddy is hiding behind a thick black fog. Every time I think I know what I'm feeling, the numbness gobbles it up. Kai though, he's being crushed. It seeps from his eyes and echoes in his voice. Seeing him like this hurts me more than my own emotions. The second after his clean shirt slides over his torso, my arms tighten around it. I hate that I can't take this away or fix this for him. Nothing I say or do will make this better.

"We should go," he murmurs with a broken-hearted sigh.

Uncle Bennett is waiting for us in the basement. "Later tonight we'll come back to finish up. Now though, we need to get to the house and call the police."

He never told us how they died. Just that they had. "What happened?"

The ceiling holds his gaze until he finally meets my eyes. "Micah and Azalea had dinner plans with Mr. and Mrs. Westbrook a few hours ago. The Westbrooks got worried when they didn't show up or answer any calls. There wasn't a response at the house either, so they called me."

"You found them?" Kai asks. Uncle Bennett looks like he might break down at any minute when he nods.

Frustration jerks my lips into a frown as I cross my arms. "I meant *how* did they die?"

They both look at me as if I've grown horns like Princess Sparkle. "Are you sure you want me to tell you right now? It's truly horrible."

While Malakai's eyes are begging me not to push this, I have to know. "Yes."

Uncle Bennett glances between us, opening his mouth three times before any actual words come out. "Azalea's throat was cut. Micah had been injected with something—most likely formaldehyde. It looked a lot like a murder-suicide."

Usually when I get angry, I feel hot enough to spontaneously combust. This time though, it's freezing. It's so cold that it turns all my organs into icicles. Daddy would never have left us.

This was Mommy.

I push between them both, grabbing Princess Sparkle to race up the basement stairs.

"Adriel, wait!" Malakai misses my arm as he reaches for me. His pleading gets quieter every time my feet land on a step.

The cool night air hits my face the minute I burst outside. Never looking behind me, I cut through people's yards to make my way to the park.

Uncle Bennett must be playing a mean trick on us. She

wouldn't have done this. I know she was sad a lot, but how could she take Daddy too? I don't understand.

"She hated you from the second you were born."

My body immobilizes at the sound of a girl's voice. I search the playground with wide eyes while the swing set chains *clink* together in the wind.

The stars catch my attention, momentarily distracting me from the girl who spoke. They look funny. The stars are... green? Moving faster than normal, they dance together in the sky. I rub my eyes when the girl speaks again.

"It's not your fault. It wasn't hers either. You just aren't the kind of person people love. You're the kind of person people hate."

Whoever this girl is, she's hiding. "Hello?" I call out.

Tiptoeing to the tunnel slide, I check to see if she's in there when she adds, "Except Malakai, your daddy, and us. We all love you."

I spin because it sounds like she's behind me. "Who are you? *Where* are you?"

"I'm one of your best friends, and I'm right here. Come on, if we hurry, we might get to see their bodies."

Movement in my hand makes me jump in surprise. I shift my gaze down to Princess Sparkle who is smiling at me with sharp, pointy teeth. My scream is inaudible, trapped inside my chest. The only thing I can do is stare. Holding my breath, I lift her up.

I'm not sure what I'm seeing.

She's different than she was minutes ago. Her plastic doll face has morphed into skin, moving like a person's. The horns burrowed deep into her forehead appear to have grown naturally instead of being hot glued.

"Princess Sparkle?"

I squeeze her with both hands in front of my face. Her teddy bear fur is coarser than it ever has been. The rip on her stomach is now a missing chunk of torn away flesh, allowing me to see her skeleton and pink muscles. Red, swollen skin puffs around the crude stitching on her missing eye. Pretending is fun, but this is…

"Don't squish me that hard. It hurts!"

Howling fills my ears, making me drop her to cover them with my hands. My eyes snap shut. This isn't real, this isn't real, this isn't real. It's just been a scary night.

Smell the flowers, blow out the candles.

After three big breaths, I lift my eyelids, almost kicking her because she's still alive, staring at me and waddling around my feet. When I reach down to grab her, I cover her mouth to stop her from talking. "Don't bite me."

Forcing my brain to focus on the sound my shoes make as they hit against the concrete, I walk the rest of the way home. The stars have returned to motionless white dots, helping to normalize my heart.

Malakai paces next to the hearse in the driveway, his shoulders visibly falling in relief when he sees me. He meets me halfway, taking my hand. "Are you okay?" I hold my breath as I lift up Princess Sparkle, fully prepared for him to freak out. His eyebrows scrunch in question. My stomach feels heavy once I realize she's turned back into a toy. "What?"

She came alive, I just saw it! I open my mouth to explain, but every word falls back down my throat. If I tell him, he'll think I'm just like Mommy.

Shaking my head, I walk toward the house. "Nothing."

His hand grips my arm. "Wait. You ran away before we decided on a story. Tell the police we were at the park when Uncle Bennett came to talk to us, okay?"

"Okay."

There are oodles of strangers behind the door, scurrying through my house. The sight crawls over my skin like bugs. I drop Princess Sparkle on the hall table and rush past the people to go to the morgue, only to find the top of the steps blocked with yellow tape that says *'SHERIFF'S LINE: DO NOT CROSS'* in black letters.

A hand softly touches my back. I spin around to see a man in a worn-out suit looking down at me. "That's an active crime scene," he grumbles. "You can't go down there yet. Are you…?" He looks at his phone. "The daughter? Adriel?"

I don't answer him as my eyes find Kai. The moment he's beside me, he takes my hand and asks, "When can we see our parents?"

A toothpick wobbles between the man's lips. "They need to be taken to the morgue and—"

"Is that a joke? They're in a morgue right now," Malakai snaps.

"The police morgue."

He tells us his name is Sheriff Knewzy. Sheriff Nosey is more like it, asking us a million questions about Mommy and Daddy. I'm happy that Kai answers most of them.

People are here for so long that Uncle Bennett goes to the Burger Bin to get us food. Even though I usually like that place, I only eat a couple fries. I'm not hungry. All I want to do is go back to the church to finish with Mr. Jasick.

It's boring me out of my brain waiting like this. Cuddling next to Malakai on the couch, I rest my head on his lap.

Ding, ding, ding, dong. Bing, bing, bing, bong.

Bong!

Bong!

Bong!

My eyes fly open at the grandfather clock's chiming. *Bong! Bong!* The hysteria lining Kai's whispers has me jolting upright. His gray irises burn with panic.

"Dad's secretary will be at the church in less than three hours. We have to—"

"I know, okay?" Uncle Bennett glances toward the hall.

"Well, then what the fuck is your plan?" Kai snaps in a low voice.

How many *bongs* were there? I look at the short hand pointing to the 5. The police people are still here? That's very, very bad. Now we'll have to find somewhere to stash the body until we can use the retort downstairs.

Luckily duckily, I know just the place.

"Uncle Bennett, may I please have some ice cream?" My brother and uncle both look at me like I'm bonkers. "I want the yummy bubblegum kind you had in your freezer last summer." I lean forward, raising my eyebrows to hint at what I'm implying.

Realization hits Malakai first. "That's a really good idea," he says with a slow nod, urging Uncle Bennett to agree.

When it finally clicks in to his skull, his eyes widen and his mouth forms an O. I look to Malakai when Uncle Bennett stands to pull his car keys out of his pocket. Where the heck does he think we're going to put Mr. Jasick? In his trunk?

He hands Kai the keys. "Meet me in the car. I just want to tell them we're leaving."

"I'm going to get Scabecca first."

Uncle Bennett raises an eyebrow at Malakai, who waves him off. "Her doll."

Hurrying up the stairs, I snatch her off the shelf. My shoes pound on the wooden steps as I run outside. I don't like being here with all these people I don't know.

Safe in the car away from listening ears, Uncle Bennett scoffs with a dry chuckle. "We are so fucked."

"We're not fucked," Kai says. "We just have to be smart about it and keep our shit together." Uncle Bennett stays silent, so he snaps, "All right?"

He glances in his side mirror. "Yeah, I got it."

"Stop by your place first. I didn't get anything to clean with, so we'll have to work with whatever you have."

With bleach, trash bags, and rags packed in his trunk, we are finally ready to go back to the church. I buckle Scabecca next to me in the back seat, watching Kai's reflection in the passenger window. His face creases as he loses himself in whatever thoughts he's having. I wish so badly I could be in his mind to feel the things he does.

The second Uncle Bennett shifts the car into park, Malakai jumps out, running to the trunk for the supplies. I have to jog every few steps to keep up with him as he rushes to the church basement. His urgency is relevant. We need to have the body gone and this place spotless in less than two hours.

Scabecca lies next to me as I kneel on the concrete to scrub at the stray blood splatter with bleach. Blood puddles in spots on the plastic that need to be soaked up.

Uncle Bennett is completely useless. He just stands in the corner dry heaving. I don't understand his problem. He works at a *mortuary*, for goodness sake.

After one last inspection, I feel a lot better that at least the cleaning part is done. I set Scabecca on top of the body bag, giving me use of both hands to help lift the overweight cadaver.

As we struggle to carry it up the stairs, Uncle Bennett groans, "I can't believe I'm actually doing this." The corpse's timing is perfect when it chooses this moment to release gasses, letting out a moaning sound. In his shock, loses his grip on the body, almost dropping it. "Goddamn it."

It takes forever for us to get him out of the church. All three of us grunt with the final shove that stuffs Mr. Jasick in the trunk. Kai runs back inside for the trash bags, and I look up at my uncle, wiping my hands on my skirt. "There. Almost done. See? That wasn't so bad." He just glares at me, so I climb in the back seat with Scabecca to wait.

While it makes me a little nervous to drive with a body this way, Uncle Bennett is a skittish ball of anxiety. He grips the steering wheel so hard his knuckles are white the entire drive back to his house. Every two seconds, he looks at the rearview mirror. Even with Malakai trying to reiterate that we'll be fine, his shoulders don't relax once.

His garage sits catty-corner to his house, allowing him to park in between. Malakai's hand rubs across my back as we follow Uncle Bennett inside the garage to the large, black chest freezer. White clouds puff up into the air when the door is lifted.

"Do you know how many Omaha Steaks I have in here?"

Kai rolls his eyes. "Your meat collection is the least of my worries." Assessing the space, he shrugs. "We can try to fit as much as we can in your kitchen freezer. The rest we'll have to put on top of him."

Uncle Bennett hauls as many frozen steaks as he can

carry into his house while Kai and I finish emptying the freezer. I keep wishing Mommy and Daddy were here to help us. Thinking about them only makes me feel yucky though.

The body bag scratches across the concrete as we drag it up the driveway, quieting once we're inside the garage. On the count of three, we heave him onto a work bench. I unzip the bag to expose the body and help Kai break the rigor mortis. After trying to get him to fit in the freezer twice, we break his neck to finally bend him the right way.

Frozen meat is piled on top of him before Uncle Bennett sets a box labeled 'Photos' on the lid. Trash bags filled with Saran Wrap and our bloody clothes are the next thing Kai hides. He stuffs them in a cardboard box that has 'Video Games' written across the side.

With a sigh, he leans against the wall. "We should get back. Until we can use the crematorium, there isn't anything else we can do."

I tune them out on the way home, humming *Ring Around the Rosie* to Scabecca. She doesn't have a head, but her dress is pretty.

The *Courtenay Family Funeral Home* sign passes by the window. Though there are a lot fewer cars here than when we left, some are still parked in the back.

It surprises me how quiet and empty the house is, meaning they must all be downstairs. Uncle Bennett mumbles he's going to sleep on the couch, disappearing into the living room.

Kai's hands wipe down his face on his way up the stairs. "I need a shower."

A shower would feel nice, except I'm not ready to wash his come out of me yet. Instead, I follow behind him to change into clean panties and a nightgown.

My throat is dry, the absence of moisture scratching the

back of my mouth. Juice sounds yummy. Hesitantly, I walk downstairs, stopping in the hall to glare at Princess Sparkle lying on the table. She hasn't come alive again since earlier in the park. The only thing that makes any sense is that I imagined it. It sure didn't feel imaginary though.

With my juice glass emptied, I return to the hall. Before I even realize that my feet have kept walking, I'm standing in the display room. My fingers trace across the large mahogany casket that's right in the center. It's lined in off-white satin with a fluffy, laced-trimmed pillow.

Daddy always said he wanted to be cremated when he died, but Mommy never told me what she wanted. I wonder if she will be put into one of these. She always said embalming was beautiful; it wouldn't surprise me if that's what she wanted for her own body.

The presentation table the casket is displayed on lifts it up too high for me to climb inside. In the hall closet, I find a step stool that's the perfect height. I unfold it and climb up. It's been a long time since I've been in a coffin. Mommy yelled at me when I was little for playing in them, so I never did it again.

She can't yell at me now.

I lie down, sighing at the comfort of the quiet coffin. It's very cozy in here. Safe. Reaching up, I close the lid. Blackness covers me in a soft, warm blanket. The echoing of my deep breathing is like a lullaby singing me to sleep.

Coffin

Malakai

18 years old

The ice-cold water rains from the shower head, pelting my back in beaded shards. I'm shaking, though I have no idea if it's from the temperature or my sobs.

Both of my parents are gone. Forever.

It's a fact I know, yet I can't help doubting it's true. Or maybe I'm just holding on to the hope that someone, somewhere, got it wrong. I'm irate at my mother for doing this to us. My emotions ping pong between that and the smothering terror for me and Adriel. What will happen to us? Will she be sent to foster care? Am I meant to be on my own?

My chest aches, throbbing to the point that it hurts to breathe. Pushing open the shower curtain, I kneel by the cabinet to search for my knife.

Relief in the form of steel.

The destruction of my skin gives me the solace I crave. Slowly, I regain a steady breath. I dry my face and get dressed before going to Adriel's room. It's empty. Any other night that wouldn't bother me. Tonight, though, it makes my heart drum with anxiety.

What happened with us seems like light years ago. I'm pissed at myself for getting upset with her…tonight of all nights. She isn't in my room which leaves only one bedroom to check.

It's unsettling how I can almost still feel them, as if their energy stained the walls and soaked into the carpet. The bed barely squeaks when I lower onto it. Everything appears the same as it did when they were still breathing. Curiosity spins in my head, wondering what items she kept close to her when she slept. Opening my mother's side table, I pick up the photos inside. They're of me. All of them. A tiny jar in the corner piques my interest. It *tinks* when I move it.

Malakai's Baby Teeth, the label says.

Anger at my mother for not having a single drawing or report card of Adriel's has me tossing the jar down, slamming the drawer shut.

I continue my search for my sister, panic cracking through my bones when I check the entire living space to only find Uncle Bennett asleep on the couch.

Air *whooshes* in my lungs the moment I cross over to the funeral home side. A stepstool sits in front of the center coffin in the display room.

If I wasn't so heartbroken, I would laugh. She always wanted to get in the caskets, but we were never allowed to. Lifting the lid causes my lips to raise in a small smile. Adriel is fast asleep inside, peaceful and free from all the horrifying events consuming our lives right now.

Careful not to wake her up, I slip in behind her. It's a snug fit, yet calming to be so close and confined with her this way. I need this comfort right now. In this small space, her intensified smell inundates my mind with memories of the mausoleum.

I know I said we could never be together that way again,

and it definitely needs to stop, but right now, it feels like she's the only thing that will keep my mind from going in a hundred opposite directions. The silk of her nightdress is smooth to the touch. Her small breast fills my palm, and she shifts with a sigh the moment I squeeze through the fabric. The taste of her skin on my lips hardens my erection growing against her ass.

Why do I want her so much? It isn't fair that I feel this. I can't control it. Maybe it's my grief or the shock that's making me so confused. Even as I question myself, my hand slips beneath her nightie to touch her panties.

Wet arousal seeps onto my fingers through the cotton. Fuck. I rub faster, waking her enough to earn an erotic moan.

I whisper, "Is this okay? I really need you right now."

Her breathing quickens in little puffs. "I need you too. All the time."

My hair falls in my face as I shift my position to hover over her. Am I really going to do this again?

Almost as if my body has separated from my thoughts, I lower the waistband of my sweat pants before pushing her nightie up to her stomach. I reach between her legs, going more off feel than sight. Guilt tries to claw at me as I tug her panties down, but I ignore it.

I need this.

Either the cramped space or her tight body is making it really hard to push inside. Hurting her is not what I want. I just need one good thrust, then I can ease up.

"Be quiet. We can't wake up Uncle Bennett." She nods while I hold on to the edge of the casket for leverage. I shove, feeling the moment I break inside. A choked cry jumps from her lips, so I cover her mouth. "Shhhh. It's okay."

Two more little whimpers escape before she quiets down

to rapid breathing. I slow, going deeper to truly feel her body encasing mine.

"What are we gonna do, Kai?" she whispers, tenderly pressing herself against me.

I wish I had the magic words, the solution to this huge fucking mess. In truth, I'm just as clueless about what this means as she is.

"I'll do whatever it takes to keep us together. I swear."

Her body stills with her cracked voice. "You think they'll try to separate us?"

I don't have the answers, so I kiss her. She relaxes as the silence settles, the rhythmic sound of our breathing allowing my mind to focus on the euphoria my body is feeling. With my steady pace, a buildup of pressure prickles my skin. The arousal will overtake me soon. I can't exactly come in the casket, and considering I already finished inside her one time too many tonight, I can't do that either. The coffin squeaks with my last few thrusts. Damn it. I have to stop.

Reaching down, I pull her panties away from her body and quickly slide out. I moan into her neck as my orgasm throbs for an abnormally long time, filling up the inside of her cotton underwear. God, I wish I could see what that looks like. After I secure them into place, I yank up my sweats.

She scoots over, giving me room to lie behind her again. "We can't sleep in here. Uncle Bennett finding us wouldn't be good...for a few reasons."

With those words, culpability crawls across my skin. I swear to myself that this was the last time. I can't live with the guilt that comes with this perversion.

She nods without showing any indication of moving. "Just a few more minutes."

I wrap my arm around her waist and blow out a breath. A few more minutes won't hurt.

"Guys! What the hell? This is a twenty-five-hundred-dollar casket!"

I jolt awake at the aggravation in Uncle Bennett's voice. It takes a few seconds for the events of last night to settle back in my memory.

My parents are dead.

I fucked my little sister—twice

And there's a body in my uncle's freezer.

Right now, my mind can't decide which is the most horrifying.

"It's not Kai's fault," Adriel says sleepily, rubbing her eyes. "I just wanted to know what they would feel if they were buried."

My eyes quickly scan over each of us to make sure our clothes are where they should be. Swallowing the lump in my throat, I clench my fists. How could I have let things go so far?

What kind of brother does that make me?

Uncle Bennett's shoulders fall as he waves us on. "Just get out, okay?" After we obey, he inspects the coffin for anything that might show we were in there. Scratching behind his ear, he stares at us like he's about to break down. "The investigators are gone." Relief overflows my veins at being able to dispose of Mr. Jasick once and for all. "Are you guys hungry?"

Oddly, I kind of am. Even with my insides in knots over my parents and Adriel, my stomach feels empty. As much as I want to get rid of Mr. Jasick, doing so on a full stomach doesn't sound like the worst idea.

"I want blueberry pancakes! And peaches and cream," Adriel declares. "I just need to shower first."

For years I've wondered how I can feel this way about her, why I have this abominable desire. Then her maniacal energy will consume me like a storm, and in those moments, my feelings make sense.

Uncle Bennett pours a cup of coffee while we wait for her. The uncomfortable silence sits and decays until finally he says, "Did you know that I'm your Godfather?"

Even though I've heard the term before, I have no real knowledge of what it means. "I didn't. What is that...exactly?"

Endless minutes of him staring out the window pass before he finally answers. "It means that I'm responsible for you. The both of you. However, you're eighteen which gives you more choices than it does Adriel. We need to talk to your parents' lawyer. I'm hoping there are finances in place that will make this easier on all of us." He sips his coffee, and I think the conversation is over until he adds, "I don't know what the fuck Micah and my sister had you kids doing, but it's over."

I nod as Adriel's black Mary Janes stomp down the stairs. She arrives in the kitchen wearing a pink dress with rainbow tights, carrying one of her toys under her arm. Her color splashes across my destroyed life, giving me a hiccup of happiness.

Clapping her hands, she says, "I'm ready for pancakes!" as if this isn't the first morning of all mornings without our parents.

Once we arrive at the Lettleton Pancake House, Uncle Bennett waits until he has his coffee, I have my soda, and Adriel has her cocoa before speaking. "I'm not completely sure how this is going to go, so for now, let's assume your mother left the business to me. Hiring another mortician is a must.

Regardless, I'm going to sell my house and live with you until both of you finish high school. Once you've both graduated, we'll see where we're at." He raises his eyebrows. "Do either of you plan to go into mortuary science?"

"Yes," Adriel replies almost immediately.

I realize that I can do whatever the hell I want. There is no 'family business' anymore. Half the family is dead. They both look to me, and I can't do more than shrug.

"I don't know."

The rest of breakfast consists of bullshit conversation about curfews and who will do what chores until Uncle Bennett pays the check.

Adriel holds my hand, dragging me to Uncle Bennett's Camaro. She's ready to get this finished as much as I am.

Mr. Jasick's frozen body is heavy and a little tricky to get in the body bag, but we eventually get him in the trunk. Too bad we didn't have the foresight to bring the cot and the first call van. Double checking the freezer for any blood or hair, I grab the bags of cellophane and our clothes before meeting Adriel and Uncle Bennett in the car.

As soon as we pull in our driveway, a relieved sigh blows from my lips. Uncle Bennett's shoulders tense the moment he turns off the car at the mortuary entrance.

"So, walk me through this." He rubs his forehead violently before looking at us in the rearview mirror. "Azalea would find people that she thought deserved to die, and you'd what? Just kill them?"

"Yes," Adriel snaps, squeezing my hand so tight my fingers crunch together. "That's exactly what we did. They weren't good people. They were very, very bad. So, walk *me* through this, Uncle Bennett. Are you gonna take care of us or just keep judging us?"

With a deep inhale, he turns in his seat, looking older than I've ever seen him. "I'm not judging you, Adriel. I'm trying to understand this crazy shit. I love you guys. I'm not your enemy."

Yanking her hand from mine, she storms out, slamming the car door and stomping with her doll all the way inside.

He groans as I tell him, "Try to understand, we were always told that what we were doing was holy work. Adriel's always been proud of it. She thinks you're belittling that—making it something wrong."

His disbelieving laugh bursts from his mouth. "It *is* fucking wrong, Kai. Tell me at least you believe that."

"I don't know what I believe at this point." I get out after her, hearing Uncle Bennett shutting his door behind me. Inside, Adriel's eyes blaze in fury as she watches him pass by to get a cot. My soft steps take me to her. "Are you okay?"

"Uncle Bennett is bad and he's mean."

A cold, biting shiver consumes my body when her eyes go vacant. I know her mind is traveling somewhere twisted. "No, he isn't. He's sad and scared. All he wants to do is help us." I nudge her shoulder so she will look up at me. Whispering, I plea, "Please don't do anything to hurt him."

Her sweet smile loosens my chest as she holds my arm, nodding her agreement. "I won't. I promise."

While there are things about her I either don't want to or am not comfortable confronting, I know her willingness to take my emotions into account is significant. And I love her for that.

I kiss the top of her head as Uncle Bennett pushes the cot

past us. We follow him to help move Mr. Jasick. The second we get his body in the cardboard box and onto the lift, I feel much better.

We watch his corpse burn in silence for so long that Uncle Bennett's voice sounds odd when he says, "Do either of you have any idea what would happen if anyone found out about this?"

As if I haven't thought about it a million times. "Not exactly, but I'm guessing it involves life in a cage."

It frustrates me that he's forcing our minds to that, now, with everything happening. Adriel glares at him, nodding toward the ceiling. "I'm going to my room."

She leaves the crematorium, and I step to follow her when Uncle Bennett grabs my arm.

"I need to talk to you for a second." His next words are not what I expect. "You know, I always liked your dad. He kept Azalea tethered. She was a balloon, and he was her string. You and Adriel are a lot like that. You need to keep her tethered. Understand?"

I get what he's saying, yet for some reason, him comparing us to our parents makes me uncomfortable.

"I understand."

Corpse Tea

Adriel

8 years old

"Would you like some more raspberry tea, Ms. Topplebottom?" I pretend she says, '*Yes, please,*' and pour the invisible tea, holding the cup up to her frozen lips. She's lying on one of the embalming tables in the prep room, so I have to stand up for this tea party. I like to play with the bodies Mommy works on because sometimes I want friends that are people. It's easier to play make believe this way.

I take the red lipstick I got from Mommy's dresser out of my dress pocket. Ms. Topplebottom's hard lips make it hard to not smear. With the yellow ribbon from my ponytail, I tie it around a patch of her hair. "You look so pretty today!" I imagine she tells me, '*You do too*!' After tipping the cup against her lips again, I gently dab her mouth with a napkin.

"What the hell are you doing?" Mommy yells, making me drop the cup. "How many times do I have to tell you? This is not a playroom, and the corpses are not your toys! Now, go to your room,"—she nods behind me— "or I'll stuff you in one of the cold lockers and leave you to freeze."

My eyes widen at the threat. She wouldn't really do that…I don't think. Still, I don't want to risk it, so I grab my tea set and run from the morgue before she yells at me more.

Once I'm safe in my room, I look out my window to see if I can find Kai. He's been gone all day. I cross my arms, pouting when I can't find him.

It's so lonely sometimes. I should make a new friend! Kai won me a pig stuffie at the arcade, plus I have the plush spotted puppy dog Uncle Bennett got me for Christmas.

I sit on the floor, using scissors to cut off the heads and tails of both toys. Threading a needle, I start sewing the pig head to the puppy body. The final touch is the curly piggy tail. I smile at her when she's finished. She's so cute.

"Hello, Piggypup!"

Mommy's cries drip into my room, filling up my ears. Sneaking into the hall, I see light shining from under the bathroom door. I wish she wasn't always so sad. Every time I try to hug her, to make her feel better, she pushes me away and tells me not to touch her. The carpet is scratchy against my ear when I try to see between the space under the door.

I hope she's okay.

She screams at someone to be quiet. I don't hear anyone else with her though, and Daddy's at First Bethel.

"Just fucking stop!" she cries.

A loud *crash* makes me sit up to put my hands against the door. "Mommy? Are you okay?" I fall forward when she yanks it open. She reaches down, gripping my collar to drag me down the hall.

"I just need a few goddamn minutes!" Jerking open the closet door, she shoves me inside so hard that I hit my head on one of the shelves. "I'll come get you when I can stand to look at you."

Darkness drowns me when the door slams. I was just trying to help. She cries a lot, and I really want to make her happy. As hard as I try, she just doesn't like me. There's a *click,* so I know she locked me inside.

It gets so boring in here. I wish I had a clock because I know how to tell time all by myself. I don't even need Malakai's help anymore! Pressing my ear against the wooden door, I try to listen for him. He will help me.

My eyes start to feel heavy. Without light, I'm getting sleepy. My knees curl against my chest as I lie under the bottom shelf. Growling in my stomach reminds me of how hungry I am. She got mad at me when I asked her for something to eat this morning, so I haven't eaten since yesterday. At least I know I won't be in here all night. Daddy will be home soon. He'll come looking for me if Kai doesn't save me first. Too bad I don't have Piggypup with me, then I wouldn't be all alone.

A *thump, thump,* makes me sit up. Bright light from the hall floods the closet, so I cover my eyes.

"Are you okay?" Kai's voice always makes my cheeks stretch with my smile.

"Yes. Mommy put me in here to get away from me."

Slowly opening my eyes, I see his mouth drooping in a frown. He reaches down to take my hand.

"I'm sorry. I should have been here—I know how Mom is. I was just excited to use my new camera. Are you hungry?"

At the mention of eating, my stomach flips. "Will you make me a peanut butter and jelly? Mommy yelled when I asked her."

His arm hugs my shoulder as he leads me down the hall. "I'll make you a sandwich *and* chips. How does that sound?"

Ooh, chips! Maybe he'll get me a soda pop too! I rub my tummy. "Yummy! Hey, can I ride on your back?"

He grins before turning around to kneel in front of me. "Hop on."

My arms wrap around his neck as he takes off running down the hallway. It's so fun bouncing up and down on every step that giggles hop out of my mouth.

When we get to the bottom of the stairs, I slide off his back to run into the kitchen. Seeing Mommy sitting at the table suctions my feet to the floor, causing Kai to bump into my back. The second she lifts her head, her face lights up like my Care Bears nightlight.

"Kai! I missed you today, baby."

Rushing over to him, she doesn't even look at me. She wraps him in a big hug, kissing his head. My fists tighten at my sides. Why won't she do that to me? I look over at the clock. Daddy will be home soon. He loves me, and he will hug me.

I won't tell him about being in the closet today, and Kai won't either. She locked me out of the house one time when it was raining, and Daddy found me walking on the side of the street soaking wet. That night, he screamed at Mommy for a long time. He said it was all her fault when I got sick. It didn't do anything besides make her hate me more. She's better at hiding it now and is only mean to me when he's not here.

Kai glances at me over her shoulder. "We're hungry. I'm going to make some sandwiches."

She finally lets him go, flashing me a glare on her way to get her coffee mug. "Your dad will be home soon. Why don't you grab a small snack so you don't ruin your dinner?"

Walking to the fridge, he grabs two bags of fruit snacks, two juice boxes along with a box of animal crackers. Mommy turns her back to me, speaking only to him. "I have some things to finish up downstairs. Come get me when it's time to eat."

The moment she leaves the kitchen, I skip over to Kai for

the snacks. "Let's go eat these in my room. I miss my friends. I haven't got to see them for a long time."

He follows me as I run up the stairs. After dropping the food on the bed, I go to my desk for my tea set. I wasn't done playing when Mommy stopped me.

"Can we have a tea party?" I hold up the tray at his arched eyebrow. "Please?"

He rolls his eyes with a smile and sits on the floor. "You're lucky I love you."

I clap my hands. He's the best big brother in the world. Using the juice to fill up the pink teapot covered in purple stars, I look at the tray holding the matching pieces. "Will you put the treats on the plates?" Once I fill four tea cups with juice, I set the teapot back on the tray.

"Who are the other two cups for?" he asks.

"Our guests, silly! They'll be here soon."

I stand up and walk to my shelf where I pick up Piggypup and Snegasis. Placing them in their spots, I use my manners to introduce them. I make Piggypup *oink* her hello, feeling so good when it makes Malakai laugh. Snegasis is a snake with wings, so I wave him in the air like he's flying. His hello sounds more like a *hiss*.

"It's so fun to have real food and drink. I usually have to pretend."

"Can I ask you a question?" Nodding, I sip my juice with my pinky in the air like a lady. He picks up Piggypup, running his finger over the stitching on her neck. "Why do you do this to your toys?"

I never really thought about it before. "I dunno. None of the kids at school like me, so I create my own friends. They won't fit in anywhere besides with me. Just like I don't fit in anywhere."

His face softens as he tilts his head. "Adriel...you fit in with me. I don't have any friends either. I just don't care. Who would want to be friends with those shit heads anyway?"

I almost choke on my juice. "S-H-I-T heads? That's a bad word!"

A *tap, tap, tap* on the door pulls our attention from our tea party. Daddy smiles at us as I jump up to give him a hug. It makes my body so warm when he squeezes me back.

"Hey there, kiddos. You want to help me make dinner? I got stuff for tacos."

Kai shrugs, but I love being Daddy's helper. Putting Snegasis in my dress pocket, I use one hand to hold Daddy's and the other to hold Malakai's all the way to the kitchen.

While I set the table, Kai rinses the vegetables. Daddy asks, "Did you guys have a good day? What did you do?"

Malakai looks at me, asking with his eyes if we should tell. I shake my head before grinning at my daddy.

"We had a tea party!"

Morgue

Malakai
18 years old

It's cold in here. I wring my hands in my lap as I sit next to Uncle Bennett, waiting for them to come get us. Self-doubt nags at me, making me question my reason for asking to do this.

These past four days since they died have been the longest of my life. It's important to me that I personally verify their bodies. I want to be sure it's true. But now that I'm here, I'm thinking this might be a mistake. I'm terrified to see my mom and dad reduced to meat bags.

My knee shakes violently when a man dressed in blue scrubs meets us in the sitting room. "You can come on back."

We follow him down the freezing hall to a set of double doors. The temperature drops significantly as it tends to do when walking into a morgue. While I'm aware of the other bodies in the room, my focus homes in on only two of them.

Soulless and lifeless, my parents' bodies are nothing more than skin containers, lying on the slabs in front of me. They don't look like themselves. Closer to an idea of them. There's no way to deny the truth of their deaths after this. Spinning on my heel, I shove open the doors to the hall, passing the technician that took us to that godforsaken room. My feet pick up speed, carrying me outside. I don't stop until I'm on the other side of the county medical examiner's parking lot. Tightening in my throat forces me to double over and hold my knees as the world spins around me.

Smell the flowers, blow out the candles.

Uncle Bennett's arms wrap around me, slowing my heartbeat. "I understand what you're going through, kid. Both of my parents are dead and now my big sister..." He swallows. "Can you imagine seeing Adriel laid out like that?" As soon as the terrifying words leave his mouth, he backs away. "Shit, I'm sorry. I shouldn't have said that."

It's too late though. My mind fabricates an image of Adriel's dead, lifeless body on that cold table. Her once supple skin hard and void of color, her beautiful gray eyes turned milky white...

The entire drive home, all I can think about is her dying. The melody of Twenty-One Pilots' *Neon Gravestones* isn't even enough to distract me from the horrific mental pictures poisoning my thoughts.

As Uncle Bennett turns onto our street, he says something about needing to get ready for a meeting in his office, but I'm not really paying attention. I don't even wait for his Camaro to come to a stop in our driveway before jumping out and running inside. I need to see her, hold her and make sure she's still breathing.

The moment I find her, sitting on her bedroom floor, talking to her creations, my heart starts beating again. My legs lose strength, and I fall to my knees beside her. Grabbing her arm, I pull her onto my lap, crying with relief against her shoulder.

I don't know why his comment made me so scared. Even logically knowing there wasn't any reason she wouldn't be all right, it felt like when I have a nightmare. Once I wake up, I need to be sure it isn't real.

"What's wrong?" She turns around in my lap to hold my face, locking me in her gaze.

"I just needed to know you were here with me."

Her lips lift ever so slightly as her hand caresses me over my jeans. "I'll always be with you."

I feel guilty for wanting this so badly after avoiding her all day yesterday and dodging her every kiss. I've been losing my mind thinking about what we've done, but right now, my craving for her touch overpowers the knowledge of how disgraceful this is. I need her more than anything in this moment.

Silky, warm lips move against mine. "Where's Uncle Bennett?" she whispers.

I kiss down her neck with my response. "In his office. He has a meeting."

As she falls open for me, I begrudgingly pull away long enough to shut and lock her door just in case.

Having sex with her has to stop. All of it does. Still, I need to feel her body in some way. She leans back on her elbows, spreading her legs wide to show me her blue panties with a blonde Disney princess right by her pussy. God, I love that she only wears dresses.

"Will you lick me again? It felt *so* good."

I adore how she can pull me back when it feels like I'm trapped. Uncle Bennett was right, except for one thing: When I need her to be, *she* becomes the string to *my* balloon.

I lie on my stomach, grinning at her request and facial expression. Allowing myself to tease her a little, I rub her over the cotton. Her impatient bucking makes me chuckle.

Yeah, she's exactly what I need right now.

Pulling her panties to the side reveals her smooth, pink cunt. My tongue straightens, dipping into her little hole. She moans softly with her toy held tightly to her chest. Little jolts of pain on my scalp from her other hand gripping at my hair has my cock straining in my jeans. I never knew someone's body could taste so fucking good. Two of my fingers fight their way into her entrance as she pushes my head down, releasing a gasped moan from her lips. I pump my hand harder, focusing on my tongue pushing against her clit with repetitious pressure. Her little pussy suctions around my fingers in quick succession, her arousal dripping down my hand.

"You're making me come, Kai."

When her pulsing stops, I remove my mouth, licking my lips. "We can't keep fucking, so let's try something different." Her eyebrows narrow but raise when I yank her panties down her legs. "If I'm not inside you, it's no different than holding hands. It's just two body parts touching each other."

I lay on top of her, lowering my jeans to release my erection. Though her grin tells me she knows I'm full of shit, she goes along with it quietly, gripping her fingers into my back. I spread her adorable, puffy lips, placing my aching cock between them. Thrusting slowly at first, I pick up speed when my tip slams against her clit.

She gasps, "Wow. This is…" Her back arches to push herself closer to me. We rock against each other's bodies, never letting go of our hold on each other. Shuddering beneath my weight, she moans, "I love you."

"I love you too," I breathe. "More than anything."

Her wetness coats me and smears across my abdomen. Tensing, I thrust faster. Her pussy feels so damn incredible. My breathing halts as a warm heaviness settles over my body.

Sitting up, I stroke myself until come streams across her dress and face. Goosebumps spread over my flesh when her tongue darts out to lick the semen from her lips.

I'm so grateful for her, for this. Regardless, just like before, my ejaculation is tied with my contradictory emotions.

The second it's over, I'm suffocated by guilt. It's as if her touch helps in the moment, yet makes it worse in the long run.

As soon as I'm drained, I scoot away from her. "I'm sorry."

"Why?" Her head tilts to the side as she crawls toward me. My come is still on her cheek, glaring at me. "Stop feeling like this is bad. It's not."

"Yes, it fucking is!" Jumping to my feet, I right my jeans. "It's sick. Just like what I did with Mom. I know I'm the one that came in here. This is my fault, and I'm sorry. This has to stop though, Adriel." It feels like I'm using her, and that's the last thing I want to do. From the crushed look on her face, she's feeling it too. "I'm sorry." I say again as if it will make anything better. If I wanted a cop out, I could say that seeing Mom and Dad's bodies fucked me up, but these feelings have been at war long before they died. I need to get away from her and the proof of my deviance dripping down her face. Backing out into the hall, I lamely say again, "I'm sorry."

Returning to my room allows the air to expand from my lungs as I lean against the door. My gaze goes to my bed where I know a knife waits for me.

Without remembering the steps that brought me here, I'm lifting my mattress to wrap my fingers around the blade. I slowly squeeze until pain zaps through each individual digit. Adrenaline lights my veins on fire steadying my thoughts. The steel cuts into the skin of my hand, the blood dripping down my wrist. Reprieve showers over me, and I drop the knife, sighing as I stare at the cuts. Small, deep wounds are on each finger and a long slice reaches across my palm.

Crimson falls in droplets on the floor as I make my way to the bathroom. Avoiding my reflection in the mirror, I wash the wounds and wrap my hand in gauze.

Once I finish using a wet rag to clean the blood out of the carpet, my eyes glance down the hall toward Adriel's room before I shut myself back in mine. Exhaling a deep breath to empty my lungs, I fall backward on my bed. I stare at the door and half expect my mother to walk through. The infuriating mix of heartbreak and relief at the fact that will never happen again tightens my chest.

Freedom and abandonment threaten to swallow me whole.

Hopped To Death

Adriel

17 years old

"He's just sad about your mommy and daddy. He'll get better soon."

The skin around my eyes stretches wide as I whip my head around to my bed. Pegamy is sitting on the edge, swinging her feet and smiling at me. She is one of my more special creations because she was hard to make. Her puppy dog head is plush with a plastic doll body, making the sewing hard. I had to use a nail from the garage to make the holes in her neck, plus she's partly stapled. Since the Pegasus wings are also mostly cloth, I used the same technique to attach them to her back. The dress she's wearing is the one she came in, so I made holes in the back for the wings.

It feels like there's something in my throat. I swallow it down as my heart drums in my chest. Why are they choosing now to talk to me?

In the end, my curiosity at what she will say wins. "B-but what if when he's better, he doesn't want me at all?"

Her wings flap, and she barks before asking, "Do you

want him to be himself or to touch you?" Jumping to her feet, she uses my bed as a trampoline. "Because I don't think you can have both."

She's making me angry. I grab her wings to throw her against the wall by my door. She squeals in pain before running under my bed to hide. What if she's right? Once the sadness about Mommy and Daddy is gone, will he ignore what I know he feels for me? I can't believe that. We loved each other this way before anything happened to our parents. He's not touching me just because he's heartbroken, he's doing it because he wants to.

I huff as I slam my head against the pillow. He went to the morgue today. I almost asked if I could go too. Maybe if I saw them that way, then they'd really seem dead, because in a lot of ways they don't. Part of me keeps expecting Daddy to come in here to ask me if I'm ready for dinner. He isn't going to though. Because of Mommy.

My anger at her boils so hot, my skin beads with sweat. She never loved me. I truly realize that now. I think I've always known. Either I denied it or I wanted to believe it would happen eventually.

Now, I don't care if she hated me because I hate her more. She took my daddy and hurt my brother. My fists ball at my sides as I jump to my feet. Pacing the floor, I search for somewhere to release this black fury bleeding inside me. I wish she would come back to life just so I can kill her myself.

She was the sinner.

The acceptance of this has me storming down the hall to my brother's room. As soon as I shove open the door, I find him taking pictures with his camera.

"They are dead, Malakai. And that's not my fault. It's *hers!*" I've never screamed at him like this, and I'm so angry that I don't care. "Do you not want to touch me because I'm your sister or because I'm not Mommy?!"

As soon as those yucky, mean words leave my mouth, I wish I could suck them back in. He stumbles, looking at me with the most devastating gaze I've ever seen. In two large steps, he's in front of me.

"Fuck you for saying that." He slams his hand against the wall next to my head, and I realize it's bandaged. Oh no...what did he do to himself? My heart aches with the possibility he did it because of me when he yells, "You know how much I hated her for making me do that shit!"

My skin weighs too much to keep standing, so I allow myself to fall to the floor. "I'm sorry...I didn't mean it..."

He kneels down in front of me, but his rage hasn't dissipated. "I don't care how mad at me you are. Don't ever fucking bring that up again." I nod while he scoffs. "Get the hell out, Adriel."

Stumbling over my feet, I do as he says. His door slams in my face, and my eyes burn like I'm finally going to cry.

No tears fall though.

I'm so angry at him right now, and I hate it. I'm also mad at myself for saying that. I'm just frustrated because he's the one who's initiated it almost every time between us, yet he continues to get upset as soon as it's over. It's not fair!

Back in my room, I lie on the floor to look under my bed. I feel bad for being so mean to Pegamy earlier. She was just trying to help. She's still there, but she isn't alive. Her skin has returned to plastic, her fur replaced with fabric.

"Pegamy?" She doesn't move, so I sigh. "I'm sorry, I shouldn't have thrown you. Will you forgive me?" There's no response, she doesn't even blink. Huffing at her stubbornness, I snap, "Fine! Don't talk to me!"

I leave her under the bed and stomp downstairs to the

garage where I pick up Daddy's hammer. Slamming the side door of the garage, I walk down my driveway. There's a farm not far from here where I go to play Foo Foo when I get mad sometimes. I once got caught by the farmer who said I could come over to play whenever I wanted.

He hates mice.

Holding my hammer tight, I keep an eye out for the little critters. "*Little bunny Foo Foo hopping through the forest. Scooping up the field mice and boppin' 'em on the head!*" I sing as I walk through the corn crops. This game helps me because I have to work so hard to bop them. Mice are really fast.

I need to fix things with Kai. We hardly ever fight, and I can't stand it. If I really thought he didn't want to be with me, I wouldn't be so upset. Imagining having to go through these next few days without him makes me dizzy with nausea.

Squeak. Squeak.

I look down to see a little white mouse staring up at me. He wants to play. As soon as I lift the hammer, off he goes. He's a worthy opponent. I'm zigzagging everywhere after him for what feels like forever. My laugh rises up my throat. I think I'm feeling better. I don't lose sight of him, but I think he might win this round. Regardless of the fact that I hate tennis shoes, I'm going to need to start wearing them to play this game. My white socks are covered in dirt while I run as fast as I can. I'm coming up behind him so I jump... Got him!

Bop!

Bop!

Bop!

The next few are not nearly as difficult as the first. With my dress covered in mice guts and my lungs out of breath, I carry my bloody hammer back home. I'm not even going to put it back. Daddy isn't here anymore to ask about it.

The doors that separate the house from the funeral parlor are closed, and I hear people talking. Hopefully that means Uncle Bennett is too busy to notice me and ask questions. I sigh when I see Malakai's door is still closed. He won't want to talk to me. I don't blame him after what I said.

My steps are slow to my room. Dropping the hammer on the floor next to my desk, I pull out my purple sparkly pen, stickers, and glitter perfume. I rip a piece of paper from my notebook.

Kai,

I'm very, very, very, very, very, very sorry. What I said was really stupid and mean. Please forgive me? I don't care if we never do that stuff again, just please don't stay mad at me. I'll do anything to make this better.

I love you,

Adriel

I get a little bit of blood on it, but I add stickers so it's pretty and spray the glitter perfume to make it smell good. Folding it up, I go to his door, kneeling on the floor to shove it underneath. What if it doesn't help? Even though I didn't realize I was purposely trying to hurt him, I was. Because he hurt me first. He said we were *sick*.

What if I ruined things for good? My hands press against the carpet to push me to my feet. As soon as I'm upright, his door swings open. He doesn't look angry. When he sees my bloodied dress, he rushes to my side. I can't help it; I have to smile.

"Are you okay? What happened?"

Laughing, I hug him. He still loves me. "I'm fine, I was just playing Foo Foo."

His eyes narrow before glancing toward the stairs. "Did Uncle Bennett see you like this?"

"No. He's still in the funeral home." My arms fall from his waist as I look in his eyes. "I really am sorry."

His unwounded hand cups my face, and the moment he grins, I get that falling feeling in my stomach. "I know. I got your note." His face tightens, hinting at torment when he kisses the top of my head. "I am too. Come on, let's clean you up before Uncle Bennett sees."

I gently hold his bandaged hand, kissing where the bloods seeps through. "Are you okay?"

The smile he gives me is sad. "I'm fine." I raise an eyebrow. "Really, I swear."

Knowing I'm risking upsetting him, I still ask, "Will you shower with me?" Then I get scared and quickly add, "Just to get clean. I promise."

His shoulders lift with his heavy breath. "You're sure Uncle Bennett doesn't know you're home yet?" I clasp my hands, nodding fast because he's about to say yes. "All right, hurry up."

I don't waste a second as he locks the door. My dress hits the floor the moment he turns around, staring at me in my panties and bra. He closes his eyes, breathing deeply before crossing the bathroom to kiss me. "I know I'm giving you whiplash. Believe me, I'm giving it to myself. It's just..." he groans, "no fucking, okay?"

Excitement tickles me as I nod. "Okay."

I bite my lip, watching his muscles move as he grabs the hem of his shirt to tug it over his head. The tightening is back between my thighs while I kiss his hard chest. He caresses my back and unhooks my bra, the gauze on his cuts scratching my skin.

Our lips touch again as his thumb rubs lightly over my nipple. Since we just made up, I'm feeling braver. Taking his hand, I slide it down the front of my panties. Air shudders from between my lips when he makes his way inside. I grip his shoulders and ride his fingers, pressing my face against his neck.

A protesting whimper falls from my lips when he removes his touch to turn on the shower. He unwraps the red-soaked gauze, letting it drop to the floor. I smirk at the hitch in his breath as I take off my panties.

The warm water hits me the instant I climb in. Feeling his cock pressing against my lower back causes my guts to flutter. He's kissing me the second I spin around. He takes my hand, placing it on his erection. I just love how it feels. Soft on the outside, hard as marble on the inside.

When I get a rhythm that he likes, he stops guiding me to squirt shampoo in his hands and massage it into my scalp. I'm in a bit of a dilemma because every time with him could be my last. I want to do it well, make it feel amazing for him, but I also don't want him to finish too quickly. Closing my eyes as he rinses the shampoo, I slightly tighten my grip and go a little quicker.

His groan makes me clench. I stroke fast a couple of times before stopping to rub the tip with my thumb. After combing the cool conditioner through my hair, he washes his own. White suds fall over his closed eyes as he rinses out the soap, bucking his hips between my fists. His breathing picks up, and he reaches out to use the wall of the shower for support. Water drips down his gorgeous face, his lips pressed together to stifle his moans.

"God, Adriel. Why are we so fucked up?"

He's still thrusting as his words come out in a choke. It hurts my feelings that he thinks that. I move my hand faster, kissing his neck when I feel the warmth of his come squirting across my stomach.

Brushing my mouth across his chest, I whisper, "I think we're perfect. It's everyone else who's fucked up."

Deceased Childhood

Malakai
13 years old

I wave at Adriel through the window as she gets into the car. Dad doesn't take me on special outings like he does her. They call it a 'father-daughter date' which is weird if you ask me. They go to fun places, like tonight he's taking her to McDonalds and Sports World. I would have liked to go. I still don't understand why they can't take me. Dad never brings me out for 'father-son dates' which sounds at least six times weirder, but I wouldn't hate having some guy time with him.

He's good to me, as far as dads go, yet I can't help feeling that Adriel is his favorite. I'm probably just overthinking things, he says I do that sometimes. It just seems like he loves her a little more than me. If I'm being honest with myself, though, it's the same with Mom, except opposite. She is an amazing mom to me. I never feel anything less than special when she's around. Then, watching how she treats my sister, breaks my heart. How can she not love her like Dad and I do? Adriel's the most special, pretty girl in the world. I hate that Mom doesn't see it.

What really sucks is I could use a distraction right now. School's been getting worse. I despise the other kids. All of them. Their dislike toward me doesn't make any sense. I've never done anything to make them detest me as much as they do. This weekend is Tony Wallace's birthday party, and everyone got invited besides me.

I huff, going back to my room for my camera before walking down to the morgue to see my mom. I've always loved taking pictures. The world takes off its mask when I look through the lens. When I was nine, I got my first camera from Uncle Bennett. To this day, that was the best gift I've ever gotten. I took photos of everything. My toys, my food, Adriel, the T.V. show I was watching… It was a Cannon Power Shot A550. I just replaced it a few months ago with this one.

Mom is in the embalming room, so I take some shots of her with the corpse. Her head lifts, smiling at me. "Malakai?"

"Yeah, Dad just left with Adriel."

Her smile widens as she nods upstairs. "Perfect. I'm almost done. Why don't you order some Chinese and pick out a movie? We'll eat on the couch tonight."

Yes! We never get to eat in front of the T.V. "Even *The Avengers?*"

"Whatever you want, baby."

Grinning all the way up the stairs, I grab her credit card to order a ton of rice, eggrolls, lo mein, and chicken. We don't ever get to use the T.V. trays. I've always wondered why we even have them. I set up the trays with our plates in front of the couch, pushing *The Avengers* Blu Ray into the player before I put my camera back in my room.

She's still not up yet, so I pour her a glass of wine. Sneaking a sip makes me gag. Gross. How does she drink that? The Dr. Pepper fizzes as I fill my glass, sighing at the taste washing away the bitterness on my tongue. The menu for the movie is flashing Captain America and Thor across the screen when I carry our drinks back to the living room. I snatch up the remote to watch the trailers while I wait for her.

I'm only on the third one when she walks up behind me and kisses my head, telling me she'll be down after a quick shower.

My stomach growls at the *ding* of the doorbell. Luckily, the delivery man doesn't bat an eye at my scribbling her name across the receipt.

Hauling all the food into the living room, I set the chopsticks next to our plates. I'm starving, so I quickly thank Jesus for my food and shovel in my first bite.

She comes down in her long, silk nightgown, her bare feet quiet on the floor. "It smells wonderful."

I grin at her with a mouth full of lo mein. "It tastes even better." Her rich laugh is such a rare sound, it sends a shiver across my neck.

She chews slowly while my food is gone after a few bites. I can feel her gaze on me through the movie until I finally look at her. "What?"

Her fingers comb through my hair as she scoots closer. "You have grown in to such a beautiful boy."

She's staring at me, but she's not looking at me. She's seeing something else. All the Chinese food rolls in my stomach while my throat closes. The hairs on my neck stand up as she shifts to press her lips to mine. Her mouth moves, deepening her kiss and setting off my panic.

My voice shakes along with the rest of me when I whisper, "Why would you do that?"

A smile stretches across her face when she lifts her nightgown enough to straddle me. What the hell is she doing? Her kisses burn my neck while her hands find their way inside my shirt. I'm finally able to get a hit of oxygen allowing me to sob, "I don't like this, Mom. Please, stop."

"Mmmm. I know, baby. I feel it too."

What is she talking about? My heart pounds in my temples when her fingers tug down my sweatpants. My skin tightens over my bones as I tense at her touch. This can't be happening. I shake my head, and she either ignores it or doesn't see the tears streaming down my cheeks. I don't want her to do this! Why does she?

The moment comes that asphyxiates me with terror. I shake my head again, pleading, "No, Mom. Please…" My words and cries are snuffed out when her palm cups my face.

"It's okay, don't be scared."

Her body slides down to connect with mine, murdering my innocence. Tears roll down my neck as my eyes snap shut. I refuse to watch what's happening to me, even if it's blurry through my tears. A layer of sweat coats my skin. Nausea attempts to climb its way up my throat, so I keep my mouth closed tight.

I grip her waist to push her off, but I can't do it. I can't move at all. Whispers of lies and delusions fall from her lips. She doesn't stop. I silently pray that God will send my dad home. My shoulder blades hit the back of the couch each time she rocks her body. Eventually, I know I can't force away the disgusting pleasure I'm feeling. For the first time in my life, I truly hate her.

The war between terror, arousal, repulsion, and heartbreak shreds something deeper within me than I've ever felt before. More than my heart is being pulverized. Even my soul screams with agony when I cry out my release. Her moans force out more sobs.

When it's finally over, she simply climbs off of me. "Do you want some cocoa? I'm making some coffee for when your dad and sister get home."

I wipe my tears and pull up my sweats before mumbling, "No, I have homework."

Up the stairs, I make it to the toilet in time to throw up all the Chinese food I just ate. I refuse to look in the mirror as I rinse my mouth with wash. Going to my room to lock myself inside, my crying becomes erratic. I'm choking. My nails claw at my throat as my head fills with air. The room spins around me, and I trip, knocking my lamp off the table. Ceramic shatters against the edge, sending blue shards sprinkling across the carpet. It's impossible to catch myself. When my shoulder slams against the floor, hot pain erupts across my arm.

Suddenly, my lungs expand, allowing me to breathe again. My gasping is loud in my ears. Watching the blood drip down my arm somehow normalizes my vision.

Smell the flowers, blow out the candles.

The breathing mantra pushes my thoughts to the past. To a time when my mother was safe. Tears drip off my face to the carpet as the memory clouds my thoughts.

The chlorine burns. Mom told me not to open my eyes under water, but I like watching people swim, and I forgot my goggles. This is the first summer I'm allowed to go in the deep end. I use my arms to get far enough to reach the bottom. The moment my feet touch the scratchy concrete, I push off to get back to the surface.

Something wraps around my ankle, keeping me from moving. Looking down, I see Tommy Wallace holding on to me. I kick and flail, but he's older than me. He's too strong for me to get free. My chest burns because I need air. The thumping *of my heart gets faster and faster the longer he holds me. I try to scream, but it sounds gargled.*

Just when I think I'm going to die without seeing my parents and sister ever again, he lets me go. I don't know if I can make it above the water. I push my arms and feet until the cool breeze hits my face. As hard as I gasp for breath, I still can't get my throat to open. Water splashes around me as I fight going back under. The only sound in my ears is Tommy's terrible laugh.

Arms wrap around me as a soft voice whispers, "It's okay, baby. Momma's here. I got you."

I hear myself wheezing. Why can't I breathe? My mom lifts me from the pool, sitting me on the ground. Her hands hold my face. "Deep breaths, sweetheart. You have to calm down."

I try to do as she says, it just doesn't work no matter how hard I try.

Adriel runs up to us in her Powerpuff Girls *swimsuit. "No running!" the lifeguard yells at her.*

Ignoring him, she kneels next to me. "Malakai? What's wrong?"

Words refuse to form, even with my mouth moving. My mom holds my face making me look at her. "Baby, pretend like your smelling flowers. Just a big sniff." I do as she says when she adds, "Now, pretend like your blowing out the candles on your birthday cake." I feel the air flow from my lips and my chest opens a little. "Good. That's good, baby. Again. Smell the flowers, blow out the candles."

After three tries, my heart slows, and I'm finally able to get enough air to talk. "Thank...you."

Adriel's wet eyebrows scrunch with worry. "Are you okay?"

I nod when my mom hugs me against her. "Good boy, baby. Good boy"

I cry harder as I pick up one of the larger shards. When I fell earlier, the pain from cutting my arm loosened my panic. Staring at it any longer will change my mind, so I bring it across my wrist. It almost makes me laugh, the immediate relief it gives me.

Just when I think I'm feeling better, despair wraps itself around my lungs again. It's like everything I thought I knew about her isn't real. She wouldn't listen to me! She just let me cry as she took what was never hers. While it was happening, I wanted my dad to know so he would put an end to it.

Now, I can't imagine ever saying it out loud.

What should I have done differently? I should have screamed or left or *something*. Maybe if we hadn't eaten Chinese or if I had picked a different movie. The Avengers is—*was* my favorite. Now I want to smash it into a hundred pieces. I'll never watch it again.

My skin feels greasy and sticky. I need her grime off of me. Slipping back in the bathroom, I turn on the water, silently screaming when I can't get it hot enough to wash away the filth covering me. My skin is red and scrubbed raw before I finally get out to return to my room. Laying on my pillow, I let the tears soak the fabric.

She gets confused sometimes. Maybe that's what happened. Maybe she doesn't even know she did it. Maybe it'll never happen again.

Please, please, God. Don't let it happen again.

I realize that I'm praying to someone who either doesn't exist or doesn't care. The 'loving Father' my dad constantly preaches about is a myth. Any God that would allow that to happen to me is a sadistic one.

A soft tap jerks my head to look at the door as Adriel's high-pitched voice asks, "Hey, are you awake?" My heart leaps so hard it feels as if it lifts me off my bed and across the room. I nearly knock her over as I hold her tight, my tears wetting the strands of her hair.

"Kai? Why are you so sad?"

I want to tell her, but I can't conjure up the sentences. My legs go weak, bringing me to my knees. Hugging her waist, I cry against her stomach.

She doesn't ask any more questions as her fingers gently stroke my hair, and she sings, "*You are my sunshine, my only sunshine. You make me happy when skies are gray.*"

Mourning

Adriel

17 years old

Mommy and Daddy's funeral is tomorrow. It took the investigators nine days to get them back to us. Uncle Bennett organized everything. He brought in a mortician from Dubuque to prepare Mommy and Daddy's bodies for the service. Even though I've been around lots of dead people growing up, seeing my own parents stiff with death will be completely different.

The mortician that Uncle Bennett brought in is old and grumpy. I glare at him as my fingertips get hot. My anger bubbles up as I imagine how he must have ruined them.

The most important part of my entire job is to recreate the essence of who they were when they still had breath, I once heard Mommy say.

He didn't even know them! How is he supposed to do that? Regardless, when I squeeze tight to Malakai's hand and we walk up to the caskets, I can almost pretend that they're only dreaming. Their cheeks are so pink I find myself waiting for them to breathe.

"They look nice." It's the only response I can come up with, so I'm relieved when Kai answers.

"Mom would have been impressed."

Daddy apparently decided to be embalmed and buried with Mommy. He always did what she wanted instead of what he did. Why should death be any different? She never truly appreciated him. When I realize what he did for her, my hate blazes. She didn't deserve him. In this moment, I decide I will deserve who I love.

Kai...

I know he's struggling right now. Our parents haven't even been gone for two weeks yet. He hasn't touched me once since our shower or spoken of it. He's being devoured by misplaced guilt. It hurts that he feels that way, thinking what we've done is bad and evil. He's wrong. We were born siblings for a reason. I know that. And God doesn't make mistakes. I believe He thought it was so important that we were together that He made sure we grew up in the same home. The only thing between me and Kai is love, and God is love. That can't be wicked or dirty. I just have to help him see through the lies the world tells. He has to see us in our purest form.

As I look up at my brother, I watch the tears roll down his face while he stares into Mommy's casket. Since we're alone, I tenderly touch his cheek, allowing a tear to bead onto the pad of my fingertip. His gaze heats up my skin when I stick out my tongue to taste his sadness.

"I wish I could eat more than your tears. I wish I could gobble up everything you're feeling. I hate it when you're sad."

Suddenly, he's holding me. His head rests against my shoulder as he releases a sound that pretends to be a laugh, but it's really a sob.

"I love you so fucking much. You know that, right?" he cries.

I nod quickly, wrapping my arms around him in a hug.

There's never been a moment in time that I didn't love and completely, truly know him. Yet now he suffers in a way I can't make myself understand, no matter how much I try to. Defiance is his armor, anger his shield. I've only seen him truly break once. Right now, it's like he's about to crumble into dust. He cries so hard, his body tremors against mine. My fingers clench his hair, holding him up and keeping him close.

I have emotions like everyone else. It's only, some of them hide behind a blurry glass. I can sense them; I just don't experience them like Kai does.

He's told me since the beginning that he hated what Mommy made him do. I've known that's how he felt, but it isn't until this moment that I think I'm starting to understand that she hurt him in many more ways than physical.

"Are you happy that she's gone?" I ask.

I think he's mad at me, the way he shoves us apart, composing himself into a glare so quickly. He opens his mouth, releasing a scream. He screams and screams at the top of his lungs. It's so loud that I have to cover my ears. Suddenly, he stops as quickly as he started, his arms falling limp at his sides.

Uncle Bennett rushes into the chapel, panic all over his washed-out face. "What happened?! What's wrong?" he pants.

Malakai looks at him as an enormous grin spreads across his face. A loud, booming laugh breaks through as he doubles over in a fit of hilarity. I don't know what's happening, and Uncle Bennett looks just as confused as I am. When Kai falls to his knees, his breathing starts to even out. I rush over to him to hug him close, rubbing his back with my hand.

His beautiful silver eyes are wet. They meet mine as his voice comes out cold.

"Yes."

R.I.P.

After Kai's, what Uncle Bennett referred to as 'mourning' today, he seemed mostly normal. Just really tired.

I love watching him sleep. His chest rising and falling is mesmerizing in the moonlight. The wooden chair beside his bed gives me a perfect view of his face. He's beautiful when he's awake, but when he sleeps, he takes the breath from my lungs.

Llumi Star, my blue llama with a plush, glittery unicorn horn, sits between my legs. I find myself rocking against her. Kai's hand rests on his chest as my gaze goes to his fingers. I can almost feel them if I imagine hard enough. Spreading my legs, I pull my panties to the side, never taking my eyes off my big brother. Even though Llumi Star's horn is soft and bendy, I'm super slippery, so it's strong enough to slide inside of me.

It's easy to pretend I'm fucking him instead of my toy with his perfect body dreaming right in front of me. I grind against Llumi Star, her soft fur tickling my clitty when Kai lets out a sigh. The chance that he could wake up and find me this way makes me move faster. I bite my lip to contain my moans. With each leg draped over the armrests of the chair, I spread them further.

"Kai," I whisper.

The tingle starts in my toes, working its way up my legs until it's between my thighs. I start shaking involuntarily while I whimper, trying to push Llumi Star deeper.

"Yes, Kai..." I say louder this time. My skin explodes, consuming me in prickling pleasure.

Thud.

"What the fuck are you doing?" I jerk my head to Kai's

bedroom door. Uncle Bennett's whisper is angry as he glares at my position. His lips curl in repulsion before he quietly snaps, "Kitchen. Now."

My cheeks burn in embarrassment as I hurry to right myself and pull down my nightgown. I hold on tight to Llumi Star as I make my way downstairs, finding Uncle Bennett sitting at the table with his face in his hands. I say nothing, taking a seat in the chair across from him. Silence has never made me uncomfortable, but right now, I wish he would just speak.

When he lifts his head, his eyes find Llumi Star sitting on the table. He scoffs, "Do you want to explain to me what I just saw, or would you rather I assume the worst?"

"What do you think you just saw?" I'm not going to tell our secret without being sure he already knows it.

His eyes bulge, and his cheeks puff out with fury. "I think I saw you rubbing your pussy to your goddamn brother! Am I fucking warm?!"

I narrow my eyes at him. Yelling at me isn't going to do anything besides wake up Malakai. "He's my brother, and I love him. I don't feel bad about that."

"I'm burying my sister tomorrow. I honestly don't have the energy for this shit. From now on, you are forbidden to be alone with him until I say otherwise. Now, go to fucking bed."

Though his voice is low, rage punches out in each syllable. He's not the only one that's mad though. I ball my hands into fists before banging them on the table and standing to face him. "NO! You can't do that!"

He jumps up to match me with clenched teeth. "Go to your *motherfucking* room now, before I decide to let the state deal with you."

The knife caddy sits on the counter as I pass to go to the hall. As soon as I see it, a man's voice speaks in my ear.

He's trying to keep you apart! It sounds different from when my creations talk to me, like it's closer.

Over and over a woman whispers, *Do it! KILL HIM!*

Spinning in a circle, my heart picks up speed. There's nobody here besides Uncle Bennett. I glance at the knives again, but shake my head.

I can't. I made a promise to Kai.

Six Feet Under

Malakai

18 years old

Since I've helped Uncle Bennett with funerals in the past, I have two suits to choose from. I don't know how long I've been standing here staring at them, unable to make a decision. Not that it matters, the suit I wear won't alter the fact that my life is about to change permanently.

Adriel hasn't come to my room this morning. I really thought she would have at least checked up on me by now. I have no idea how she's handling things today, and yesterday's freak-out might have made her nervous.

I need her with me through what's sure to be the worst day of my life. Not even my run this morning could clear my head. The floor creaks beneath my feet on the way to her bedroom where her toys stare at me from the shelves with their creepy eyes.

Pounding down the stairs, I continue my search. Food from people sending their condolences surrounds my uncle who looks convincingly put together, sitting at the kitchen table in his suit.

"Hey, Uncle Bennett, have you seen Adriel this morning?" I get a glass to fill it with juice. When I turn to him, I'm surprised by his expression. His face has lost its color, while at the same time it's so twisted up, he looks like he could blow a fuse at any moment. "Uncle Bennett?"

Standing to walk to the sink, he places his mug inside. "We need to have a conversation after the service about your sister." I sway on my feet as my thoughts jump to the worst possible scenario. What the hell did she do? Unable to speak, I nod my understanding. As he leaves the kitchen, he looks over his shoulder and spits, "I think she's in the chapel."

With an hour until the funeral, I pray we have the privacy to discuss what this is about. I walk as fast as possible without breaking into a run the whole way to the chapel. Air rushes through my lips when my feet cross the threshold, and I see Adriel sitting alone on the front row, staring at the boxes that hold our parents. Slowly walking up the light gray aisle lined in teal roses, I take my seat next to her on the pew.

"Are you gonna say anything today?" My voice seems to echo, breaking the dense silence.

Her Mary Jane clad feet swing as she shrugs. "I don't know. I think whatever I have to say should be to them. Not a bunch of people that didn't know them like we did."

That's something that's been bothering me. What I want to say to them can't be said in a chapel. Her not speaking will hopefully make my lack of eulogy less noticeable.

My shoulders tense when I whisper, "Did something happen with Uncle Bennett? He wants to talk to me…about you."

She shuts her eyes as her teeth worry her lower lip. "I don't want to upset you more today."

With my building anxiety, keeping my voice down isn't easy. "It will be worse to wonder. Just tell me."

The torn lace of her three-legged doll's dress worms between her nervous fingers. "Um...he caught me doing something last night."

"What? What were you doing?"

"I-I was touching myself...you know," her gaze falls to her lap, "there...while I was watching you sleep." Slowly, her eyes rise to meet mine. "He says we aren't allowed to be alone together anymore."

My jaw is made of lead as I gape at her. She did what?! What was she thinking? My anger at her for allowing herself to get caught is tainted by the image of what she must have looked like. I hate my body's reaction to her in this moment, my erection growing right in front of my dead parents.

Her hand softly rubs over the bulge in my pants. I shove her off as I nearly fall out of the pew. "Are you fucking serious? This..." I gesture between us, "is way past done."

Even as I storm out of the chapel, I fight with myself. The further I get from her, the harder it is to not go back to her. I feel bad... I mean, I do want her just as much as she wants me, and it's fucked up to act otherwise. Still, we've got to stop this. I can't believe getting caught wasn't enough for her to realize this could ruin our lives even more.

Waiting for the funeral to start in my room is the safest option right now. I go upstairs to lay on my bed, staring at the ceiling until Uncle Bennett knocks on my door and lets himself in.

"We're about to start."

Sitting up, I rest my arms on my knees. "Uncle Bennett?" He tilts his head in question as I blurt, "We don't need to talk about Adriel. I took care of it. Nothing like that will happen again. I swear...You really have nothing to worry about. She's just struggling to process all this."

With a slight nod, he shoves his hands in his pockets. "I hope so."

The chapel is filled with most of the congregation along with a few people Mom had worked with over the years. If they only knew a fraction of the truth about my parents, these seats would be much emptier. I follow Uncle Bennett up the aisle, stopping to nod at the blur of meaningless condolences.

Adriel is waiting by herself on the front row. Now that I've hopefully diverted my uncle's worries, I feel guilty for speaking to her that way, on today of all days. The moment I take my seat, I squeeze her hand between us, sneaking a quick kiss on her fingers.

Uncle Bennett takes his place at the front while I lean over to whisper, "I'm sorry I yelled."

A small smile from her is all I need to know that I'm forgiven. As our uncle thanks everyone for coming, she leans her head on my shoulder. A few scriptures are read, and music is played. When Uncle Bennett begins his eulogy, my composure weakens.

Sorrow creeps up my gut, sticking in my throat to hear him speak about my mother before I was born. I never knew that woman. The woman he speaks of is not the same one that raised us.

He opens it up for others to talk if they choose. Stares burn the back of my neck. They all expect me to speak. As if sensing my restlessness, Adriel scoots closer, holding tight to my hand.

We listen to people speak words that are impossible to relate to. My parents were strangers to me.

Six feet.

That's how far inside the earth they will rot for eternity. They'll fall to pieces as they decompose into nothing. Teal roses are placed on each coffin one person at a time. Sunlight breaks through the trees as my parents' oak caskets are lowered into the ground. Mr. Westbrook, First Bethel's gray-haired associate pastor, begins to pray in his baritone voice, overpowering the orchestra of quiet sobs coming from parishioners. Adriel kneels in her black dress, digging her fingers into the dirt bucket, tossing a handful into each plot. The sound of it hitting the coffins is a shrill ring in my ears.

My mother took everything from me, yet I'm meant to mourn her. She thought her pain was more important than us or the rest of our lives. She's always been like that, I realize. Her feelings were more significant than mine when she made me be with her. She never cared about anyone other than herself. As a result, me, Dad, Adriel, and Uncle Bennett are paying the price.

I need to get out of here. A raven's high-pitched call sounds like it's saying, *Run! Run! Run!* My hair itches my face, so I shove it away, sprinting from the cemetery as fast as possible. I don't stop until I've reached the grassy patch at the other side of the church.

Just like pushing my head above water, once I'm away from the burial site my lungs inflate, allowing me to fully breathe again. I drop to my knees, gulping in the air.

It's over. It's finally over. No more nights of being scared to fall asleep. No more tensing up at every noise in the dark. That fear left a hole that I have no idea how to fill.

Adriel's footsteps come up behind me at a fast pace. "Kai? Are you all right?"

Looking up at her, I take her hand to pull her down next to me. "I couldn't take it anymore."

She lifts my arm to drape it around her before she lays her head against me. "You don't have to. It's over now."

I smile as I brush her hair from her face. "It's over now."

Will And Testament

Adriel
17 years old

"Okay there are a few things we need to go over." Uncle Bennett pulls out a big, white envelope, removing a stack of papers. "This might feel soon, but if we get it out of the way, we can spend our time figuring our lives out now."

I quietly chew on the breakfast casserole someone dropped off. It's super yummy. Kai's cut hand rests on the table. It's finally healed enough that he doesn't need gauze anymore.

"I spoke to your parents' lawyer yesterday, so I'm just going to lay it out there, and if you have any questions, just ask." He clears his throat, his eyes scanning the documents before they flip to me. "For the next ten months, I'm your legal guardian, Adriel. During that time, you are to follow and respect my rules. On your eighteenth birthday, you'll get the twenty-thousand dollars they left you." Turning to Malakai he says, "Since you're already eighteen, you'll get yours once you graduate."

His eyes stretch wide. "They left me twenty-thousand dollars?!"

"Actually, your mom had another nine thousand just for you in a separate account." Kai's face goes blank as his empty stare settles on the kitchen sink when Uncle Bennett adds, "You should know, its purpose was college tuition."

The muscles of Kai's crossed arms bulge beneath his shirt. "I'll keep that in mind."

Straightening the papers on the table, he slides them back inside the envelope. "The funeral home is mine until one or both of you decide you want to take over, whether in part or as a whole." Uncle Bennett's fingers play with the envelope flap before tapping on the tabletop.

"There's something else I want to mention... Your dad once told me he hadn't spoken to his family since before you two were born. I'm assuming you aren't aware of them?"

I look at Kai just as he turns to me. We were always told Daddy didn't have any family. It was never something I thought about.

Our heads shake simultaneously.

"Well, I received a letter from his brother's son. Actually, you did. A private courier delivered it yesterday. He sent his condolences along with three hundred dollars for each of you. I'm using it to open both of you your own bank account. You need to start learning money management."

Wait...we have a cousin? This is oodles of information to process. I want to know why we've never heard of him when Kai asks, "What's his name?"

Uncle Bennett stands from his seat, going to the letter holder to pick up a paper. He hands it to Kai. "Mikkel. His name is Mikkel Courtenay."

Uncle Bennett shifts on his feet, his cheeks turning red

as he changes the subject and stares at me. "One last thing… Kai's more than welcome to stay here as long as he pleases. However, if you pull any bullshit like the other night ever again, he has to leave. Got it?" I nod quickly. He's obviously uncomfortable with this conversation, deeming that an acceptable response. "Okay then." Turning back to my brother, he asks, "Are you sure you want to go back to school already? It's still really soon. Nobody would blame you for taking some more time." Tilting his head in consideration, he adds, "On the other hand, it would keep you from falling behind."

"Yeah, we wouldn't want our dead parents to interfere with our schoolwork," Kai snaps.

Uncle Bennett rubs the back of his neck with an irritated sigh. "I'm trying here, guys. Just tell me what you need."

"Right now, I need to go to bed. I have school tomorrow." Kai stands, walking out of the kitchen without another word.

"If he's going to school," I say, "then I am too. He shouldn't be there by himself."

"I don't know what the fuck I'm doing here, Adriel. Being your uncle is one thing, but being responsible for you two is something else entirely. I wasn't ready for this, so I'm just trying to do the right thing by you kids."

Following Kai's lead, I stand up. "Then don't ever threaten to separate us again. I need him, and he needs me. More than either of us need you."

My bracelets *jingle* as I slip my arms through my pink backpack straps on my way down the hall. Kai's door is cracked open enough for me to peek my head inside. His back is to me, sitting at his desk.

"Kai? Are you ready for school?" He turns in his seat, holding a paper in his hand. "What's that? Mikkel's letter?"

"Yeah. He seems nice. I don't understand why Dad lied."

"Can I read it?" Nodding as I walk to him, he hands me the folded note. It's typed on thick, textured paper.

Mikkel Courtenay
6 West Orleans Ave
Grand Isle, Louisiana 70358
(985) 678-8600

Malakai and Adriel,
I'm sure this letter must come as a shock to you as I doubt you are aware of the existence of me or my family. Your father was my father's brother. We are profoundly saddened to hear of your parents' passing, and we offer our deepest condolences. I understand that you may not be prepared to speak at the moment, but I want to extend the offer to help you in any way I can during this tragic time. Enclosed is a check for each of you. I felt it was the least I could do under the circumstances. Please do not hesitate to reach out at any time. Day or night. I hope to hear from you.
Mikkel Courtenay.

Curiosity itches my brain as I hand it back to him. "Do you want to call him?"

He tosses the letter on his desk before grabbing my hand to pull me on his lap. My heart does somersaults, hoping he will kiss me. I feel like he's been avoiding me ever since our shower, and it's been worse since Uncle Bennett caught me in his room with Llumi Star. His lips softly press against my arm.

"I don't know, maybe in a few weeks. There's enough going on right now." Turning my head to face him, I lean forward. The moment my lips touch against his, he moves away. He doesn't look at me when he says, "It's getting late. We should go." My disappointment closes my throat, locking away any response I might have. I get off him when he moves to stand, kissing the top of my head.

He doesn't want you.

Sick, sick, sick!

He loves you more than anything.

I fight the urge to cover my ears as I walk out his door. Passing my uncle, I frown at him before waiting for Kai in the hearse.

I wish I could turn the voices off. They just confuse me. After he climbs in, I try to see if Kai'll change his mind. "Are you sure you want to go to school? We could always skip and go somewhere else...anywhere else."

"No. School is normal. I need some normalcy right now."

We don't speak about our parents, our surprise cousin, or school. Heavy silence makes me uneasy until he tightens his grip on my hand, raising it to his lips. That makes me smile. His touch always shifts my mood.

It only lasts until we pull into the Lettleton High parking lot though. He takes a big breath, giving my hand one more quick kiss before picking up his backpack and getting out of the car.

This is the last place I want to be. I only came for Kai. Sitting in my seat, I stall as long as possible until I groan and force myself to follow after him.

Most of the day goes by in a blur. It's weird that Bridgett and her coven leave me alone. The strangest part, however, comes at the end of the day.

"Hey, psy—Adriel, wait up."

Turning slowly, I glare at her. "What do you want, Bridgett?" Her clone friends stand behind her. They look so different without sneers twisting their faces.

"It really sucks about your parents...Not even you deserve that."

"Thanks," I deadpan.

"Well, I'm having a candlelight vigil party for them at my house tonight. You and Malakai can come if you want."

I shake my head without giving her a response as I walk toward my last class. I have no intention of going to that...I don't think. Aside from her family being part of First Bethel's congregation, she barely knew my parents. She obviously can't be trusted.

Everything my English teacher says sounds garbled while I watch the clock. All I want is to be back with Malakai.

The final bell isn't even finished ringing when I jump from my seat, hurrying to the senior hall. He's at his locker when I rush over to him, squeezing him with my hug.

"Something bonkers happened today," I inform him. "Bridgett invited us to a party. It's for Mommy and Daddy."

Even his scoff makes me wet. "Yeah, I heard. Fucking stupid."

Holding my hands behind my back, I rock on my heels. "I've never been invited to a party before...and it is for our parents."

He freezes mid movement with raised eyebrows. "You're not seriously saying you want to go, are you?"

I guess I want to more than I thought I did. "Maybe? I dunno... Only if you go though."

Groaning, he slams his locker. "This isn't going to end well. You can't say I didn't warn you."

"Do you think Uncle Bennett will let me use some of the money Mikkel gave me to get an outfit? I want to look pretty."

"You'll look pretty no matter what you wear." Once the comment leaves his lips, his face goes impassive. "Sure, I'll ask."

Draping his arm over my shoulder, he walks me outside to the hearse.

It's so strange going home from school knowing Mommy and Daddy won't be there. Even the smell of formaldehyde is gone now.

Uncle Bennett is vacuuming the carpet in the lobby when we get home, turning it off once he sees us. "Hey, guys. How was school?"

"It was…interesting." Kai raises his eyebrows, stuffing his hands in his pockets. "We got invited to a party tonight."

Uncle Bennett's eyebrows jump in surprise. "Oh?"

"Is there any way we can have some of that money from our cousin to get Adriel a new outfit? She'd like to wear something special."

His hand flies into his pocket. He knows we never do things like this. "Yeah, of course." Pulling out a black, leather wallet, he digs out four twenty-dollar bills. "Will this be enough?"

Kai looks at me, and I nod. I'll definitely find a pretty dress with that. "Yeah," he says, taking the cash. "That's great. Thanks."

With the money in his back pocket, he turns to go upstairs with me right behind him. As soon as he crosses the threshold to his room, I walk up to him, gently resting my hands on his biceps. The muscles in his arms flex under my palms. It's been almost two weeks since he's touched me. It's driving me bonkers. I think I've been patient long enough.

Lightly brushing my fingers over the front of his jeans, I murmur against his mouth, "Thank you for getting me the dress money."

He crushes my wrist as he yanks my hand away. "You have to stop it, Adriel. Me and you? Like this? It won't ever happen again, okay? You need to get that through your head."

Liar! Liar! Lies, lies, lies! A man's voice screams in my brain.

I shake my head to get the voice out, hearing myself growl. He can't keep going back and forth like this! Fucking me when he's sad, turning me away when he's guilty.

You're just like your mommy.

'Fala lala la lala la la.'

I want to scream at the voices to be quiet! How can I think with them jabbering and singing? Ripping my wrist free from his grip, I stand on my tiptoes to get as close to his height as I can.

"Stop acting like I'm the only one that wants this." I stomp to his door, snapping over my shoulder, "We need to leave in ten minutes to get me a dress."

He makes me so mad! If I were any other girl, he wouldn't act this way. The very thought enhances my fury. He's ashamed of me, his own sister, yet if it were some girl he barely knew, he wouldn't hide his feelings for her at all. It doesn't make sense!

I slam the door to my bedroom. The walls shake around me as small, pink lights sprinkle from the ceiling. Why can't I stop seeing this stuff?!

Falling on my bed in a huff, I feel paralyzed when a sluggish voice sounds in my ear. "You need to make him jealous."

I jump up to look around my room, nervous to find the

source of the voice. My eyes fix on Sluma who is using her long arms to swing her way down from my shelf. She's a six eyed, stuffed sloth that wished she was a mermaid, so I chopped off her legs and gave her a purple mermaid tail.

I hear something trickling, like running water behind me. Turning around, I almost fall off my bed. Midnight black liquid seeps from the ceiling, walls, and outlets, quickly filling my room. I want to scream for Malakai. There's already enough liquid on the floor that when Sluma lets go of the bottom shelf, she splashes into it, swimming to my bed.

Using her lengthy arms, she unhurriedly pulls herself up my bed skirt to finally sit next to me on my comforter. She flaps her fin, black droplets landing on my arm as a wide grin fills her face.

"All you have to do is pretend to like another boy at the party tonight." All six of her eyes blink at different times.

My pulse steadies with her slow-paced words. At least she's trying to help me. "How do I do that? I don't really know any other boys."

Waving an arm at me in a plodding way, she giggles. "Easy peasy, bunny squeezy. Most boys will do anything if you offer them your sex hole!"

"What if it doesn't work? What do I do with the boy?"

A knock on the door makes us both look up, Malakai's voice floating across the black ocean surrounding my bed.

"Hey, can I come in?"

My ears burn. He's always just walked in without knocking. Him changing that now brings my frustration out in my voice.

"I guess that's up to you!"

"You have to remind him how much he wants you," Sluma whispers.

Kai sighs and pushes open the door. The liquid doesn't pour into the hall like I expected, instead it stays confined to my room. His shoes disappear beneath the fluid as he walks further inside. My heart jumps up and down in my stomach when he neither acknowledges the black sea around us or Sluma sitting up next to me, tapping her mermaid tail on the bed.

"I don't want to fight, okay? Will you just forgive me? All I'm trying to do is protect us both."

Sluma grins with an approving nod. Pushing off the bed, I hesitantly lower my feet to the flooded floor. I can feel it, but it doesn't soak through to my socks. "Okay, let's go."

When I walk by him, he doesn't take my hand, leaving me to cross my arms all the way to the hearse.

Heriotza

Malakai

18 years old.

She'll barely speak to me, and I can't say I blame her. My constant inconsistency with us has got to be infuriating. I know it's driving me up the damn wall. It still upsets me that she's making this so difficult on me when she knows I'm just trying to take care of her.

I've ached for her touch, tormented until I'm alone in the shower and free to let my mind roam. Feeling her lips around me is something I regret not doing with her. It consumes my every sexual thought. She's pouting right now because she's mad. It's adorable. All I want to do is fuck that petulant mouth. I hate when she's angry with me, but it looks so beautiful on her. My hands clench the wheel, so I don't reach out to touch her plump, pink bottom lip. Against my leg, my erection grows. I try to hide it, thinking of how much this party is going to suck, to kill my arousal.

We were only invited for one of two reasons. Either they actually have some type of a conscience guilting them into inviting the kids whose dead parents are being used as an excuse

I'm praying it's the former.

The moment I park in front of her favorite store, Heriotza, she jumps from the hearse. I follow her inside where she predictably goes to the dresses. She's never been the type to take too long to shop, she knows exactly what she likes. After a few minutes, she has her first choice draped over her arm.

I lean against the wall outside the dressing room, watching her feet under the door. When she emerges a few minutes later, I inwardly groan at the throbbing in my jeans. She's wearing a pastel blue dress with white polka dots. It's sleeveless, fitting tight around her torso with pale pink ruffles trimming along her shoulders down to her waist where the dress flares out. The hem ends high on her thigh, showing her bare legs.

"I want this one," she states, spinning in a circle so the skirt lifts around her. Her yellow panties flash for anyone who is looking to see.

Even as my cock twitches, I snap in a whisper, "Adriel, stop that! I can see your underwear."

Ignoring my scolding, she holds up a finger. "Oooh! I should get matching panties!" Once she's changed back into her clothes, she picks out pink cotton ones and a pair of white ruffled socks. The clerk hands her the shopping bag as I pay, grinning at her lifted spirits. She skips next to me on our way to the hearse. "What do you think it will be like tonight?"

"A lot of drunk, horny idiots is my guess."

"Oh, come on, grumpy guts!" she squeals as she hops in with her shopping bag. "It's our first party! It'll be fun."

Her expectations for this make me nervous. She doesn't always react well to disappointment. "Well, we're gonna find out."

I'd rather swim through glass shards than go to this stupid thing, but she's obviously excited, and I don't need to give her another reason to be pissed at me.

Uncle Bennett has Mexican takeout spread across the kitchen table when we get home. Immediately, she pulls out her dress to show him. "Isn't it pretty?"

"It looks a little short..." She frowns, making him clear his throat. "It's a nice dress, Adriel."

I can hear her feet pounding up the stairs to put her bag away. Seconds later, she's back in the kitchen with a doll. Uncle Bennett piles his plate full of food, shoving a large bite of rice into his mouth,

"Uncle Bennett!" Adriel shrieks. "You didn't even pray!"

Swallowing his entire bite in one gulp he stutters, "Uh, yeah, sorry."

He goes to church most of the time, though I've always thought he saw it as more of a business opportunity. I'm pretty sure he's not one to pray on a regular basis, judging from the way he stumbles through it.

The moment he says, "Amen", Adriel takes three quick consecutive bites. I smile at her eagerness while Uncle Bennett raises a questioning eyebrow. "I have to get ready," she mumbles around her quesadilla.

"Where is this party at?" Uncle Bennett asks.

"Bridgett Matthew's house," Adriel answers.

Wiping his mouth with a napkin, he leans back in his chair. "Just so we're clear, I'm not dumb, okay? I know how these things go. Just be home by midnight, and call me if you drink. Do *not* drive drunk. Understand?"

I nod. "We understand."

It isn't long before she announces that's she's finished, nearly sprinting from the kitchen. After helping Uncle Bennett clean up the food, I kill the next couple of hours with my headphones and camera. When the clock on my phone reads nine-thirty, I drop my head on my desk. I just want to get this over with.

My door hits the wall when it swings open behind me. Turning around, my eyes widen at the vision of her, and my heart pounds with a hard *thud*. She's wearing her new dress with her white socks and black Mary Janes. Her hair is curled, half of it tied up with a pink ribbon. I've never seen her with makeup on before. She's...fuck, she's gorgeous. Small, glittery stickers are scattered by her eyes above her cheekbones.

"Are you ready?"

"Y-you look..." I really am trying to not give her more mixed signals. I just want her to know that I notice her efforts. "Incredible."

Her blushed cheeks brighten further with her grin. "Thank you."

I'm secretly relieved she isn't holding one of her creations. I would never ask her to leave them, they're part of who she is. I just know bringing a toy to a party would give the assholes at school even more ammo to tease her with.

In the car, she bounces in her seat, humming to herself until we pull up to Bridgett's house. Over fifteen cars are parked on the lawn. A huge, hand-painted sign hangs on the front porch with an arrow pointing to the back yard.

PASTOR MICAH

AND

AZALEA COURTENAY

CANDLELIGHT VIGIL

→

Shoving my hands in my pockets to keep myself from touching her, I follow the sound of voices to the back of the house. Everyone must have carpooled considering the human to vehicle ratio. Candles sit on any available flat surface. Awkward greetings are tossed our way as we walk to the beer keg.

"Are you going to drink?" I whisper to her.

She's always had her own sense of morality, and as far as I know, drinking falls into the 'sin' category.

Her blue painted nails are bright against the red solo cup when she picks it up with a shrug. A kid in her grade helps her tap the keg before she brings it to her lips, swallowing a big gulp. The disgusted expression twisting her features siphons a laugh from my mouth while I fill my own cup.

More people continue to arrive. I can't believe there hasn't been a single person that's said something rude. Maybe being orphaned took the target off our backs.

My mom's wine is the only alcohol I've ever tasted, and after my fourth cup of beer, I start feeling a buzzing warmth swarming through my body. Adriel drifts off, wandering through the party to survey our classmates.

Bridgett Matthews, the skank that makes Adriel's high school life hell, stands on top of her patio table with a cup in one hand and a candle in the other.

"Hey, bitches!" Whoops and hollers sound all around me. "Let's remember why we're here before we're too drunk to." Their laughing at her insensitive joke grates on my nerves as she holds up her candle. "For Pastor and Mrs. Courtenay!" Everyone follows her lead, holding their candles in the air. Flickering flames rise toward the sky, spotting my vision with orange dots. "Now let's get our memorial on!"

Yelling extinguishes the silence before someone turns the

music up loud. Looking around for Adriel, I spot her in her blue dress walking into the house through the open back door. Why did she wander off anyway? I thought she wanted to be here with me.

After topping off my cup, I follow her inside. The heavy, oval table in the dining room is littered with food, soda, and hard liquor. It feels like over half the party is in here, judging by the way I have to zigzag around the groups of people to get to the living room.

My eyes stick to Adriel the moment I turn the corner. Nausea threatens the beer I'm drinking when an ire like I've never experienced burns straight through me.

She's sitting on the couch, way too fucking close to Stefan Marks, an asshole who's in half of my classes. I can't hear their conversation, but their smiles say they're flirting. Her fingers fondle her ruffles before she touches his arm, whispering something in his ear. My cup crinkles as I grip the flimsy plastic, forcing myself not to make a scene. It isn't fair for me to stop her. Even though the very thought makes my throat close up, I know she needs to like other guys.

Just not Stefan motherfucking Marks.

She stands up, allowing me to exhale because I think she's about to walk away…until she faces him and lifts her skirt. My jaw drops. Although I can't see them, Stefan is obviously getting an eyeful of her panties.

What the ever-loving fuck?!

My head spins with alcohol fueled fury. I don't know what she says to him, but his eyes widen as he nods. Grabbing his hand, she pulls him off the couch, leading him into a hall.

Yeah, the hell that's happening. I slam back the rest of my beer, dropping my cup on a table as I storm after them. She's not letting that piece of shit touch a single part of her. They're stepping onto the landing at the top of the stairs when I catch sight of them.

"Adriel!" I yell, my voice booming in my ears. They both stare at me as I pound up the steps, my chest heaving. "What. The. *Hell* are you doing?"

Her eyes blaze. She wants this to hurt me, and it does. It motherfucking does. Softly touching his chest, she bats her mascara-painted lashes.

"This is my new friend, Stefan. He wants to see inside my new panties."

Yep. I'm going to kill him.

Stefan's eyebrow raises at me, questioning my response. Being irate is a perfectly acceptable reaction…I think. A normal brother would be furious at this too.

Smell the flowers, blow out the candles.

Forcing my voice to appear even, I say, "Get out of here, Stefan. Then maybe you won't spend the night in the hospital."

He throws up his hands, scooting past her to go back downstairs. "I'm out. Fucking the psycho isn't worth it."

My teeth grind as I clench my jaw. If I wasn't so ready to tear into Adriel right now, he would be paying for that comment. Glaring at her in silence, I ball my hands into fists while Stefan descends the steps. Her stare dares me to say something. I grip her arm, pulling her into the first door I see, slamming it behind us.

I thought I could do it. Will myself to not want her, but I can't. I can't be around her every day without touching and kissing her. And I definitely can't watch her with someone else.

She's been right all along; I desire her just as much, if not more, than she does me. I proverbially throw my hands up.

I'm done fighting the inevitable.

Tombstones

Stefan was easy. He isn't popular and has the reputation of hooking up with anyone. A little flirting, giving him a flash of panties, and the mention of sex was all it took. I just wish I could have seen Kai's face when I lifted my skirt.

I can see it now though, and it's hardened in fury. The rage in his voice is making me tingly. Stefan mumbles something about me being psycho, but I don't really hear it. I'm focused on my big brother, waiting for his reaction. I don't know if it worked or if I just made him mad at me again. Suddenly, he jumps into motion, yanking me into a bedroom.

It takes five seconds to realize we're in Bridgett's room. Her pictures, cheerleading trophies, and pop star posters are a dead giveaway.

"What the hell were you thinking? Stefan Marks?!"

"Why do you care?" I scream. "You don't want to fuck me, so I found someone who would!"

Nearly popping my wrist, he pulls me to Bridgett's bed, tossing me on the edge. In one movement, he lifts my dress to rip my new pink panties down my legs.

"That's bullshit." I reach for them, and he shakes his head before stuffing them in his back pocket. "I've been dying to fuck you again, and you know it." Leaning forward, he rests his fists on the bed next to my hips, bringing us eye to eye. "That's why you've been tormenting me."

His lip raises with a smirk as he stands upright. The sound of his zipper tearing open makes my mind catch up to what's happening. My heartbeat becomes wild as I smile at him.

It's happening! Sluma was right! I jolt at his sudden touch. His fingertips rub up and down my slit.

"You're fucking soaked. This was your plan all along, wasn't it?"

"Yes."

With a scoff, he slides two fingers inside me. "Well, it worked." He pumps his hand quickly, kissing my jaw as he murmurs, "Lie on your stomach and face me."

I do what he says immediately. Biting my lip, I watch him shove his jeans and underwear over his butt. His cock springs free, giving me a rush of excitement at how hard it is. I can't wait to feel it inside of me again. The tip is shiny and a little pinker than the rest. Raised veins decorate his shaft, leading to the small patch of dark hair at the base. He fists his hand around it as my eyes shift up to his.

"Will you…put it in your mouth?"

I've been wanting to do this for a long time. Licking the hole, I nod. His body shivers when something slightly salty lands on my tongue. I trace along a large vein before opening my mouth. The head is silky when I close my lips around it. Sucking hard and fast as if drinking from a bottle makes him moan, so I try to take more in. His pelvis pushes forward, forcing him deeper. He slams against my throat causing me to gag, but I won't let it stop me.

We work together to get a steady rhythm, his hands gripping my head while he groans out his question. "Would you have really slept with Stefan? If I didn't stop you?"

I take my mouth off him, making a *pop* sound. "Ewe, no way. I never ever want to feel anyone besides you."

He bends over, smashing his lips against mine while flipping me over so I'm lying on my back. My legs spread automatically for him. He settles his hips between them, moving his kisses down my neck. Groaning, he thrusts his cock between my pussy lips.

As he lines himself up with my entrance he whispers, "Are you ready?" If I nod any harder, I'll break my neck. With this angle, he's able to slide all the way in on the first shove. "Fuck. You feel so incredible."

He does too.

My hands clasp onto his back while his butt raises with every thrust into me. I hug him tight, pressing my body against his to feel him deeper. He lifts my leg higher to do the same.

"Don't ever turn me away again," I whisper against his neck. "Please."

He shakes his head. "I won't, I swear. I'm so sorry." There's somewhere deep inside that he keeps hitting, and I clench around him. My skin does the tingling thing that tells me my orgasm is coming.

"Harder, Kai. Keep doing that, but harder." The heels of my Mary Janes scrape against his thighs as he grunts, ramming as violently as he can, just like I asked. My body glows as the pink lights that were in my room float around us. I usually hate when I see things, but this time, it adds to my euphoria. Stars dance across my vision, mixing with the lights as I come, making me cry out in pleasure.

"Oh my God! This is so fucked up!" Bridgett's laugh

seems to eject him out of me and off the bed. We both look at her, standing in her bedroom doorway, holding up her phone as if filming.

Kai frantically yanks up his pants. "Please, Bridgett, you can't tell anyone." His expression breaks my heart.

Black liquid pours from her eyes and darkens her teeth as she laughs. "Are you kidding? This is gold!"

Fury and fear threaten to tear me to bits as they fight for my attention. If she posts that or even tells anyone, Malakai will be ripped away from me.

Dead girls can't speak, a soft voice whispers.

They'll take him!

Cut off her fingers, cut out her tongue, do it before your secrets are sung.

I don't know what's happening. Regardless, just like Sluma, these voices are right. Without thinking, I jump from the bed to grab a cheerleading trophy off the shelf. Swinging the base against her head, Bridgett falls to the floor with a groan. The pink lights shine brighter around me, illuminating the room to the point it's almost blinding. My arm pulls back behind my head, preparing to land another blow, when Kai's hand grasps my wrist.

"What are you doing?!" he screams.

"She's gonna tell!" There are times I almost think I'll be able to cry, and this is one of those times. "You'll be taken away."

"So, you just jump right to killing her?!" Bridgett shifts on the floor, holding her head as she cries black tears. He tugs on my arm, pulling me from the room. "Come on, we've gotta get out of here."

I fight to get free from his grip. "What about the phone?"

Just then, Bridgett's boyfriend, Gavin Guerin, appears

in the doorway. "Whoa! What happened?!" I'm on my knees, scanning the floor trying to find her phone, when Kai grabs my arm, using Gavin's distraction with Bridgett to get us out of her room. He doesn't say anything to me or anyone else as he drags me through the house and out to the hearse.

Once he peels out of the yard and we're back on the road he barks at me, "I can't believe you tried to bash in Bridgett's brain! What the shit was that?"

"She's mean and evil!" I scream. "She wants to hurt us!"

"She's not fucking evil, Adriel, she's just a bitch. You have to stop this. Family nights are over. I can't constantly be worried your gonna kill every goddamn person that pisses you off!"

I don't know why he's so mad at me. I was just trying to protect us. If she shares that video, everyone will know, and the only person left that matters to me will be gone.

"I just don't want to lose you."

He sighs, taking my hand. "I know."

"What do we do if she shares that video?"

Groaning, he scratches his eye. "I have no idea."

He's not driving in the right direction to go home. It isn't until he turns on Corbillard Street that I realize he's heading to the church. "Why are we going to First Bethel?"

"Because we're gonna tell Mom and Dad. About us."

What good is that gonna do? "But...they're dead."

The hearse pulls right in front of the cemetery. "I need this, Adriel, all right?"

Sitting in the front seat for a moment, I watch him make his way through the plots. I don't know why he thinks this is important. Regardless, since he does, I do too. I join Kai at our parents' resting place where he's already kneeling.

"You fucking bitch!" he screams at our mother's

tombstone, making me jump at his unexpected outburst. "How could you do this to us?!" Lowering next to him, I put my hand on his back. His fingers clench in the dirt beneath him as he yells at our father's grave, "Now do you know what she was doing?! She fucked me up so much that the only girl I want is my own goddamn sister!"

His words freeze me solid. My chest hurts. He hates his feelings for me. It despises him that he loves me, that he desires me. I'm a sickness to him, a disease. It makes me wonder if Mommy hadn't made him be with her if he would even want me at all. The idea turns my stomach as I jump to my feet.

"I didn't know loving me caused you so much pain." As angry as it makes me that he feels that way, I also don't want to be the same as my mommy. I don't want to be the cause of a single ounce of his hurt. "You don't ever have to touch me again. I don't want you to."

Without Kai, I'll be alone forever. Knowing this makes the tears that refuse to fall burn behind my sockets.

The chilled night air blows my hair back as I run through the cemetery. I pass the hearse and keep going even when I reach the street. Just as I'm about to cut through a backyard, his strong grasp closes around my arm before I'm pressed against his hard, warm body.

His chest raises against my cheek with his labored breathing. "Loving you is the only thing that takes the pain away, Adriel." Cupping my cheeks, he lifts my face to look at him, the street lights casting shadows across his expression.

"Why is this so confusing for you? It's driving me bonkers!"

His laugh carries no joy. "Because the world sees this as wrong."

"The world sees a lot of things as 'wrong.' Do you really *feel* like it's bad, or are you just going off of what you *think* is right?"

His smirk makes me press my thighs together. "How did you get so smart?"

Manslaughter

Malakai

18 years old

I don't get a moment of sleep. Tossing and turning in my sheets replaces the dreams I'd normally have. My thoughts keep traveling to the video Bridgett took tonight. Proof of mine and Adriel's relationship will destroy us. Uncle Bennett will kick me out, not to mention, I have no idea what the legal repercussions might be.

The only way to know if Bridgett posted it is if I break down and create the social media accounts I've been avoiding for years. People treat me like shit at school, I didn't need them doing it online too.

Reaching over to my night table, I pick up my phone. There are definitely sites I hear more about, so I start there. Using my own name would be stupid, so I enter the bogus information that's required to sign up. My breathing steadies after two of the sites don't show anything of us on Bridgett's pages. Once I find her third account however, my heart stops.

The video of us in our most intimate moment already has over one hundred and fifty views. Sweat beads on my burning skin. I cover my mouth, attempting to stifle the bile turning in my gut. So many people watching my darkest secret makes me want to scream. A ton of vile comments ranging from '*I knew it!*' to '*That's fucking gross*' continue to pour in every few minutes.

I'm going to throw up.

My trash can is just close enough to release the sick that spews from my throat. This can't be happening.

Fuck, fuck, fuck!

What about school on Monday? That's if, somehow, Uncle Bennett doesn't hear about this before then. My fingers clench the phone as I fall back onto my bed. Bridgett had been filming for a while before she made herself known.

Once the initial blow of knowing that this is online for all the world to see wears off, I can't stop watching myself giving in to my deepest desires. Replaying the video, my former self moans in pleasure while I feel Adriel's mouth for the first time. I'll never forget how intense that was. The horror of my situation morphs into lust, heating my flesh. My night pants lift with the hardening of my cock. Adriel's little, white, lacy socks and black buckle shoes in the air is one of the sexiest things I've ever seen. Pushing down my waist band, I release my erection. Seeing us together is more arousing than I could have ever imagined. It's pointless to try to deny it. Tonight made me realize that she's it for me. There's never been anyone else, and I don't think there ever could be.

I know Adriel's got issues, but really, how could she not? We've been murdering people with our parents' coercion and blessing for the past four years. The things she's seen… I can't really blame her for her darkness. If I'm being honest, her darkness is one of the things I find beautiful about her. She's humanity at its core. Lust and violence. Yet at the same time, her imagination keeps her innocent. She sees things through a different lens than the rest of us. I'd be lying if I said I didn't want to go to her room to finish what we started earlier. I just can't push our luck with our uncle.

In the video, her face contorts in pleasure. As her back arches with her orgasm, I'm pushed over. My come hits the screen, dripping down my fingers as I moan.

"Fuck."

After I clean myself, I pull up the search bar for the laws on incest in Iowa. I need some idea of what I'm up against.

My stomach leaps into my chest when I read the words on the screen: *Class D felony*. Blood pumps through my veins so hard it *whooshes* in my ears. We could both get up to five years, and that's if the judge sees her as mentally sound. If not, I'm looking at a whole other set of charges.

Oh, God… Tossing my phone on my bed, I push off the sheets. What was I thinking? At a party? My fingers nearly rip the hair out of my scalp as I pace the floor, trying to come up with a solution that doesn't involve wearing a jumpsuit behind steel bars. The more I contemplate, the more anxious I get. It feels like I'm about to have a heart attack. Frantically, I search for my knife, slicing it quickly across my wrist. In my haste, I cut deeper than intended, making blood pour from the wound down my arm.

Shit. In a frenzy, I hurry to the bathroom, cleaning the cut before wrapping it in gauze and lowering my sleeve. I can't go to prison, and imagining Adriel locked away sets my cells on fire. The finality of what we have to do is a cinder block to the chest.

Run.

We have to leave. I have no idea where, I just know we can't be here when this blows up. With the video being online, the police might already know.

Running down the hall as quietly as possible, I push open Adriel's door to find her asleep in bed. She's in a baby doll nightgown that feels smooth beneath my fingers.

"Adriel! Wake up," I whisper. She rolls over, mumbling and rubbing her eyes. "Come on, we have to go. I'll explain in the car."

"What?" She sits up in bed with a yawn.

"Get as much as you can in your backpack. We aren't coming back, so take what's important."

Her voice shakes when she looks to her shelves. "But... what about my creations?"

There isn't time to argue. We can't be hauling her toys around. On the other hand, I know I'm taking her by surprise. "If we don't leave soon, things are going to get very bad. Do you trust me?"

Nodding, she pushes off her blankets to pick up her pastel backpack. She dumps its contents on the floor as I head back to my room. Once my own bag is stuffed half full of clothes, I return to the bathroom where I pack our toothbrushes, some toilet paper, and soap.

Adriel meets me in the hall with her bulging Rilakkuma backpack. "I'm ready. Where are we going?"

Her hand clutches mine as I lead her downstairs. "I have no idea, somewhere away from here."

On our way through the hall, she stops at our family portrait, taking it off the wall. She removes it from the frame, folding it and slipping it into the front pocket of her backpack.

"You get some water and snacks while I grab Uncle Bennett's wallet and keys," I tell her.

Luckily, he has the habit of leaving them both on the counter, and tonight isn't any different. She's still rummaging through the cabinets behind me when my hand wraps around the metal keys. His black leather wallet feels thick between my fingers. I hope it's from money.

"What's going on?" Uncle Bennett's yawning voice stops me cold. Adriel looks to me for guidance while I'm standing here, immobilized. His gaze moves to my hands. "Why do you have my keys?" I can see his brain processing our actions with the tilt of his head. "And is that my wallet?!"

He was cool about the sinners, considering. Maybe he'll help us with this too. "We...we fucked up bad, Uncle Bennett. At the party tonight..." This is really hard to say out loud.

"That's why we're leaving? Because of the video?" Adriel asks.

I nod at her questioning, narrowed brows. "Bridgett posted it online."

Just as she opens her mouth, Uncle Bennett cuts in. "What video?"

With an irritated sigh, she snaps, "The video of us having sex." She ignores his dropped jaw as she turns back to me. "Will they take you away?"

"They could take both of us away for a long time. We'll go to prison. I won't see you for years." I hold my hands out to my uncle. "That's why we have to go. We need money and a less conspicuous car than the hearse."

Shaking his head, he points to Adriel while keeping his glare on me. "I knew she was fucked up, but I thought better of you."

Though I don't think his anger is misplaced, it infuriates me that Adriel has to listen to him talk about her that way.

"Watch it, Uncle Bennett."

He scoffs. "I don't think you're in any position to threaten me right now."

Every minute that passes increases our chances of getting caught. "We're running out of time! Either help us or get out of our way."

Adriel holds my hand to lead me out the door when Uncle Bennett grabs my arm. "You can't spend your life running. This is different from the guy at the church. This was a conscious decision made by the both of you. If there's a video, there's proof. You have to accept the consequences."

Standing between us, Adriel lifts herself up on her toes. "Why should we be punished for something that only affects us? It's not fair!"

He's in her face when he barks, "What about when he knocks you up with a deformed kid with health issues? Does that only affect you?"

She steps back, squinting her eyes, doubting the truth of his words. When she looks over her shoulder, it's as if the empty space behind her is suddenly more interesting than this conversation.

I shake my head. This is all irrelevant right now. He's just stalling. I'm about to walk out when his fist grasps at my shirt. "I'm not letting you leave, Malakai."

My hand wraps around his wrist to get him off me at the same time Adriel kicks him in the shin. He yells in pain, releasing me. She uses his distraction to push him in the chest with all her might, grunting when her palms slam against his body.

Stumbling backward, he has nothing to hold on to. I reach for him and our fingertips touch before he falls away from me. I hear a loud *crack* as his skull slams against the edge of the counter, snapping his head forward. Standing frozen, I watch his body drop to a heap on the linoleum floor.

Moving or breathing is impossible. Adriel runs to me, holding my face and frantically begging for me to look at her. But I can't. My eyes won't peel away from my uncle.

"I'm sorry, I'm sorry! It was an accident! I promise I didn't mean to! Please don't be mad at me!"

Her desperate pleas snap my focus back to our situation. The truth is, I don't have the luxury of time to mourn my uncle. Even though it was an accident, we're about to be fugitives on the run. How many additional years will we get for manslaughter?

I grab her arms, giving her a quick kiss to calm her. "Listen to me. No matter what happens, you can't ever tell anyone about this, okay? If it comes down to it, we're saying I did it." She shakes her head, looking as though she's about to start arguing with me, so I move to our now dead uncle, tucking my arms under his. "Come on, help me move him."

In silent obedience, she grabs his feet. Dragging him down the hall to the stairs, we carry him as fast as we're able.

"Go turn on the cremation chamber," I order.

My uncle's unmoving eyes stare aimlessly. I once read that the brain continues to function on some level for up to ten minutes after death. Is he aware of what we're doing? That he's dead?

"I'm so sorry," I whisper just in case he can still hear me.

Adriel returns, running up the steps to help me lift him. Halfway down, he slips from my grasp. His head slams against the stairs, sending his lifeless body falling the rest of the way down.

"That makes it easier," she says.

Her coldness jars me. Giving her an incredulous glance,

I run to the landing to get him off the floor. We bring him to the crematorium, and it isn't until we finally heave him onto the furnace lift that my anxiety simmers. I don't think we have the time to wait for his body to turn to ash, and I'm not willing to risk it. Once I set the adjustable control system, I take her hand, leaving our uncle to burn.

"We've gotta go. Come on."

Looking over my shoulder one last time, I wish I could tell him I loved him. I never wanted him involved at all.

Blood Lust

Adriel

17 years old

His silence is scaring me. He said he wasn't angry with me about Uncle Bennett, yet he's barely spoken to me since we got in the car. The gas light comes on, and he mumbles, "Shit," under his breath. At the first station he sees, he pulls in, frowning at my clothes. "You're still in your nightgown. Stay in the car."

"Will you get me a Fun Dip? And a cherry soda pop?"

He nods. "Sure."

My finger taps my phone screen as he walks inside. I'm curious how he felt watching the video.

I know what Bridgett's favorite social media site is because she talks about it all the time. The video sits at the top of her feed with hundreds of terrible comments. I want so badly to respond to each of them and tell them exactly what part of their body I want to chop off.

Watching his bottom lift with every hard shove into me tenses the muscles between my legs. Our conversation can be heard as clear as day. I don't like that. That was supposed to be private.

And they're mocking it.

By the time he gets back, I'm ready to scream. It infuriates me that people see us the way they do. They've never liked us, but they downright despise us being together.

"They're wrong." I toss the phone on the console. "We looked beautiful together."

"I know." He picks up our cells. "We need to get rid of these, though." Taking them to the little trash can next to the gas pump, he wraps them in a paper towel before shoving them beneath the other trash.

As he jumps back into the car, he asks, "So, is there anywhere you want to go? Pick a direction."

The first thought I have is our cousin. He said he wanted to help us. Right now, we need it. "Do you still have Mikkel's letter?"

"It's in my bag." Doubt laces his voice. "Do you think that's a good idea? We don't know anything about him."

The possibility of meeting a cousin I never knew existed excites my curiosity. I shrug. "Now seems as good a time to meet him as any. If he won't help us, then we'll be in the same situation we are now, but maybe he will."

With a heavy sigh, he says, "South it is." He rubs my fingers with his thumb to the beat of the low music on the radio. "I took as much money as I could off of Uncle Bennett's credit card and our accounts. It'll have to be enough. I'm worried it'll leave a paper trail if we keep taking out money." He sighs, switching lanes to merge. "I still can't believe Uncle Bennett is dead."

My chest hurts to hear him sound so heartbroken. It's my fault. I really didn't mean to push him; it was more like I felt like I *had* to. I was being screamed at to do it by the people I keep hearing. I definitely didn't mean for him to die.

"How much did you get?"

"Almost eleven hundred. Even though it sounds like a lot, we need to be careful. It won't be hard to burn through that."

"What about the money from Mommy and Daddy?"

"I don't know how to get to it," he murmurs. "It's in a different account."

"I'm sorry you're sad about Uncle Bennett."

His head whips toward me with a frown. "Aren't you?"

Even knowing I should be, I'm just not. I don't really care that he's dead. I only care that Kai is hurting because of it. "I'm sad you're sad." He doesn't say anything to that, so I switch the subject. "Can we change our hair? Maybe I can cut mine or dye it pink!"

"Altering our appearance is a good idea, but first we need to find a different car. They'll be looking for this one."

"How are we gonna do that?"

"I don't fucking know," he snaps. "I've never been a goddamn fugitive before."

Ripping my hand back, my breath catches in my throat. "You think this is my fault."

"No, I don't. I'm just tired. I'll drive for as long as I can, then we'll find somewhere to crash. Somewhere cheap that takes cash without a credit card." His hand reaches over, caressing my cheek with his silent apology. Gently, he brings his fingers under my chin to turn my face toward him. "We'll figure this out, okay? I won't let anything happen to you."

"I know you won't."

We ride in silence for an hour before sleep starts yanking me down. With his hand in mine, I shut my eyes, drifting off to the song playing on the radio.

I feel myself moving, and it takes me a second to remember why. My balled fists rub my eyes before I turn to my brother, who's obviously struggling to stay awake. The sun is barely peeking out, giving everything a bluish tint. Looking at the clock tells me we've been in the car for more than six hours. Kai must be super sleepy.

"Where are we?"

"Missouri. We just passed somewhere called Bowling Green," he yawns.

"Are we going to stop soon? You need to sleep."

"Yeah, I just wanted to get as far as possible. I don't know how long we have until someone notices Uncle Bennett is missing."

We can't stay at just any hotel, so I keep my eyes peeled for something inconspicuous. After another hour on the highway, we finally find a motel that looks so destitute we aren't even sure it's open until the green 'Vacant' sign flickers. It's called *Roll of the Dice Motel,* which is perfect since that's exactly what we'd be doing by staying there.

"I'll be right back."

He disappears inside the lobby while I open my bag. I brought my toe tag book and as many of my creations that would fit with my clothes. They all stare up at me, though none of them are alive right now. I wonder what will happen to the ones I left behind. Taking out Beddy, I watch Malakai jog back to the car.

"It's an hourly rate, so I paid for six—" His eyes shift to my backpack. "Oh my God, Adriel. Tell me you packed more than your toys."

"I did! I have dresses, socks, and panties. Don't be mad. I already had to leave so many behind."

His hands wipe over his face with a groan. "Come on, let's get some sleep."

Carrying our backpacks along with the plastic bag of food

I took, we walk up to the long pathway where the rooms are. He takes out a key, sliding it into the lock of room six. The light buzzes, flickering every few seconds. Either the stained carpet or the water damaged walls have created a mildew smell.

Opening my mouth, I stick out my tongue. "Yucky."

"It's just for a few hours, you can handle it."

His backpack *thuds* when he drops it on the table by the window. Immediately walking to the bed, he yanks back the blanket, sending a big, shiny, black bug scurrying across the stained sheets. I really, really don't like bugs. They are one of the very few things that make me cringe.

His tired laugh warms my skin as he shakes out the sheets. "I know it's gross." He kicks off his shoes, leaving everything else on when he climbs on the mattress. "But I'm too fucking tired to care."

I set Beddy and my bags down next to his, so I can go potty. The bathroom is just as disgusting as the rest of this place. Walking back into the room, I find him already dreaming, his chest slowly rising and falling. I'm not really sleepy since I slept in the car.

The car. We'll need to get rid of it soon. I feel guilty about Uncle Bennett, and I want to make it up to Kai.

Beddy and the keys are all I take before slipping outside. Malakai won't be up for a while, so I should have plenty of time.

Even though I know how to drive, I don't do it very often because Kai always does. After buckling Beddy in with the seatbelt, I start the car. I know the direction we were heading, so I go the opposite way. The sun is out now, stabbing my eyeballs with its rays when I turn right down what looks to be a less traveled road.

"How long are we going to drive? Don't forget, we have to walk back to the motel."

My heart picks up. When am I going to get used to this? Beddy's Barbie body is now real skin, and she's wiggling her toes. She blinks her three beady eyes, waiting for my answer.

"Just a little further."

"Thank you for bringing me. I would have missed you so much!" With a *click*, she takes off her seat belt, climbing up the door to look out the window.

"I'm sad that I had to leave some of the others behind, but you're extra special. You remind me of the first time with Kai."

Giggling, she sits next to the door lock, kicking out her legs. "I remember."

"Did that make you mad?"

"Mad? No, silly! All of us want you and Malakai to be together."

I grin at her. "Why won't any of you come alive for him?"

Her bear head tilts to the side. "Because his brain is different than yours."

"I'm sick, like my mommy."

"Don't say that! You're not sick! You're *special*. Like your mommy."

We drive for thirty more minutes before I feel like it's far enough. Since Beddy's turned back into plastic, this is going to be a boring walk. Leaving the keys in Uncle Bennett's car, I pick her up and skip along the side of the road, kicking the rocks in my way.

It's warmer here than it was in Lettleton. I'm glad I'm still wearing my nightdress because it's thin and feels good when the wind blows.

The loud rumble of a car cracks through the stillness

behind me. I can tell it's slowing, but it isn't until it stops next to me that I get nervous.

A man rolls down the window, his salt and pepper hair sticking out around his leathery face. "Hey there, little thing. Would you like a ride?"

It would be nice not to have to walk the rest of the way. I look to Beddy, who gives me no sign of life. Nodding to the man, I say, "Yes, please."

He pushes open the door of the large, gray car, waiting until I'm buckled up before he says anything. "Are you all right?"

"Yes, I'm just trying to get back to my brother."

"Where are your parents?" As his large fingers change the radio station, I notice movement beneath his tanned skin. I try not to stare at whatever it is that's traveling up his forearm. It looks like there's a big bug crawling around inside his flesh.

"Dead."

When he nods, I swear a small smile peeks out. "I like your doll."

The hand that was just fiddling with the music reaches across the car to rest on my thigh. Gaping at him, I shove his hand away. "Get your big, yucky hand off me!"

His stupid laugh only makes me angrier. "How old are you anyway?" Tilting his head, he considers his question. "Actually, never mind. It's more fun not to know."

The knot is still moving. It wiggles to hide under the sleeve of his striped, button-down shirt, then appears again above his collar to crawl up his neck.

"Let me out."

He pulls over, but when I reach for the silver handle, he locks the doors and squeezes my arm. "Not yet."

The sound of him unzipping his pants prickles my ears.

Reaching into his jeans, he releases his ugly, red erection. It sticks straight up as he strokes it. The moment I try to lift my leg to kick him, he fists my hair. He's unexpectedly strong, so no matter how hard I push against his hands, he's still able to force my head down. The rushing of blood in my ears is so loud it sounds like I'm next to a waterfall, snuffing out the happy music floating from the speakers.

I keep my lips pressed together tight, shaking my head in an attempt to stop this from happening. One hand grips my neck while the other pushes me down. No, no, no!

The restless skin bug seems to be chasing me when it slithers down his stomach to the head of his penis. I keep expecting something to crawl out of his come hole.

My teeth cut the inside of my lips when he slams himself against my closed mouth. I scream around his shaft the second his dick breaks through. He's being so rough! I can't stop gagging, made worse by the movement in my mouth from the skin creature. The bushy hair on his pelvis rubs against my face and itches.

Dirty! Dirty! A woman's voice sobs in my ear.

Another girl screams, *Bite!*

Without thinking, I listen, baring my teeth and chomping down. Blood pools on my tongue as his bellows fill the car.

He's a sinner. You know what happens to sinners.

Since he's more concerned with his mangled genitalia, he doesn't see it coming when I grab Beddy. I shove her legs as hard as I can into his eye, enchanted by his screams of agony. I take a deep breath, the noises coming from him quiet my nerves and sound so nice in my ears. Feeling calmer, I do the same to his other eye. He's a bloody mess, but whatever lived under his skin has stopped squirming.

While he continues to freak out, I search the car for

something sharp. I've heard breaking someone's neck is a lot harder to do than it looks.

Vines with large thorns crawl from the edges of the glove box, bulging until it pops open. Peeking inside, I smile. The vines wrap around a silver pocket knife, lifting it up to drop it in my hand. The creeping plants *snap* as they continue to slither up the dashboard and across the windshield.

He's still wailing next to me as I tap my chin to the beat of the music and think about what to do next. It will be much easier to move him when he's alive. Even though there hasn't been another car since he picked me up, I still need to hurry.

As I reach across him to unlock the doors, he gasps for air between his cries. With Beddy in my hand, I jump out, racing around the car to open his door.

"Come on, get out."

"What the fuck are you doing to me?!"

I think that should be fairly obvious by now. Tugging his arm, I pull him out, and he stumbles to the ground. "Stand up, stupid!"

Hurry!

He can't run because he's blind, so he just lets me lead him to the line of trees about a yard in front of us.

'Make it hurt, make him cry, it's time for him to die, die, die.'

I should have buttoned his jeans because they fall down as we walk, making him fall. "Hurry up!" Sobbing, he forces himself to his feet. Once we're hidden enough that nobody should be able to find him too soon, I stab him in the stomach. The blood feels warm on my skin. "You picked the wrong girl to face fuck."

I wish I had more time to play with him. I don't, though, so I only stab him five more times before finally slitting his throat.

Homicidal

Malakai

18 years old

I reach out to hold her, my fingers finding only empty bed sheets. The sun shines through the threadbare curtains, lighting up the quiet motel room.

"Adriel?" I nearly trip over the blankets in my haste to check the bathroom. The open door reveals the light is off. My blood pumps so hard my vision blurs. "Adriel!"

Sprinting to the motel room door, I swing it open, praying she's just outside getting fresh air. The only thing in front of me is a barren parking lot. Uncle Bennett's car is gone.

What the hell is she doing now?! I know she didn't ditch me, but what if she gets caught or hurt? Or fucking kills someone else?

I slam the door, ripping my hands through my hair as I walk across the room to grab my shoes. Who knows how many people have seen her?

As fast as I can without running, I go to the lobby. The same man from last night is staring at his phone when the bell *dings* at my entrance.

"Hey man, you still have a couple hours left. We don't give refunds."

"No, I'm just curious if you've seen a girl? She has dark hair and was probably holding a doll?"

He shakes his head. "Nah, I haven't seen anyone."

Fucking Adriel. "Thanks."

I can't believe my goddamn little sister ran off with our car. Back in the room, I flip through the channels, hoping I don't find what I'm looking for. The worst part about this is not having any idea how much the police know. We could be way ahead of them, or they could be right on our asses. Which is why we need to keep moving.

With every tick of the clock, my heartbeat doubles in speed. I'm really starting to get fucking scared, and sitting here doing nothing is driving me crazy. I need to go look for her.

Her backpack is stuffed so full. It's partially unzipped, so I'm trying to close it as the door opens. Sunlight streaks across the motel room, illuminating the girl that holds my sanity in her pretty little clutches.

Relief presses against my chest in overwhelming waves. In two strides, I'm in front of her, slamming the door before shoving her against it. Blood streaks from the corners of her lips. As I scan down her frame, I see more scarlet scattered across her nightgown and legs. The doll in her hand looks like its legs were dipped in crimson.

She's always been stunning in blood.

"Are you hurt?"

She shakes her head, dropping the doll to slide her hands beneath my shirt. I taste her mouth and whoever's blood this is, eating her soft moans as I cup her face.

Nipping at her bottom lip, I break our kiss. "Don't ever leave without me again." Her silky nightdress bunches beneath my palms as I push it up her thighs before my hand finds their way into her panties. "You scared the shit out of me."

She's so slippery, two of my fingers easily glide in. Her response to my touch seizes my breathing. How could I have ever denied her? Metallic sweetness hits my tongue as I lick inside her mouth, pumping my arm. I need to know where the blood came from. As I pull away to ask, she interjects.

"I need to tell you something." The way she says that sobers me. I start to take out my fingers when she grasps my wrist. "Don't stop." Rising body heat burns my neck. The expression on her pretty face is unsettling. With one hand inside her, I use the other to caress away her frown. I'm not sure if it's worse when something akin to embarrassment crosses her features. "I got rid of Uncle Bennett's car…I…" Her voice catches as she bucks against me. "Had to walk back. A man saw me," the sound of her moan hardens my cock, yet her temperament sets off every alarm in my mind, "and offered me a ride." Reaching down to stroke me over my sweatpants she continues. "He was a bad man." The further she gets into this story, the harder she fucks my hand. "I'm sorry, Kai. He made me…"

The air leaves my lungs at her words. Jolting back, I look down at her. Fear is not an expression I'm used to seeing on her face, and I wonder if it's because of what she's telling me or what she thinks my reaction to it will be.

The last thing I want her to think is that any of my anger is directed at her when the boiling in my gut makes me scream, "He made you what, Adriel?!"

"I…" Her eyes close as she rolls her hips. "Please don't stop, Kai."

"Tell me!" I can't sit here and fucking finger her with my mind running through horrifying scenarios. Backing away, I clench my fists. If I didn't know any better, I'd think she was about to cry. My arms wrap around her, holding her against my chest to kiss her head. "Are you okay?"

"I am now. He got what he deserved."

Thick, wet spots of blood cover her pink nightgown. I trace my finger through them. At least I know her well enough to know he suffered. "This is his blood?"

She nods. "And his car is in the parking lot."

I can't believe how proud of her I am. She is so much more capable of protecting herself than I give her credit for.

"Did he rape you?" As soon as I ask the question, I know it's an asshole thing to do. I need to let her tell me when she's ready, but I'm about to go mad.

The shake of her head helps shift the tightening of my muscles. Her eyes darken as her posture straightens. "He made me suck his dick, so I bit it off. Well, tried to anyway."

"And he's dead?" If he's not, he's about to be.

"Yes."

With hesitant fingers, she tugs on my waistband. Fuck, we really need to go. Nevertheless, it's important to be who she needs me to be right now.

Taking her hand, I lead her to the table, shoving our bags to the floor. With her palms flat on the laminate top, I walk behind her to push her nightie over her head. I focus on my touch being gentle regardless of my urge to give in to the fury, which takes a lot of effort since my blood feels like lava burning through my veins. My hand pushes between her shoulder blades, bending her over the table and forcing her to stand on the tips of her toes.

It's impossible not to think about what she just went through. Even though we were raised the same, we react to things in very different ways, and I don't know how she's feeling about what happened. I want us both to forget our fucked-up reality for a few moments and just be together.

My lips sprinkle kisses down every bone of her spine. Lowering my pants enough to wet myself with her arousal, I allow her body to consume mine. The pace is slow. I want both of us to feel every second of this.

We don't speak as we listen to the melody of our bodies fitting together so perfectly. My nails leave indentions in her shoulders as I slam her against me harder. Moans and grunts are all that leave our lips until she gasps, "Will you come in my mouth? I want his taste gone."

My sweet Adriel. I squeeze my eyes shut, nodding against her back. After a few final thrusts, I remove myself from her body. She looks so precious on her knees. Taking her time, she slowly licks, kissing softly in between each stroke of her tongue. When her mouth wraps around me, I rest my palms against her head to thrust deeper down her throat. Her little hands jerk me while she sucks with eagerness.

The pressure of my upcoming orgasm tightens my skin, and I push her head harder. "Okay, it's about to come out," I groan.

Her suction and speed intensify, exploding every cell as I empty myself down her throat. She doesn't stop, even when I'm drained, making me hypersensitive to her touch. I slowly take myself out of her mouth, watching her lick her lips as she looks up at me.

"So, you're not mad at me?"

I kneel in front of her to lift her chin. "I'm definitely not mad at you for what that dead fuck did. I just hate that it happened. You can't go out alone anymore. It's too dangerous."

Her lips, still shiny with my come, lift ever so slightly. "I promise I won't do that again."

Standing, I lift my pants. "Take a quick shower. We need to get going."

With her spirits clearly lifted, she picks up Beddy off the floor to bring her into the bathroom. I take an outfit out of her bag before carrying our things to the car she stole.

Opening the unlocked car door reveals a set of keys and a small knife laying on a bloody seat.

Well, fuck. This isn't an ideal situation.

Cadaver Cake

Adriel

11 years old

I am so excited! Today we get to go outside for science class. Mr. Martinez hands out the nature walk bingo cards along with markers. I look at what things I have to find to get a 'bingo' and pick a prize from the box. Some of the stuff will be easy, like the mud or flowers. Things like an 'active nest' will be harder. Last time I looked in the prize box, there was a whole book of stickers that I really want.

Once we all have our cards, Mr. Martinez orders us to get in line by the door. I open my backpack, whispering to Moonfish that I'll be back soon.

My spot is fifth in line because my last name starts with a C. Jordan Davis stands behind me, kicking my ankles. "Stop it!" I tell him, but he just kicks me harder.

"Are you gonna tattle to the teacher, loser?"

I frown at him. I've never been a tattle tell in my whole entire life. We all shuffle outside, walking on the sidewalk in single file as Mr. Martinez leads us to the nature park behind the school.

"Don't wander off too far, and meet back here in thirty minutes. Have fun!"

I look at my card. There's a spider web, a baby frog, a soaring bird, and lots more stuff, so I set out on my hunt. Something makes a *crunch* under my feet. Looking down, I clap with glee to see an acorn on the ground. I use my marker to make an *X* through the acorn box.

Ashley Radcliff's laugh is loud as she gets teased by Martin Brewster. He's holding a bug, pretending like he's going to throw it on her.

"Gross, Martin!" she shrieks.

Walking toward them I ask, "What did you find?"

Martin sneers at me, holding up a big insect with wriggling legs. Ashley leans over to whisper something in his ear, and he chuckles while she runs over to me. I think she's going to hug me, which is weird because she doesn't like me. Instead, she jumps on me, knocking me to the ground.

"Do it!" she screams.

Her shoes smash the fingers on both of my hands as she holds open my mouth. Martin straddles me, hovering the squirming bug between my lips. "Bon appétit!" he laughs before dropping the insect into my mouth. I can feel it moving down my throat, its little legs tickling my esophagus, making me gag.

I can't speak because the moving critter eats all my words. Their laughs ring in my ears while I try to swallow. They finally let me go free, and I instantly get on my knees. Coughing, I dry heave, saliva dripping onto the grass.

Their laughs get farther away. They must be done picking on me for now. I can't feel the bug moving anymore, so I push myself to my feet. It confuses me why they don't like me. Every time I try to be nice, they just get meaner.

All by myself, I walk through the trees. I step over a log, and what I see makes me gasp. Moss! That's one of my boxes! I check it off, determined to get a bingo.

I try to not think about it when they're mean to me, even though it just makes me do it more. Maybe they don't understand how they are making me feel? If I let them see how much they are hurting me, maybe they'll stop.

If not, then they deserve to suffer.

Flipping through my brand-new sticker book, I try to decide who I will teach a lesson to first. While it may have been Ashley's idea, it was Martin who made me swallow the bug. First, I should decide *what* I'll do, then I'll choose to who.

A whole page of pretty rainbow stickers makes me smile. I pick a small one to put on my cheek.

My fingers touch the cold stone of the angel wings on the headstone in front of me. "What do you think, Eliza? Should I make them eat bugs? How would I do that?"

"Talking to Eliza?"

At the sound of Malakai's voice, I jump up to run around Eliza's plot. The gate *creaks* closed behind him as his dark hair falls over his eyes and his warm smile brightens his face. This is the first year we've ever gone to different schools. I hate it. He's in middle school now and gets out thirty minutes later than me.

Squeezing him with all my might, I say, "Do you think she can hear me?"

He kisses my head with a laugh. "I don't know, maybe. If she can, do you think she can understand you? She'd be two for eternity."

I take his hand as we walk to the mausoleum. "I think she understands me. She was two when she died, but she's been an angel for over a hundred years."

Grinning at me, he pulls open the door. "You have a point." It's much darker in here. The dim light casts a shadow across his face while he sits on the floor. "Your rainbow sticker is cool."

"I won a whole book at bingo!" The pages flap when I shake it in front of his face.

His eyes glitter with his smirk. "Sounds like you had a better day than I did."

It makes him sad and mad every time I tell him what the kids do to me, so I try really hard not to.

"Why? What happened?"

He clasps his hands, resting his arms on his knees. "Just the same old shit." He shouldn't say bad words. I used to tell him so, but he never listened. Something flashes across his face, and he raises his eyebrows. "Oh, yeah, I did overhear a crazy story today. I think you're gonna like it."

"Okay!"

"Apparently, there was a guy in Florida somewhere that was murdering people, then serving them in the food at the restaurant he owned. How messed up his that?" He shakes his head with a shudder. "So disgusting."

My eyes go wide, and I clap my hands. "That is a good story!"

Not only that, but now I know what Martin's lesson will be.

Looking into the hole, I wait for him. He's going to have to come out eventually. Daddy said he wants him dead because he's ruining the yard. My fingers tap the cool metal of Malakai's baseball bat.

"Come on, little groundhog. I just want to talk to you!"

The sound of Mommy's van makes electricity crackle through my stomach. It's been difficult finding time to be alone with the bodies the last few days. Not very many people have died lately, and I have to get to them before Mommy embalms or cremates them. She'll get mad if she finds me in the morgue, but she hardly ever leaves.

I sneak inside the front door, taking off my shoes to tiptoe down the stairs. Peeking my head through the cracked open morgue door, I watch as she wheels a woman's body in through the back entrance. She immediately lifts her head onto a block before she writes her information on the white board and attaches a band around her wrist. My impatience causes me to shift my feet as I watch her take off the lady's clothes. Finally, she covers her with a sheet and puts her in one of the coolers.

Since I don't want to get caught, I go upstairs until she leaves the morgue. In my room, I get my crayons and a coloring book. I bring them to the kitchen, coloring pretty pictures while I wait. Malakai is with Daddy cleaning the church, so when I hear Mommy in the hall, I run to see where she goes. Her steps are slow as she climbs the stairs to the top floor. Listening really close, I don't move until I hear the shower going.

I need to hurry.

With a napkin and a pair of big scissors from the kitchen, I run to the morgue, jumping off the third step from the bottom. The cold air from the cooling locker hits my face as I tug the woman's body out a little. Using the scissors, I try to cut off her big and second toe. It's too hard, though, so I have to snap the bones by hand. I'm so excited my skin is tingling.

Once the toes are wrapped in the napkin and the locker door is closed, I'm able to safely sprint up to my room.

I look at the severed toes, deciding the best way to make Martin eat them. I'll need to separate the skin from the bones. Then I can hide it inside something.

When my door opens behind me, I jump, hurrying to cover the napkin. "Hey, whatcha got?" Kai asks on his way over to me.

I open my mouth to tell him, before changing my mind. It will be a much better story after it's done. "Oh, nothing…Will you help me make cupcakes?"

Lunch is usually one of the worst parts of the day. Today, though, I've been looking forward to it since I woke up. Even Mommy screaming at me last night doesn't bother me. She'd said she knew I took the toes, but no matter how mad she got, I wouldn't tell her where I had them.

I swing my pink Barbie lunchbox, skipping to the table that Martin is sitting at. Throwing my leg over the bench, I sit down and open the box.

"I don't want to be seen with you, loser. Sit somewhere else."

His comment doesn't upset me even a little bit because of what I'm about to do. This is making me feel better already.

"You can't have the whole table to yourself. Besides, I'll hurry. I've been excited to eat my cupcake all day."

Opening the plastic Tupperware, I make a show of licking my lips at the strawberry toe skin cupcake. "Mmmm." Just as I'd expected, he reaches across the table, snatching it out of my hand. "Hey!"

His big teeth show with his cackle just before he sinks them deep into the pastry. Half of it is gone in one bite.

I grin at him as a repulsed frown pulls down his face. He forcibly swallows and tosses the cupcake on the table. "Ugh, that's nasty. What the hell is in that?"

Lacing my fingers, I lean forward, keeping my voice low. "That was really mean of you to make me eat that bug. So, I made you eat something yucky too." His eyes widen in question. I can't tell him without giggling. "It's the skin from a dead lady's toes."

He tries to get away from me so fast that he falls over the bench, unable to stop his vomit from spewing onto the floor. I stand to leave, picking up what's left of the cupcake.

My smile is firmly in place all the way out of the cafeteria. I'll eat my lunch in the bathroom again.

Cut Off

Malakai
18 years old

"*Bang! Bang! Maxwell's silver hammer came down upon her head. Bang! Bang! Maxwell's silver hammer made sure that she was dead,*" Adriel sings along with the only radio station we could find with a clear signal. "I like this song. I wonder who sings it."

I'm trying to pay attention to what she's saying, but I'm running on very few hours of sleep. We still have a few more days until we get to Grande Isle, and I'm not comfortable with the idea of sleeping at motels the whole way. It seems too obvious if the police are looking for us. Plus, we keep stopping to use the bathroom or eat, so the drive is taking longer than I'd like.

"We need to find somewhere to stay soon. Like an abandoned building or something. I need to rest."

Her eyes flicker with excitement. "Can we do that the whole way to Louisiana? I like that oodles better than staying in nasty motels. This should be an adventure anyway."

I laugh through my exhaustion. She's always been the

type to be animated in her joy. While I constantly fear that she's like our mother, in reality, she's the exact opposite of her. My mom rarely expressed her emotions. Adriel screams them.

We drive through a whole lot of nothing for another fucking forty-five minutes. After crossing the Arkansas border, I'm about to suggest we just sleep in the car when she taps on her window with a gasp. "Hey, look! That might be abandoned."

I follow her finger to a little building set back, away from the road. It's too small to be a house, yet too big to be a shed. Turning on my blinker, I follow the makeshift road that leads behind the structure to a dirt lot surrounded by foliage.

She jumps out, slamming the car door while hollering, "Come on!"

I follow her to the front where we find a wooden, hand-painted sign that reads, '*Connie's Book Café*' nailed to a closed serving window. Using the bottom of my palms, I push up as hard as I can, but it doesn't budge. We walk to the side, both looking through the dirt covered windows. There's nobody inside, and it doesn't look like there has been for a while. Adriel keeps exploring while I try to see through the glass. From what I can tell, it looks like a storage room.

Crack! Crash!

"I got it!" she hollers from the back, near where I left the car. Turning the corner of the building, I find her holding a long, metal piece of an air conditioning unit. She beams up at me as she pushes open a small wooden door. As I step inside, I look down at the hole she made above the handle. It's just big enough for her to slide her hand through.

Three rows of shelves, some labeled, some containing a book or two, are lined up behind the serving window. What I think is a kitchenette sits to my left, and I'll be damned if there isn't a cot on my right.

"This seems like a weird place to have a bookstore."

She picks up the hardcover resting on the 'Children's Fiction' shelf, blowing off a cloud of dust. "It gets kind of boring in the car after a while. Maybe this was for people riding in the car like me." The pages flip beneath her fingers when she says, "I think it's a good idea."

"Obviously not too good or it wouldn't be out of business." She squints at me, so I add, "Besides, there's no one like you." That earns me a grin. There has to be at least six inches of dust covering everything in here. "God, this place is filthy. You were turned off by the motel, how is this any better?" She shrugs as I fall onto the cot, watching dust clouds fill the air. "Well, I don't care either way. I'd sleep just about anywhere right now." Holding the book, she lies down beside me. "What did you find?"

"The Secret Garden. Will you read some to me before we go to sleep?"

I kiss her head as I take the book. "No more than a chapter."

Covering her mouth with a sleepy yawn, she says, "Okay." Her head rests against my chest while I turn to the first page.

"When Mary Lennox was sent to Misselthwaite Manor to live with her uncle, everybody said she was the most disagreeable-looking child ever seen..."

For the second morning in a row, I wake up with Adriel missing. It's either late enough in the morning or early enough in the evening for the sun to add some light to the space, allowing me to see she's nowhere in here. I hear her speaking before I even reach the partially open door. Her voice doesn't give off any hints of danger, so I quietly peek outside.

She leans against the car with her arms crossed as one of her creations, I think she calls her 'Sluma,' is lying on the hood.

Adriel shakes her head, throwing up her arms. "I don't know. Whatever happens, it's worth it to try." After a moment of silence, she frowns. "Don't say that. He won't ever let that happen."

The air turns thin around me, making breathing difficult. There is nobody else around. She always talks *for* her toys, but this is different. With a small smile, she shrugs. "Forever."

I don't know if the tears falling down my cheeks are from fear or heartbreak. It's happening like I've always feared it would. How am I going to protect her without knowing what she's seeing or hearing?

My hand wipes over my face before I walk out the door. "What's forever?"

She jumps away from the car, glancing to her toy as she shakes her head. "I—I was just...um...thinking."

I can't hold back my scoff. She's lying to me now? "Don't fucking bullshit me. Not after everything. What did your doll say?"

With wide eyes, she slowly turns her head toward me. "You can hear her? And see her moving?"

Holding back my sob is becoming increasingly more difficult. "No, but you can, can't you?"

Her face doesn't give away even a hint of emotion when she straightens. "Yes. Ever since Uncle Bennett told us about Mommy and Daddy."

I let the back of my head drop against the wall of the book café. It's only been a couple weeks, and an eventful couple of weeks at that. "Why lie to me? As far as I knew, you didn't do that."

She holds her hands behind her back, and when she

looks at me, her voice shakes. "Because I don't want to be like Mommy. I know you don't want me to be like her either."

I wonder what it's like. To live like that. What she sees and hears is real to her. It's not her fault. She can't help it.

"You're not like Mom. You may have the same...gift, but besides that? You're just you, Adriel." I walk up to her, lifting her up and sitting her on the hood of the car. "Please don't hide things from me." The smile that kills me every time brings her face back to life. My lips find hers, and she responds by pulling me closer. I brush her hair over her ear, leaning in to whisper. "Don't lie to me again, okay?"

Her irises flash like lightning bugs. "I promise."

I still can't believe I slept for nearly twelve hours. At least it allowed me the energy to drive through most of the day today and finally get us into Louisiana.

"What are we going to do about another car?" Adriel asks.

I've been contemplating that since she got this one. "We can't keep killing people for them. Stealing one will just worsen our situation and put the police right on our ass." Not to mention, what are the chances we'll find a car with the keys in it? I don't know how to hotwire a car. Unless I'm missing something, that leaves us with only one risky option. "Maybe we should hitchhike?" As soon as the suggestion leaves my lips, her face darkens. "Shit, Adriel, I'm sorry. I'll be with you this time. I don't know what other options we have."

Sighing at her lack of response, I keep my eyes peeled for somewhere to stay before it gets too dark. When houses begin to pop up, we both see a tall one with boarded up windows at the same time. The driveway is long, wrapping around to the back of the house. With the broken windows, it's easy to see that this home has undoubtedly been forgotten.

"Maybe we can finish breaking the glass to push you through?" I barely get the idea into words when shattering sounds beside me. She's holding a rock, knocking off all the sharp edges. "Hold on, let me get a towel from the car."

After safely hoisting her inside, she lets me in through the back door. The floral wallpaper is ripped in large sections, water stains altering its original color. A few pieces of broken furniture are scattered across the floor, accompanied by trash. I nearly trip on the torn carpet as we make our way up the creaky stairs. The upstairs rooms aren't any better, maybe even creepier than the bottom floor. There isn't a single bed to be found besides a baby crib.

"I like it!"

With a laugh I take her hand to lead her back to the car. "We should get some stuff to make things a little more comfortable. "Why don't we try to find a place to buy supplies before we settle in?"

Every time we get in this car, it makes my skin burn. I can't wait to get rid of it. Since I don't know where anything is or have a GPS, I just pick a direction. It takes about ten minutes to start seeing restaurants, houses and businesses in the town called Cut Off.

I stop at a dollar store, holding her hand as I tell her, "I'll get a few blankets and pillows. You get some food. Not too much though. We need to save money."

One of her creations is clutched tightly to her chest when she nods in agreement, skipping on her way to the food section. Finding the home goods, I choose two of the thickest blankets and fluffiest pillows I can find. We'll be fine without a heater. I didn't get too cold last night with Adriel next to me. Not only are we well into spring, it's also getting warmer the farther we drive.

As I pass several aisles looking for Adriel, I notice a girl in an employee uniform, tapping on her touchscreen. My head spins with the urge to get ahold of that phone. I need to get online. Glancing around to make sure Adriel isn't nearby, I make my way over to the girl.

She looks up, meeting my eyes as her face widens with a smile. "Hi, do you need help findin' somethin'?"

"Actually, I have a really weird question..." I rub the back of my neck, working out a way to ask this without sounding like a freak. "Can I use your phone for a second?"

"You don't have a phone?" she laughs.

"I lost mine. I'm not from here."

Biting her lip, she raises a brow. "Oh, yeah, sure."

I try my best not to rip it from her hand, typing our names along with Lettleton into the search bar as fast as possible. My eyes scan the links until one posted today makes me unsteady on my feet. The stomach acids in my gut turn sour.

Incestuous Iowa Teens Suspects In Murder Investigation

LETTLETON – Police issued an arrest warrant early Sunday morning for Malakai Courtenay, 18, and Adriel Courtenay, 17. The siblings are wanted for questioning in the murder investigation of an unidentified body.

Police arrived at the Courtenay home late Saturday evening after receiving video surveillance of the siblings participating in incestuous activity during a party at a classmate's home. Malakai and Adriel were last seen leaving the aforementioned party.

Bennett Wilkens, who became their legal guardian just days prior, is also missing. Whether he is currently with the siblings is unknown at this time—

"So, how long will you be in town?" My head jerks up at the girl, her question interrupting my reading. She places her hand on my arm. "Whoa, are you okay, hon? You look pale." My heartbeat is too loud to process what she's saying.

I feel her presence even before the sales girl's wide eyed expression overtakes her face. Adriel's energy quivers around me as I look over my shoulder.

She stares at the girl who's still touching my arm as if she can strike her dead using sheer will. That's not what's making my stomach do acrobatics though. It's the way she's holding a large kitchen knife.

Yanking my arm away from the girl's tightened grip, I slam her phone in her hands before I face my livid little sister.

"You know, Kai, if you want to fuck her," she spins the blade with a furious smirk, "I can cut a hole in her neck for you to use."

The color drains from the girl's face, and I'm certain she's going to pass out. Scorching fury rages through me as I rip the knife away from Adriel, tossing it on the nearest shelf. She taunts me with her defiant expression, flaming my temper at her constant inability to keep a low motherfucking profile. I can't keep treating her homicidal tendencies like a personality quirk. My hand squeezes her arm hard enough to hurt her, and for the first time ever, I don't give a damn. I drag her to the front of the store, finding an empty cart to hold our purchases.

"Get your ass out to the fucking car. Do not move one damn muscle, got it?"

Her expression tells me she feels the exact same way I do. She throws the food in the basket before storming outside.

The police are looking for us. There's an actual warrant out for our arrest, and she's going around threatening to stab people.

Haematophiliac

Adriel

17 years old

If I wasn't so irate, the way he's speaking to me might hurt my feelings, but really, I'm just glad that whore isn't touching him anymore. Her shrill giggle hit my spine from across the store. I was already carrying the knife that I found in the kitchen section because after what's happened, I thought it would be good for protection. The moment I saw her touching his body, the weapon sang in my hand.

The need to puncture the life out of her was almost magnetic. He was *smiling* at her, and I know he wishes he could sleep with her. I'm sure he's dying to fuck someone that isn't family. The rotten cherry on top of that horrible sundae is that he protected *her*…from *me*.

"I think he's madder that you made yourself memorable." Ponkey gallops across the dashboard, stretching her pony legs. "That ugly girl will remember you now, for sure."

I shake my head. "She touched him, and he let her."

"It was just on his arm." Ponkey rears on her back legs, so I pick her up.

"Didn't you hear her? She was trying to get him to ask her out."

Ponkey laughs, her monkey shrieks breaking up each chuckle. "*So, how long will you be in town?*" Even though her impression of the girl is horrible, and I'm in a yucky mood, it makes me laugh anyway.

The door to the store opens as Malakai storms through, bags in hand. My smile drips off my face, the rage at his encounter bursting through my limbs. After throwing the bags in the back seat, he slides in next to me, slamming the door.

"What the fuck was that?! Are you trying to get us caught?!" The car roars to life seconds before he swings around in reverse. "We'll be lucky if she isn't calling the cops right now! What the hell were you thinking?!" He roars at me so loud, I can see a vein thumping in his neck.

"Don't yell at her!" Ponkey cries.

"Are you going to fucking say something?" he snaps.

Crossing my arms, I look out the window. "Ponkey says to stop screaming at me."

He scoffs, rubbing his hand over his face. "Well, does *Ponkey* know you just threatened to kill someone in goddamn public?"

With a frown, she squeaks, "Yes, and I also know that you were flirting with someone that wasn't Adriel."

"She said that she also saw you seducing that bitch."

"I wasn't fucking seducing her, Adriel. I was trying to get her to let me use her phone. And guess what? They know about the video at the party, and they found Uncle Bennett. They just don't know it's him yet. The police are looking for us right now."

Thick silence fills my ears. I can't hear the music, or the car engine. I don't even know if he's still talking. Black liquid trickles from the windows, dripping to the floorboards. It rains down from the roof of the car and seeps out from the vents.

I can feel my chest moving up and down, yet I can't suck in any oxygen. What if they already know we're here? Panic rises up my throat, setting it aflame.

"Have they found Uncle Bennett's car?"

A low growl rumbles under his breath. "I might be able to answer that question if you hadn't threatened to poke holes in my internet source."

Ponkey steps across my lap as she asks, "How much longer was the article?"

If there wasn't a lot more there, maybe they didn't know too much. "How much did you have left to read?"

"Maybe a paragraph or two."

His answer allows my chest to expand. "Then I doubt they've found Uncle Bennett's car or the man that picked me up. There would have been a lot more written. We just need to keep going."

Ponkey offers, "Ask him if he liked the sales lady."

I sigh, scared for his answer. "Did you like her? The girl at the store? Is that why you're so mad?"

With white knuckles, he squeezes the steering wheel like he thinks it's my throat. "Are you delusional? I love *you*. I want to be with *you*. What part of this road trip from hell makes you doubt that?"

I know there were kind words that fell from his lips, yet the loudest one repeating in my brain is *delusional*.

"You think I'm bonkers like Mommy. You think loving me makes you sick. Is it really that insane to wonder if you might want to feel a cunt that isn't related to you?!"

"You want to know what I thought of the moment I saw her? That she had a phone. I thought about keeping you safe.

I don't give a fuck anymore that you're my sister, and it pisses me off that you still do."

"I don't! I never did." Apparently, he feels there's nothing more to add, so I say, "My mind is broken. That's how you feel, isn't it?" He opens his mouth to respond when I remind him, "You called me 'delusional', Kai."

"And you won't fucking quit trying to kill people!" Although he's obviously still furious, he drives no quicker than the speed limit. I wish he'd stop screaming at me though. I stay quiet, keeping my arms crossed. "Throwing a fit isn't going to save you. If you ever pull any shit like that again, I swear to God, I'll take your creations away."

"What?!" I jerk my head toward him as Ponkey gapes at his threat. "You can't do that!"

"I don't know what else to do, Adriel! You're just... you're..."

As he fumbles through his thoughts, I finish for him. "Delusional?"

His head slams against the headrest with a sigh. "I didn't mean it like that, okay? I just meant, you're so far off base. I don't really think you're insane. You're perfect."

Ponkey tilts her monkey head. "He seems like he really means that."

"Maybe," I tell her. "But the fact that I can hear you definitely doesn't help the situation."

The moment the car comes to a stop behind the old house, I get Ponkey and jump out, rushing to the trunk. It lifts open, and I stuff Ponkey into one of the bags before looping my hands through four of them.

Deep down, I know he wasn't trying to hurt me, I just can't get past what it felt like to see her hands on him, to hear that word spewing from his lips. *Delusional.*

The stairs echo loudly as I stomp up each one. While there are no beds in the bedrooms, they still seem like the best place to sleep. I drop the bags in the largest one, pulling out the fluffiest blanket, and laying it out on the floor. He bought two pillows, so I throw them down next to each other, though I wonder if he'll want to sleep next to me tonight. There is one more blanket, so I toss it over the first, crawling across the makeshift bed to straighten it out. My head drops at the sound of his soft footsteps behind me. I just want to be alone right now.

"I'm going to go for a walk with Ponkey. It's pretty outside. I'll be back soon."

A sweaty hand covers my mouth, stopping my breathing. "You're in my house, bitch."

I'm flipped onto my back when I hear a *SMACK*. Stinging tendrils of pain curl up the side of my face.

"It's been a while since we've had a guest, Carl." Although I can't see who it's coming from, the voice is scratchy, and definitely from a woman.

"We thought it was—" I'm hit again, across the other cheek.

His stench hits my nose before he comes into view. A long, greasy brown beard covers most of his face, surrounded by stringy hair of the same color.

"She said 'we,'" the lady snarls. "Is there someone else with you?" She kneels next to me, her grimy teeth rotting from her skull. A large blade twinkles in my vision as she softly scrapes the sharp tip across my cheek. "You have a pretty face. I can't wait to fuck it up."

"I'll go check to see who else is here." Carl kisses her, their tongues looking like fighting snakes. "Don't have too much fun while I'm gone, baby."

Her grin makes me gag. Using all her weight, she sits on my stomach, dropping the knife, so she can hold my arms over my head. The putrid aroma coming from her mouth rivals that of Carl's when she sticks her tongue out and licks up my cheek.

"Ugh. You are *really* smelly."

She coughs with her throaty laugh. "You'll have my stink all over you by the time we're done."

Sinner, sinner, are you gonna skin her?

"Do you want to die first, or would you rather watch me chop up Carl before I get to you?" I snap. It makes me so mad that people keep trying to hurt us. I'm sick of it.

"Whoo! Look at you! Got a little fire in there, don't you?"

Hard *thuds* sounding from outside the bedroom stops her taunting. Looking over her shoulder, I want to scream at Carl dragging Kai by his neck. "Look what I found. Two for one."

Malakai kicks, fighting hard. While he's able to make Carl stumble, he doesn't get free before he's tossed down next to me. The way his eyes are stretched in terror turns my stomach. This can't be the way things end.

Shifting my eyes to the knife, I try to communicate silently for Kai to get it. He attempts to land a hit, but Carl grabs his arms each time.

"You motherfuckers better just kill us," Kai screams, "or believe me, between me and my sister, you'll wish you had."

"Don't worry, you little shit, we'll get to that." The woman spits when she speaks. "But first I want this little whore," she grinds against me again, "to watch my husband fuck that bad attitude out of you."

"No!" Ponkey screams from the bag she's in, kicking it and making it move. "You can't let them hurt Malakai!"

Even though she's trying to help, her screaming is

distracting, and she isn't telling me anything I don't already know.

"Tie her up, baby. I want to watch you ride his face while his ass bleeds on my cock." Kai grunts, resorting to throwing his body around in uncontrolled kicks and punches.

She moans at Carl's words, thrusting against my stomach. "We have two of them, why not take advantage? Show her what her brother feels like."

From the look on her face she's expecting that to be the thing that scares me. Joke's on her.

"Pretend, Adriel! Pretend that's a bad thing! Then when she moves, you get the knife!" The plastic bag rustles with Ponkey's voice.

Fake crying as best as I can I beg, "Please, no. We'll give you anything you want. Just don't make us do that!"

You're gonna die!

La la la la la.

Carl's hands grip at Kai through his jeans. I can't take the contortion of terror on his beautiful face. "Keep crying, girl. That shit will keep me hard forever."

The woman, who he has only referred to as 'Baby', undoes her stained pants to reach inside. "Mmmm, yes, lover. I'm soaking wet."

"Let her taste it," Carl offers.

Now, now, now!

Using the distraction of her arousal, I twist from her one-handed hold long enough to grip my fist around the thick hilt of the knife. I can't see where I'm stabbing her, but once I feel the blade slide in somewhere, her weight shifts, and she gasps.

Carl lunges at me, knocking my head against the floor. His fingers scrape at mine, fighting for the knife. He's already way heavier than his wife, so when Kai jumps on his back, all the air gets blown from my lungs.

I'm going to die from being squished to death, the way Carl's trying to buck him off. Carl's big, sweaty hand clutches at my throat, squeezing tight as Malakai reaches his arm around the front of him. In his fist, Kai's holding the pocket knife I took from the man in Oklahoma. He jabs it into the side of Carl's jugular, twisting it and making blood squirt. The symphony of their screams tickles my skin.

"NO!" The lady cries as she limps toward us, gripping her stabbed leg.

Carl finally stops fighting me for the knife, so I slice it across his cheek just as I meet Kai's gaze. The beautiful blackness in my brother's eyes as he rips out the pocket knife sends jolts of ecstasy to my clitty. I wish he would embrace this side of himself more often. Carl's blood drips onto my face, and I let it fall into my mouth as he releases the hand choking me in order to hold his wounded neck.

The woman screams at Kai, and he jumps to his feet. Swinging his arm out, he slices the sharp metal across her throat. She stops mid stride, swaying as she gasps with her attempt to speak. Red sputters from her lips as she falls to her knees.

Carl wheezes, frantically stumbling over to her. Reaching down, Malakai hands me the small knife and yanks the large one from my grasp. My breath catches at the waves of rage rolling off of him.

He storms over to Carl, reaching down to fist his shirt, lifting him enough to stab him in the stomach. "I. Fucking. Hate. Rapists!" His voice is so loud it fills the room, each word punctuated with a new hole in Carl's gut.

I can't believe how turned on this is making me. My

fingers rub over my panties. The more drenched in blood Kai gets, the more drenched I get between my legs.

Carl's weight becomes too much for Kai to keep holding upright. His shoulders heave as he lets Carl fall. He kneels on all fours, still squeezing the knife inside Carl's abdomen.

I crawl on my knees to go to him. Peeling his fingers from the hilt, I look at his hardened face. He glistens in the setting sun, the blood appearing black in the dimming light. It's all over him. Dripping from his jaw and smeared across his shirt. It's the most captivating thing I've ever seen.

With a hand on each of his cheeks, I kiss him. "I love you." He swallows my whisper as his slippery hands slide to the back of my neck. His tongue slips into my mouth, deepening our kiss. Never separating from his lips, I shift around to straddle Carl's cadaver.

"He wanted to fuck us so bad." I stroke the hilt of the knife and smirk at the raised eyebrows on Kai's face. "It looks like he's ready." Moving my panties, I line the hilt of the knife up with my aching entrance, and slide down over it.

"Fuck, Adriel." His chuckle is erotically sinister.

Oh yes, I like this side of him.

His fingers tangle in my hair while he stands, undoing his jeans. They drop to the floor as he tears the shirt from his body. I clench around the knife the moment he releases his cock. Stroking himself, he smears crimson across his shaft. My hips move faster, blood covering my thighs and pussy.

"Suck his blood off me." He will never have to ask me twice. The coppery taste hits my tongue as I lick up his length. The forcefulness of his hand pushing against the back of my head causes little stars to burst in my tummy. I suction my mouth around him in quick, hard sucks. Gripping both sides of my head, he thrusts harder. "Oh, my God, yes. Suck my cock." The sound of every whispered, "Fuck," speeds up the pulse in my veins.

At his words I rub myself faster, fucking the handle so hard, the corpse beneath me jolts with every thrust. My bottom hits the fabric of his dirty jeans with how deep I'm taking the hilt.

I adore the sound of Kai's moans even more than I loved their screams. Lifting my eyes to look at him, I find him watching me. With a nod of his head, he says. "Get up here." Slowly, I take him out of my mouth, softly kissing the tip before I slide off the knife.

"See? It's hard to not kill people when they keep deserving it."

Urn

Malakai

14 years old

I miss the days when my mother's touch was nothing more than comforting. Every time we're together this way, it feels like a piece of who I was meant to be dies. I despise that even with the sick in my throat, my body burns. I become eager for my release, thankful that it means it's almost over.

She grips my arms as I close my eyes. Watching just intensifies my nightmares. The noises I make as I tremble beneath her sound disgusting in my own ears. My body detonates while her moans strangle me. With a contented sigh, she climbs off, falling to the comforter.

"Go get your sister and set the table. Your father will be home soon to make dinner. I have some work to finish up." Her fingers trace along my cuts, and I always wonder when she'll ask about them.

She never does.

"All right," is the only response I can think to give.

Reaching down, I pull up my underwear and jeans. I wish I had time to wash her off in the shower before Dad gets home.

When she's finally gone, I dig around in my nightstand for a knife. The rage that smothers me every single time I finish with her rips at my chest. I slice fast across my sensitive skin. The wounds from the night before last haven't healed yet, so their tenderness screams when the blade runs over them. I hate that I hate her.

Smell the flowers, blow out the candles.

Flipping off my light, I rub my fingers over the bumpy wallpaper in the hall on my way to Adriel's bedroom. I push open her door to find her on the floor, playing with her toys.

"Was Mommy just in your room?" she asks.

My face and neck heat up with my nod. "We need to set the table. Dad will be home soon."

At the mention of my father's return, she picks up a doll before bolting over to me. It's impossible to be next to her and not smile. Her hand tightens around mine, soothing my nerves as she pulls me all the way down the stairs.

Dad walks in just as I'm placing the forks on the napkins next to the plates. "Hey, kids, did you have a good day?"

Sometimes my life feels like it's on repeat. I'm constantly battling with myself, wondering if things would be worse if he knew. What if he thinks that I did it because I wanted to? That she's confused, and I've been seducing her? I'm too scared that she'll be taken away or he'll never look at me the same again. I eventually always come to the same conclusion: that enduring what she does is the best and safest choice.

Adriel hugs her creation to her chest as she nods. "Yes, Daddy. Did you?"

He gives me an unidentifiable look as he kisses the top of her head. "Yes, I did, baby girl." Walking over to the slow cooker on the counter, he stirs its contents. "Why don't you both go get washed up and tell your mother it's time to eat."

Adriel follows me out to the hallway, tugging on my arm. "Do you want me to go tell Mommy, so you don't have to?"

Her offer makes my throat swell. While my mother's cruelty toward her has diminished to subtle abhorrence over the years, she still treats Adriel like crap. As much as I hate to ask her to do that, it's hard for me to be alone with Mom so soon after she's been in my room.

"Is that okay?"

Her eyes darken when a small smile contradicts them. Standing on the tips of her toes, she softly puts her lips to mine before running to go downstairs.

Once my hands are clean, I go back to the kitchen. There's still half a pitcher of lemonade in the fridge, and I'm setting it on the table when Dad ruffles my hair like I'm fucking six.

"You doing all right?"

I shrug. It's not like I can honestly answer that.

His eyes narrow, moving his hand to my shoulder. "I don't deny that I sometimes make mistakes, son. I just need you to know I'm always here for you. I love you, okay?"

I swallow the unexpected tears. Our relationship has always been a struggle. While he definitely frustrates me, I know he tries his hardest, and I've never doubted his love.

"Yeah, I know."

With a sad smile, he finishes putting the food on the table while we wait for Mom and Adriel.

"I wasn't going to mention this until after we eat, but the last thing I want to do is blindside you again." All the moisture in my mouth completely evaporates, forcing me to swallow. His arm rests on my shoulder. "I'm bringing you with me to pick up a sinner tonight. We've done this with you kids three times, and you have yet to personally take a life." My eyes stretch wide, and he sighs. "It's time to rip off the proverbial bandage. I promise, the first time is the toughest."

My heart feels like it's going to explode. I struggle to get my mouth around any words as sweat beads along my skin. Finding a response is impossible, so when Mom and Adriel enter the kitchen, my lungs feel like they can finally expand. We sit at the table, and I blank out during the prayer. All I can think about is what will be expected of me later tonight.

The whole concept is still confusing. We were raised with a clear set of rules: thou shall not have any other gods before me, thou shall not dishonor thy mother and father, thou shall not steal, thou shall not kill...

What pisses me off is that family night contradicts all of those rules, making them irrelevant and my parents hypocrites. Adriel, the most obedient person I know, seems to be completely unaffected by the fact that we've been taking human lives. In fact, she's been more vibrant since this all began. Like she's more awake. While the knowledge that it's going to continue to happen sets me on edge, it seems to revitalize her. She truly loves it while I dread it. These 'sinners' aren't going to stop, so my family isn't going to stop killing them, and I'm the only one uncomfortable with it.

The end of our meal comes way too soon. My dad stands to put his plate in the sink and says, "Malakai and I are going out. You two need to be ready when we get back."

"Are we having another family night?!" Adriel shrieks.

My mother's face is blank until realization slowly hits her. "You're taking him to get her?" Her voice is unsteady as she glares at my father. "Don't you think that's dangerous?"

Wait...*her?* The last three kills have all been men. He's going to make me kill a girl? The little bit of food I just ate rolls in my stomach.

"He's more capable than you give him credit for." Even through my anxiety, his belief in me makes me smile.

"I wasn't—" She abruptly stops, standing from the table. When she walks over to me, her lips kiss the top of my head. "Be careful, baby," she whispers. Barely looking at Adriel, she adds, "Clear the table. I'm going to lie down for a bit." Dad sighs, watching her leave the kitchen.

"Can I come too?" Adriel asks.

He walks over to her and cups her cheek. "Not this time, baby girl, but I promise I'll take you at some point, okay?"

"Okay, Daddy."

He taps her chin. "Good girl." On his way out of the kitchen, his hand squeezes my shoulder. "Come on, son."

My heart fights to free itself from my chest, and I freeze. I don't want to do this! Glancing at Adriel, I see her pretty smile. She jumps from her seat, hugging me tight. "I hope you have so much fun," she whispers.

Just so she doesn't worry, I force a smile. "Thanks."

I'm slow to my feet as I follow my dad to the garage. "This never goes exactly as planned, so be prepared to improvise." He opens a cabinet above his workbench, removing a clear glass bottle labeled '*XylaMed*' and a small syringe. "This is what we'll inject her with once she's incapacitated." He fills the syringe. "We've learned through trial and error that horse tranquilizer works best. If you need to ever do this yourself, remember, no more than one milligram per one hundred pounds. If you don't, they might take too long to wake up or not wake up at all."

The room spins, so I lean against the table saw. I don't know if I can do this. He's made me hurt them each time. I've cut off an ear, scooped out an eye, burned away flesh…still, I was never the reason they died. "How did you even get that? I'm pretty sure it's not available at the Wiggle Mart."

"No, it's not." Lifting a large gym bag off the floor, he places the filled syringe inside. "I started paying someone I met online for a prescription after your mother and I learned that chloroform wasn't a reliable anesthetic." My head is starting to hurt. The amount of illegal shit we're doing just keeps piling up. If I'm really honest, it infuriates me that they're willing to risk mine and Adriel's safety for this. He walks across the garage, adding rope and rolls of cellophane to the bag before popping open the trunk. "I brought the tools and implements to the church this morning, so we'll change our clothes when we pick up your mom and sister."

"Do you ever feel guilty?" He tilts his head, so I continue, "For taking away any chance they could have had to change?"

He sighs, "I used to. Now, though, I'm certain we are removing those with souls that are so decayed, it's too late for that. Truly wicked people are unable to change, Kai. Believe me." His hands rest on my shoulders as he looks into my eyes. "Even so, I pray for them. I pray that if there is still an ounce of goodness left in them, God will grant them mercy. I suggest you do the same. My conscience on this is clear." I nod, and he returns it before walking to the driver's side. "We should get going."

The station wagon is thick with summer heat when we climb inside. I'm not as scared about kidnapping this woman as much as I am terrified to murder her. "Do I really have to kill this one? She's a girl."

"Gender doesn't make a person less evil, Malakai." He reverses out of the driveway. "I think hearing about what these sinners do isn't enough. You need to see it."

The way he says that sends fire to my fingertips. "What do you mean?"

"We aren't just going to grab her. She's under the

impression that we're going to pay her to have sex with her eight-year-old daughter. Her selfish sins are delivering her right into the palms of our hands."

My fingers turn red with how hard I'm squeezing the door handle. "What will happen to the little girl?"

"Hopefully she'll be put in a safer environment." Saying nothing, because what is there to say, I turn my head to look out the window. "I know this has been hard on you. Please believe me when I say this will change things for you."

I nod. Thankfully, he leaves me to my thoughts until we reach Des Moines.

As he takes an exit, the signal *clicks,* and he says, "The woman's name is Debbie. I told her we want to have the child together, so play the part until we're in the little girl's room. Debbie has already informed me that she will be remaining in the home. Once she believes we're doing what we're paying for, you can figure out how to make your move. The easiest way will be to incapacitate her first. I usually hit them on the head with something before injecting them."

Everything feels like it's happening really fast, and my mind frantically searches for a way to get out of this. Of course, I want to help this little girl, I'm just not ready to kill her mother yet. "But I don't even know where to put the needle."

He points to his arm, a few inches below his shoulder. "Get it in the muscle, right here. That's always gotten the most consistent results for me."

He turns down a street called Akufa Boulevard, slowing in front of a shitty apartment complex. "Alright, I'm going to get the Xylazine syringe from the trunk. Since it could take up to ten minutes to take effect, use anything you can to keep her contained until then." He grips my shoulder. "Please, Malakai,

I need you to sell this. It's the only way it'll work. Act like the little girl turns you on. Okay?"

My nervousness and apprehension over killing someone are traded for the doubt that I can pull this off. She's fucking eight. Who would want that? How am I supposed to pretend to be something I can't even wrap my head around? Still, with everything in my soul telling me this is wrong, I nod.

"One last thing. I'm going to say and do things that are going to shock you. You need to know it's just so this is seen through. All right?"

"I understand."

"I'm proud of you, and I love you, Kai."

"I love you too, Dad." I'm surprised at the emotions overtaking me. I'm confused by them actually. I want to make him proud of me, I want to save this little girl, but it still feels so horrible.

He gets out, and I see him open the trunk in the rearview. My body feels heavy and sluggish, like I have to use all my energy to open the door and walk to him. The small case with the needle inside burns in my palm when he hands it to me.

With the slam of the trunk and a final nod, he makes his way up the stairs where I follow him to apartment twenty-six. My lungs are inflating and deflating so fast I have to close my eyes to control my breathing.

Seconds after he knocks, a blonde woman opens the door. Our eyes connect, and I think I might throw up. She doesn't look like I'd imagined her. Her somewhat modest clothes are clean, and light makeup softens her face. Looking at her, I would never think she was the kind of person my dad says she is.

"Hello." Even her voice is unexpected. Its sultry with a seductive edge. "Harold Dean?"

I glance at my father who nods, his grin widening his face in an unnatural way. "And you must be Debbie Wilder. This is my son, Jeremy." I had no idea we were giving fake names which makes me nervous about what other surprises this little trip has in store.

She opens the door wider, smiling as she holds out her arm in invitation. "Well, there's someone ready to meet you. Come on in." Winking at my dad, she adds, "She's a lucky girl."

For the first time, the queasiness in my gut isn't because of what I'm about to do—it's because of what she believes we're here to do.

The second I step into the small living room, my eyes land on a little girl with flaxen hair. Her eyes look like they should be on someone much older. She glances between us, and I wish there was a way to tell her we aren't here to do what she thinks.

My dad groans, and I'm sure my eyes bulge when he grabs himself over his jeans. "Fuck, look at her."

I have to make her believe I'm down for this. Swallowing, I walk over to the girl, kneeling to her level and softly touch her arm. I try to comfort her while simultaneously appearing aroused.

"This is Millie. What do you have to say to the nice men, sweetie?"

Her eyes glaze over, making her little smile unsettling. "I can't wait to suck your cocks," she squeaks.

It feels like a stone falls to my stomach, and I'm so grateful Debbie can't see my face. I want Millie to know that I understand. That I know what she's feeling, and I won't do that to her. I grab her hand, making her eyes shift to mine. As slightly as I can, I shake my head, but her narrowed eyebrows tell me I'm just confusing her.

My father laughs, sounding nothing like himself when he says, "Oh, neither can I, sugar." I jerk my head back to look at him. How is he able to act like this? He turns to Debbie, handing her the payment. I wonder how much money is worth destroying her child's mind and soul? The idea of her being too dead to hurt this girl anymore is becoming incredibly appealing. "Is there anything we can't do?"

She shakes her head. "You can put it anywhere. Just don't hit her or leave marks."

I grind my teeth together, clenching my jaw. What my mother does to me is entangled with her actual love for me. What this woman is doing? This is purely for self-gain.

He was right. Watching her sins is much more effective than simply hearing about them. I stand with Millie's hand still in mine.

"Can we get started?" The words taste like vomit in my mouth. I can't do this much longer.

They both look at me, and Dad laughs again. "That's my boy. Impatient as ever." He grins, telling me I did well.

"Of course. Her room is that one right there." She points behind Millie.

Hopefully appearing eager, I pull her inside. Other than a bed, there's not much in here—

A couple stuffed animals and a few books. This poor little girl's situation makes mine pale in comparison.

Behind me, my dad walks in and shuts the door. When I turn to look at him, Millie's fingers fumble with my jeans as she drops to her knees. I have to bite my tongue, so I don't yell. Taking her hands off of me, I kneel on the floor in front of her.

"We aren't here to hurt you," I whisper. "I'm sorry if we scared you."

Her misunderstanding makes her look angry. "What do you mean?"

My dad sits next to me, speaking in a gentle voice. "What your mother is making you do is very bad."

Her eyes fill with tears. "I'm bad?"

"No, sweetheart. Your mommy is. You've done nothing wrong, okay?"

She chews the inside of her mouth. "Okay."

When he stands, her eyes follow him, full of curiosity at his intentions. He picks up a book then sits against the wall, patting the floor next to him. "Do you want me to read you a story?

Looking at me, she stands, still clearly uneasy about this unexpected turn of events. She hesitantly creeps across the room. When she sits, she leaves nearly a foot of space between them.

My feelings about this have completely flipped. I'm going to enjoy torturing every last breath out of Debbie.

There's nothing in here substantial enough to hit her with. I wish I would have looked for something while I was in the living room. The syringe seems to pulse in my jeans, so I take it out, returning the empty case to my pocket.

With my dad's voice reading about a giant red dog, I slowly creak open Millie's door. Since I don't hear anything, I risk poking out my head. The living room is empty, but I notice there's an urn on a shelf. Sneaking across the carpet, I cringe when the floor groans. I stop to look over my shoulder before grabbing the urn.

Dishes *clang* behind me, alerting me of Debbie's location. As quietly and quickly as I'm able to, I approach the kitchen and peer around the corner to see her. She's smoking something in a glass pipe. Thick, white smoke billows from her lips as I grip the syringe against the urn. I get close enough that I'm about to hit her when she suddenly turns, her eyes widening at my stance.

"What the fu—"

My adrenaline kicks in, and I slam the brass jar against the side of her head. The pipe shatters on the linoleum as a stream of blood trickles from her hairline. Yelling, her hand goes to the point of impact before she stumbles, reaching for something to hold. The urn slips from my grip when I lunge, tackling her. She isn't a large woman, so it doesn't take excessive effort to keep her pinned down.

"How?" I seethe. "How can you do that to your own child?!"

"You don't understand!" She weeps while fighting to get free from my grasp. "I'm sick!"

Those words almost make me falter, but I keep my hold tight. "What do you mean?" Her eyes flash to the counter where a bag of clear crystals sits on the edge. "Your drugs?"

Fucking tears fill her eyes like I'm supposed to feel bad for her because she's an addict. When she nods, I don't understand the emotion that surges from my gut to my skull. Dropping the syringe, I pick up the urn, holding tight to the narrowed neck. The fingers of my other hand comb through her hair before tangling it in a fist to jerk her head to the side.

I have more knowledge of the human body than most kids my age, so I know the pterion is the weakest part of the skull. Her screams sound far away, as if I can't really hear them, probably because I don't care about them. Slamming the urn against the space behind her temple I yell, "You're her mom!" I tighten my grip and bring it down again. "You fucking bitch!" The blood and my own tears blur the harm I've inflicted. However, the definite *crunch* when I hit her a third time tells me I've done damage. I can almost feel my mother touching me as I weep through my screams. "She's just a little kid!" The bloody urn falls from my grasp to the floor while my chest heaves.

She's not moving and barely breathing. Wiping my slick hands down my face, I move to sit next to her. Oddly, my nerves are calming, allowing my pulse to slow. Well, shit. This wasn't how it was supposed to go. As my thoughts clear, I stand to my feet to go get my dad.

Guilt eats at me knowing that my actions will cause Millie more damage when she sees me painted in her mother's blood. I open her door, peeking my head inside. Dad's sitting in the same spot, but Millie has scooted beside him to rest her head on his arm. They look up at me, and my father's face pales while hers frowns.

"Stay here, sweetheart. I'll be right back."

She grabs his hand and shakes her head. "Please don't go away."

"I promise I won't be gone long. Just don't leave this room, okay?" While it's reluctant, she nods her agreement. Once her door is closed behind us, he looks me over. "What happened? Are you okay?"

Nodding, I try to explain. "She just…she made me snap."

"I'm sorry. I heard the yelling and was about to come check on you, I had just told Millie you were playing, and I didn't want to scare her more by running out." He stalks toward the kitchen, stopping at the entrance with me behind him.

"Is she dead?" I can't tell if her chest is moving with breath.

He sighs. "If not, she will be soon. This definitely changes our plans."

Adriel is going to be so pissed at me for fucking up family

night. She's been talking for weeks about wanting to crush someone's head with the C-clamp. "I'm sorry...what she was doing to Millie, I—"

He grips my shoulder. "Believe me, I understand. It's all right." Turning to look over his shoulder he adds, "Though a witness is always a problem." What?! I shake my head frantically. "Relax, son, we're not going to hurt the girl. We eradicate sinners. Nothing else."

"Then what are we going to do?"

He scratches the back of his head. "The same thing we do at the church and pray that nobody shows up until we're done."

"And Millie?"

"Let me talk to her. I'll be sure she doesn't see the body, so there should be no reason she won't trust me when I tell her Debbie left. Wherever she ends up, it has to be better than here." He attempts to hug me without getting bloody. "I need you to know, you've made me incredibly proud tonight."

Human Creations

Adriel

17 years old

A bird chirping in the window is the first sound I hear before Malakai's steady breathing. It smells like shit in here. Actual shit. I think our dead friends had some accidents. Blue light from the early morning glows in the windows as I look down at my brother deep in sleep.

"He's not waking up anytime soon. *Ruff*! Let's play!" Pegamy's muffled voice comes from my backpack. I rush over to it, moving my clothes to see her puppy tongue hanging out as she pants. Her doll hands hold out my sewing kit as her wings try to flutter in the cramped space. I pick her up, and the moment her feet hit the floor, she drops the kit to run to the corpses. She flaps her wings, flying between them. "We should switch their heads!" Her cackling makes me laugh.

I kneel by my future creations and clap. She has great ideas. "Ooh, and I can switch their feet with their hands and give them mermaid fins!" Jumping to my feet, I grab ahold of Carl's arms. "Come on, help me drag them to the next room, so we don't wake up Malakai."

He is so heavy and bloody that I slip and fall twice as I drag him down the hall. I'm already panting before I do the same with the lady. Once I catch my breath, I sit Pegamy on my shoulders to walk down the stairs.

"Where are we going?" she asks as she bats at my hair.

"I want to pick some flowers first."

She climbs to the top on my head, looking at me upside down. "Do you think Kai will be mad at us?"

The rising sun shows a pretty patch of flowers sitting under a tree next to the car, so I rush over to pick them. "He won't be mad. They're already dead."

With a full bouquet of mixed flowers and a pile of thick sticks tucked in my arm, we walk back inside. I check to make sure Kai's still sleeping and tell Pegamy to pick up my sewing kit. Hurrying back to the room with Carl and his wife, I follow the path of blood down the hall.

Pegamy flies around singing as I sit on Carl's body to pull out the knife still in his gut from the night before. More blood coats the crusted-over residue. At least I'm still naked and won't ruin more clothes.

I rip his shirt down the middle to expose his chest before yanking off his jeans. Straddling him, I hold the hilt of the knife with both hands and lift it above my head to get more force before I stab it into his suprasternal notch. I saw the blade down his chest, stopping right beneath his ribs. The sun's warm kisses land on my face and shoulders, intensifying the floaty feeling this is giving me. His flesh squelches between my fingers as I rip away his epidermal casing. Once I cut off the excess flaps of skin and toss them in the corner, I reach down with red fingers for the flowers. I arrange them between his ribs so that all the colors are evenly spread out. Sweat wets my forehead, but my slick hands do nothing to wipe it away.

"That is so pretty!" Pegamy squeals.

"Thank you."

I scoot to his legs. The ankle bone is making this harder than I thought.

"Cut as deep as you can all the way around. Then you can break the bone."

I grin at her, doing as she says. His blood shimmers in the sunlight as I hold his foot, stomping on exposed leg bone to break his foot off from the ankle. My breathing has increased in not only anticipation, but also exhaustion. "This is really hard work!"

"*Ruff!*" Pegamy sits on my new creation's head. "It'll be worth it."

"We need to name him," I tell her.

"How about Meanie Meanface?"

She's so silly, I laugh. "Maybe."

His wrist is much easier because the bone snaps without as much effort. The broken off bones sticking out of his leg make it easy to squish the detached hand onto it. I repeat the process with his other foot. Once they're both attached, I set to sewing. My fingers are slippery with blood, taking me forever to thread the needle. Human flesh is much more supple than fabric or plastic, so the needle glides in smoothly. Next, I thread the inside of his thighs and calves together. Letting out a big breath, I stare at the last piece: the head.

Sawing through the flesh is exhausting. My sweat drips down, mixing with the new and old blood. I finally cut through enough of Carl's neck that I can twist and tug until his spine finally snaps free. His hair makes a nice handle to carry the severed head to his wife's body to do the same to her.

The sticks make wet, squishy noises when I shove them into the open neck holes. Once I have Carl's head fastened to the lady's body, I secure it with stitching and repeat the process with her.

Now that he's finished, I've got the perfect name for him.

"I think we should call him Handsie. Because he has no hands, and he tried to touch my brother."

"Yes! That's it!" she squeals.

I do the same thing to the woman that I did to Handsie except I only cut off her breasts instead of the whole chest cavity for the flowers. I think about what her name should be. Carl never called her anything besides, 'Baby.' All I really know about her is that she was mean and smelly.

"Adriel?!" Kai's panicked voice coils around me, making me jump to my feet. "Adriel?! Where are you?!"

I call for him, "I'm in here!"

He appears in the doorway, relief pulling down his shoulders. "I saw the blood, and I—" With raised eyebrows, his gaze travels over Handsie, and he asks, "What are you doing?"

"His name is Handsie, and hers is…Stinky Baby. Switching their heads was Pegamy's idea."

He stalks toward me, his naked form beautiful in the morning sun. Crouching down beside me, he looks at my work. He's silent for so long I think maybe he is mad when he says, "The flowers are a nice touch…" With a sigh, he wipes his hand over my hair. "We do need to get out of here though. Finish your project, and then go clean off in the pond we swam in last night."

Stinky Baby is getting close to being finished when he returns with a folded stack of clothes. "Everything is packed up." He lays out one of my dresses with a pair of panties and socks over the edge of the old baby crib. "We're getting low on clean clothes."

We're also running out of money. Soon, we're going to need food. Plus, we still have to change the way we look. The very idea of stealing gives me a sick feeling that I don't like. I'm just not sure we have any other choice.

Double checking Stinky Baby's threading, I try to concentrate on the last of my stitching instead of watching Kai's muscles flex as he tugs the black and white striped t-shirt over his head. He finds me staring at him, and he gives me my favorite ornery smile.

"You need to quit looking at me like that. My dick is already hard, and we need to get back on the road." He bends over, tasting the inside of my mouth with his kiss. "I've always loved how you look in blood." Backing out of the room, he nods to Handsie and Stinky Baby. "Try to hurry."

Finally, I cut the thread to the last stitch. She's perfect. They both are. I stand up to look at my first human creations. It's impossible not to grin. "*Woof*! They're absolutely beautiful! Oh, how I wish we had a camera!" Pegamy flies around in excited circles.

"Kai does! What a great idea!" I pluck her out of the air to set her on my shoulder. "Come on, I gotta tidy up."

Kai's leaning against the hood of the car with crossed arms as he stares at me. While he isn't exactly smiling, he isn't frowning either. He just looks lost in his thoughts.

"Will you take a picture of Handsie and Stinky Baby? I want to remember them."

He arches an amused brow. Every part of me aches for him. Heart, body, and mind.

With a nod toward the pond, he agrees. "Sure, go get washed."

Since he's waiting on me, I don't play around with Pegamy. I just get the blood rinsed off of us and hurry back to the house.

Back upstairs, I tell Pegamy to get my sewing kit as I yank on my dress and panties. I buckle my shoes and pick up the bloody knife that lies on the floor next to Stinky Baby, attempting to clean it off with an unsoiled spot on her clothes before going outside.

Kai meets me at the passenger door, plucking the blade from my hand. "I'll be taking this now."

The smile that lifts his lips makes me cross my ankles, pressing my thighs together. Frowning at him, I toss my bag on the floorboard. "Why?"

His eyebrows raise with an unamused stare. "Really?" The heat of his body radiates against me as his fingers dip beneath my dress, rubbing me over my panties. Soft lips kiss up my neck before his teeth nip at my ear. My body shivers at the sound of his deep voice. "You know you have a tendency to stick these into people." I try to hold my glare, but then he chuckles, sliding his hand inside my panties. I grab onto his shoulders as he rests the knife on the roof and pumps his fingers with escalating aggression. "You looked beautiful in their blood." His lips touch mine softly. I lean into the kiss until suddenly he takes away his touch. My gasp fills his grinning mouth. "As much as I want to finish this, we better go. We're wasting light."

I gape at him as he snatches the knife and runs to the driver's side door. We get in the car for the last time, pulling away from the house that is now Handsie and Stinky Baby's tomb.

He takes my hand, and I notice the angry, red scars on his arm which show bright in the sunlight. T-shirts alone are not something he ever wears. I like seeing his arms. His body sits tight and tense, causing sadness to eat at me like a disease. I didn't think about it when he got dressed, but I don't think he has any more clean, long-sleeved shirts.

Softly, I touch the raised scars from years of him hurting himself. I've always wondered when he started doing it. One day, they were just there and have been ever since. I think I kept waiting for him to talk to me about them. He never did though. While there are quite a few marks on his right wrist, there are oodles more on his left. I separate our hands to kiss them.

"You've never told me why you do this. I know it's not because you're trying to die."

He chews on his lip as if he's unsure himself. "It just feels…well, 'good' isn't the right word. I mean it hurts, just not like it does here." He taps his head. "I shouldn't let what me and Mom did bother me so much. I truly think she was confused. I hate her and love her at the same time. I was constantly pulled between being scared of her and for her. That, on top of all the stuff at school…it became a lot. When I cut myself, all the shit that rots and decomposes in my mind gets loosened. Like some of it finally releases. It's trading my emotional pain for physical pain."

Mommy never loved me, I believe that now more than ever, but she loved Kai too much. I think that may have been worse. "Have you done it since they died?"

He nods. "It's basically my go-to when I can't deal with what I'm feeling."

"Have you ever done it because of me?"

Momentarily closing his eyes, he groans, "Adriel, that isn't fair." His gray irises are lighter in the sun, glistening when he looks at me. With quick glances at the road, he reaches over, gripping the side of my face and neck. "I felt out of control with us at first. I thought something was wrong with me. It wasn't because of you, okay?"

I want to ask him to stop. The idea of anyone hurting him, even himself, makes me very, very angry. At the same time, though, he's telling me it helps him. Why would I want to take away his safety net? In this moment, I silently promise him that someday he won't need it. I'd never kill another sinner if I truly thought it would make him quit mutilating himself.

Smiling at him, I place my hand on his. "I know."

My eyes keep shifting to the clock on the dashboard every couple of minutes. We've been in the car nearing two hours, and that's how long he said we'd drive before we'd leave it.

As if reading my thoughts, he sighs. "I think it's time we continue on foot."

I drop my head back on the seat. I don't want to walk. "Maybe a little longer?"

"It's going to suck regardless if it's now or in five minutes. Besides, I'll be less paranoid without this thing." He takes an exit, driving until we find a low traffic road. After about a mile, he pulls off into the grass. "We need to attach as much to our backpacks as we can. This stuff is going to get heavy really fast."

He rolls up the blankets, tying them to his bag with some twine he found in the trunk. After doing the same with the pillows on mine, we stuff all the food we can into any free spaces in our backpack pockets.

Hand in hand, we start our walk under the burning sun.

I wish I had sunglasses; I feel like I'm going blind. It seems to take forever to get to the end of the street, and we don't see a single car along the way. By the time we reach the main highway, my dress is already sticking to my skin.

My heart *pitter patters* the moment I hear the first rumbling of a car. "What do we do? Just hold our hands out like this?" I make a 'thumbs up' at the passing car that doesn't even slow down.

Fifteen cars later, I know because I counted, we've been walking for what feels like hours. My legs are tired, and I'm thirsty. When my eyes find a gas station in the distance, a jolt of energy courses through me.

I point to it. "Can I get some sunglasses and water? Pleeease?" I whine because throwing a fit usually works with Kai.

"Yeah, I need to piss anyway."

When we finally reach the Gas 'N' Grub, I run inside. Black spots dance across my vision, the air conditioner the most remarkable cold bliss on my face. I moan as Malakai's hand brushes my arm, placing a soft kiss to my cheek. "Just sunglasses and water, okay? Get me a bottle too."

I skip to the sunglasses and take out Princess Sparkle. "I need to pick out ones that make it hard to tell who I am." She obviously doesn't feel like talking to me right now, so I talk for her. "These ones are pretty!" The glasses are pink with heart-shaped lenses. I try on a few more, but keep coming back to the heart ones. I slide them on top of my head before walking to the coolers. Kai likes Fiji water, but I like Dasani. I pick out one of each when his arms wrap around my waist, and he rests his chin on my shoulder.

"You ready? Maybe you should go to the bathroom while we're here." He's right. I hate having to squat in the bushes. I hand him the waters and sunglasses before doing as he says. It's odd that I've gone my whole life never appreciating toilet paper before. There are three rolls lined along the top of the paper towel dispenser. Taking a big breath, I reach up to grab one and stick it in my backpack. *Dear Jesus, I'm sorry for stealing.*

After washing my hands, I meet Kai at the front of the store where he gives me my sunglasses and a pack of four hair ties. They are each a different color and have a plastic star attached. "I thought you could braid your hair or put it in a ponytail. It might make you look a little different."

Standing on my toes, I kiss his cheek. "Thank you."

He holds my water as I braid my pigtails. The hair off my neck gives me more pleasure than I expected. "How do I look?"

The grays of his eyes darken with his smile. "Perfect."

Cereal Killers

Malakai
18 years old

I'm not sure how much longer I can keep going. We've been walking in the heat for hours. Every car that passes ignores our upturned thumbs. This looked a lot easier on T.V. We've seen a few cop cars along the way, and every time I think I'm going to pass out. Now that we are so exposed, my paranoia is worse than it was in the car.

I can't stop thinking about how much they've found out at this point. "Do you think that we'd be considered serial killers? I mean, if they find out about the other bodies?"

"Ooh, I want some cereal. I'm hungry."

I laugh, loving how she can so quickly shift my mood. Her comment has me remembering when she was little and thought 'serial killer' meant that there was a cereal out there that was poisoned and would kill her if she ate it.

A sign for an upcoming gas station has me groaning in relief. "We'll stop there."

As an added bonus, there's a restaurant inside, so we can sit and relax for a bit. I want something hotter than cereal.

Eggs and sausage with a side of hash browns sounds freaking amazing.

I scoot into the booth with Adriel, somehow able to refrain from biting into a sausage until after she prays.

"I saw a sign a little while ago that said Grande Isle was sixty-three miles away. If we can get a ride, we'll get there today." With my mouth full of the best food I've tasted in days, I mumble, "Thank God."

"What are we going to do once we get there?"

I gulp down my chocolate milk before answering. Damn, this is good. "We'll try to find a decent motel. Then, I don't know. I guess we'll call Mikkel. Ask if we can meet him."

Until now, I had enough to worry about without giving much thought to whether or not he will be a safe haven. Uncle Bennett knew us our entire lives and was ready to send us to jail after he found out about us. I'm not sure this is really the best choice, but I also can't think of any others.

"I hope he likes us. We don't have much luck with that."

Scooping a big pile onto my fork, I scoff. "Then fuck him. It's you and me now, okay? Anyone who has an issue with that is irrelevant."

I'm surprised at how much I truly believe that now. She's all I have, and she's all I want. When her big smile makes her gray eyes shimmer, I pray for the first time in years.

I know I haven't talked to you in a while... just please... don't let anyone separate us. Help us get out of this. I swear, I'll do anything.

Once our food is gone, we set out to finish our wayward journey. The sun beats down on us, and it doesn't take long for perspiration to wet my forehead. Just as I fear we'll be walking the rest of the way to Grand Isle, a blue Oldsmobile pulls over to stop in front of us. The driver is an elderly woman, her dark skin a harsh contrast to her white hair holding a tint of violet.

"You youngins all right? Why you out walking in this heat?"

"Our car broke down," I lie.

Adriel looks at me, though she keeps her lips pressed tightly together. The woman waves her hand, and the *click* of the doors unlocking urges on my excitement. We're finally getting out of the sun.

"Go on, get in."

I climb in the back with Adriel right behind me. As I drop my bag on the floorboard, the woman asks, "Where are you two tryin' to go?"

"Grand Isle," Adriel pipes up.

"My Lord, child. That's a long way to walk." Neither of us respond to her, so she adds, "Well, get comfortable, it's about an hour drive."

I could almost cry with gratitude. This woman has no idea how much she's helping us. "That's very generous, thank you."

"I'm just doing what the good Lord would want me to do. I'm Betty Jean Lewis by the way." She looks at us in the rearview, grinning. "Your names wouldn't happen to be Pugsley and Wednesday, would they?"

A laugh bursts from my gut. "Are you saying we look like the kids from the Addams Family?"

"Only if that chubby little boy grew up to be a very handsome young man." I smile at her in the mirror where she winks at me. Adriel's hand clenches around mine, crushing my fingers together. My gaze jerks in her direction to see her glaring at Betty Jean. She cannot seriously be mad at this little old lady. It was just a bit of innocent fun. "Don't give me that look, child." Though her words are a bit chiding, her smile softens them. "I may be old, but that don't make me blind."

Adriel's fingers loosen, allowing me to exhale. Moving my hand to her thigh, I give her a reassuring squeeze. "She can get a little protective of me sometimes." She looks up at me, uncertainty scrunching her dark eyebrows.

Betty Jean chuckles. "Ain't nothin' wrong with a woman claimin' her man."

At that, Adriel's face relaxes, and she says, "I'm Adriel. This is my bro—"

"Boyfriend," I interject. Betty Jean's already deduced that we're a couple. Knowing we're also siblings would likely lose us this ride. "I'm her boyfriend, Malakai." Her perplexed expression in the rear-view mirror tells me she senses that something is up. "Do you happen to have a phone I can use, Betty Jean?"

Reaching across the middle console, she digs through a big brown purse. "I sure do. My daughter got it for me...even though she never calls," she grumbles. "I think you must be the only young people in all of Louisiana without a cellular telephone."

My hand shakes in anticipation when I take it from her. "Thank you."

One of the first links that pops up has me holding my breath. ***Search Widens For Iowa Teens.***

Aside from Uncle Bennett's remains being identified and us being named the prime suspects, there isn't more information than last time.

"Are you all right, honey child? You've gone as white as my bedsheets."

Instead of throwing the phone out the damn window like I want to, I give it back to her. "I'm fine, thank you."

Adriel tilts her head in question, but it's not like we can really talk right now.

Betty Jean more than makes up for the conversation as I watch all the palm trees pass by. I'd never seen one in person before.

By the time we reach a big, blue sign that says, *GRAND ISLE,* I know her kids and grandkids names, her favorite television show, and all about Norma Lee, the 'high and mighty' woman from her salon.

"You kids be safe. It was nice to meet you," Betty Jean says once we're out of her car.

"It was nice to meet you too. Thank you for the ride," I say.

As we wave at her, I look around the beach community. Every building I come across is raised up on stilts. I've never seen anything like it.

"Whoa…" Adriel spins in a circle. "This is magical." She points to the Gulf of Mexico laid out in the distance. "Can we go to the beach?"

Now that we've made it, I'm anxious to speak with our cousin. On the other hand, we've had a long few days, and she deserves to have a good time for a couple hours. I drape my arm over her shoulder to pull her close. "Sure."

Her arms hug me tight as she squeals. "Yay!"

After walking so much today I'm exhausted, yet somehow, she produces a burst of energy that has her dragging me down the long, wooden pathway leading to the beach. The moment we hit the sand, she yanks off her shoes and socks, dropping her bag before running into the water.

She splashes around, not caring that she's soaking her dress. Watching her having a blast, I sit next to our things. I'll admit, this place does give me a peaceful, warm feeling, and it's not from the weather.

There are a lot of people, and I have no idea how many are tourists. I hope finding an available, cash room won't be too hard. After I feel like I've given her a sufficient amount of time to play, I call for her.

Thankfully she doesn't pout. When she gets closer, I see her skin has pinked from the sun. Her eyes are tired as she says, "I'm hungry again."

The first three places we try require a credit card and are more than we can afford anyway. The fourth hotel we attempt is unlike anything I knew existed. Instead of a building with rooms, they rent out cottages and trailers. They still require a credit card, though, so it seems like we're going to have to think of a different plan. As we leave the office, Adriel releases my hand and walks up to a man getting out of his car before I can ask her what she's doing.

He nods to her, and she runs back to me. "Give him the money. He's going to rent us the mobile home."

While I'm hesitant, worried he'll rip us off, I hand over the cash. Surprisingly, moments later he returns with the keys.

"Thank Christ," I mumble on the way to the white trailer.

It's much cleaner in here than I expected based on the dated exterior, and while it's small, it's more than enough space for us.

Adriel immediately rips off her dress and undergarments, grabbing the toiletries from my bag. "I really need a shower."

Following her lead, I tear down my filthy jeans and toss off my shoes. It feels amazing to wash off the grime of the last few days. Swimming in that pond didn't do much to make me feel clean. As the shampoo rolls down my face, my cock is consumed in a hot suctioning. I don't need to open my eyes to know her mouth is on me. God, her tongue feels incredible.

Finally, my nerves are relaxing. For the first time in days, my stomach isn't twisted in a knot.

The way she looks when I open my eyes has my erection jolting against her lips. Water drips down her face and body. Her eyelashes look so long when they're wet, making those gorgeous, ashen eyes even more stunning. Long strands of her charcoal hair stick to her petite breasts right next to those rosebud nipples. I was such a moron to think I could have lived without having her this way. How had I ever believed this was wrong?

I grip her wet head to pound against her throat. "Fuck, yes. Make me come." The vibrations from her lips when she moans are about to kill me. "I love you more than anything. Do you know that? I'm sorry I haven't thanked you for loving me back."

She stands, never ceasing her stroking. "You loving me *is* thanking me, Kai."

I tug my last clean shirt over my head before stuffing the trailer key in my jeans pocket. "They have a laundromat here, so I'm gonna grab some soap. We'll clean clothes when I get back."

She's still naked from our shower, jumping up and down on the bed with one of her dolls. "Okay. Princess Sparkle wants to know when we get to eat? And when are we calling cousin Mikkel?"

This is still taking a lot to get used to. She needs to know that I will always support her, so I try hard to hide the fact that every time she talks to her creations, it feels like a knife turning in my stomach.

"I'll get some food while I'm out, but since it's getting late, let's just chill tonight. We'll call him tomorrow."

As I approach the bed, she bounces to her knees, puckering her lips for a kiss. "Hurry up! We're hungry."

The *squeak, squeak, squeak* of the bed continues from her jumping as I shut the door. On our way here, I saw a small convenience store a little farther down that should have food and detergent.

It's not even a twenty-minute walk. This entire place is only eight miles long and a mile wide.

The shrill chime of a bell alerts the clerk that I've arrived. He holds up his hand in greeting while I pick out soap and softener sheets. Adriel likes the lilac ones.

The food selection is pretty decent, the easiest option being pizza and soda. When I drop everything on the counter, the clerk tilts his head. The examining expression he's giving me is creeping me out.

His eyes widen as he drops the box of fabric softener sheets. "Holy crap." Before I can catch up with what's happening, he reaches beneath the counter to reveal a rifle. "I just realized why you look familiar."

Shit.

It's odd how things like this can affect time. I'm not sure if I hold my hands up before or after I say, "Okay, man. Chill. You're not gonna shoot me for trying to buy some groceries."

"Nah, you're that guy from Nebraska or wherever that fucked his sister. And didn't you guys kill your uncle?"

Swallowing is the only movement I can make. My feet fuse to the floor.

"I could really use that reward."

He shifts his eyes upward, likely fantasizing about selling me out for a payday. At his small distraction, I am released from my hold to the linoleum. I push off my feet, bolting out the door. The moment I step onto the gravel, glass shatters behind me with a *BOOM*.

White hot pain wraps around my thigh. I nearly fall on my face as people in the parking lot stare. That asshole actually shot me. My adrenaline surges into effect, allowing me to continue running.

Keeping my eyes peeled for cops, I stay off the main street, taking the first side road I reach. It doesn't take long to realize that was a bad choice considering there are no other connecting streets, and it's a dead end. This place is so open, it gives me an unsettling feeling of exposure. I'm forced to risk running between the houses, trees, and hotels to head in the direction of Adriel.

Being recognized is not good at all. He seemed more concerned with the money than doing the right thing, giving me a shred of hope that he didn't call the cops. Without me, there is no ransom.

Fuck. That's a slim chance.

Slick blood seeps through my jeans, coming off on my fingers. It stings like a motherfucker.

Adriel's going to freak out that I was shot.

Deathbed

Adriel
17 years old

"Toss me up, and catch me at the same time that you bounce!" Princess Sparkle squeals.

I like this little trailer. Too bad me and Malakai can't just live here. I do as she asks a few times, laughing at the sound of her high-pitched cackle. After catching her one last time, I jump off the bed to snoop through the cabinets. She wiggles out of my arms, crawling on the counter as I look at the flower calendar pinned above the sink. It's only the 22nd.

"It feels like we left home a lot longer than three days ago," I tell her.

"Uh-oh..." Her pink bear paw points to today's square. "Look at the date. You always start bleeding before the 6th. That's bad."

It takes me a second to figure out what she's talking about. When what she's implying sinks in, I feel dizzy. With everything that's happened, I haven't even thought about my period. The desire to have a baby has never been something I've experienced, and I want one even less now. Kai would be so angry, and Uncle Bennett said if this happened, the baby would be sick.

My fingers grip the sink, wondering if I really do have something growing in my tummy, feasting on my insides. I shake my head. "That can't be what's happening."

"You have to make sure. Malakai would hate you if you had a baby that was like you and your mommy."

I'm suddenly straining to breathe. "What do I do?"

Her sharp teeth gnaw on the corner of the calendar. "Make it go away before he finds out."

"How?"

"Stab it so it dies. Use something sharp."

Fear fills up my throat. I don't want to do what she's saying. I wouldn't be mean to it like my mommy was to me. And Kai might not get mad at me. It would be a perfect person, created by us both because we love each other.

Even as I question this, my thoughts bounce back to how something could be wrong with the baby. What if we have to keep running? We won't be able to take care of it. Or worse, we get caught, and they take it away, giving it to someone evil.

Looking over my shoulder at the closet, I wonder if there are hangers in there. I know I've heard of that before.

Abomination!

Get it out!

His baby would be beautiful.

I cover my ears. This is confusing enough without the voices yelling at me too. Yanking open the door reveals three wire hangers, each with white paper wrapped around it.

"You sure this is going to work?"

Flopping on her bottom, Princess Sparkle kicks her legs over the edge of the counter. "It's the only way I can think of." She holds up her fuzzy arms for me to carry her. "Uppies!"

I pick her up before sitting her next to me on the bed. The paper rips as I tear it off and drop it on the comforter. While I unbend the metal, I examine the jagged ends. "This is really going to hurt."

Princess Sparkle crawls on her knees to bend over and poke at the sheet with her horns. "Just get it like this."

Once I straighten the hanger as much as I can, I scoot back to the headboard. She's watching with curiosity as I spread my legs. The daunting metal wire makes my stomach hurt. When I don't move, Princess Sparkle tilts her head, so I answer her silent question. "I'm scared."

She waves her paw at me. "It'll be over before you know it, but you better hurry. Kai will be back soon."

Do it!

With a big breath, I slowly slide one end inside me. It doesn't hurt at all until I hit something. Stabbing pain surges through me, as if it electrocuted me. I suck in through my teeth, tensing before I jab it a little harder.

Black covers my vision. My voice screams like I'm not in my body anymore. Sliding out the hanger, I see a little blood on it.

Smell the flowers, blow out the candles.

I reach down, my fingers shaking as I touch myself. The moment I feel how wet it is, I look at my hand covered in red. Blood drips onto the white sheets, and suddenly my skin is covered in sweat. My chest aches from my thrashing heart when I realize the bleeding isn't slowing.

"Shit," I whisper.

Her paws rest on my thigh as she looks between my legs. "Oh no! You're hurt!"

"N—now Kai will find out for sure." All my words come out stuttered. I lie back, looking at the roof of the trailer that is now littered in pink, blinking lights. My body feels weird. I'm shivering while sweat continues to thicken on my skin, my hair sticking to my face. I should try to clean up, I'm just too frightened to get out of the bed I might die in.

She cuddles up next to me, her horns poking my arm. "Malakai will be here soon. He won't let you die."

The timing is so perfect, it's as if he heard her. The door swings open, and the most beautiful boy in the world walks through. There's pain on his flushed face when he looks at me from the trailer entrance. "Are you okay?"

What do I say? I usually never struggle with words, but this…I shouldn't have listened to Princess Sparkle. I should have waited to ask him.

He steps over to the bed, walking through the lights as he puts more weight on his left leg. Why is he walking funny? Once he reaches me, his eyes widen in horror.

"Oh, my God…" Wet tears shimmer over his irises as he evaluates the sight of me. Holding my face tightly, he sobs, "What did you do?" I can feel his hands tremor as he reaches between my legs. A jarring stillness settles over his brooding expression when he grips the bloody wire. If I wasn't already lying down, he could knock me over with the look he's giving me. "Why would you do this?!" he bellows through his tears.

Chills overtake me, choking me with dread. As if I've forgotten how to speak, my lips shake without making a sound. The hanger clatters on the counter after he hurls it across the trailer.

A red spot on his thigh catches my gaze. Why is he bleeding?! The words may have refused to appear seconds ago, yet now they pour from my mouth. "Malakai! What happened?"

Answering with the same silence I did, he limps to his

backpack. Mikkel's letter crinkles as he carries it to the phone. The pain makes nausea slam into me, and I lean over the side of the bed to throw up.

"Try to stay still. I'll clean that in a minute." He doesn't look at me as he dials the number. I can tell when someone answers because he stands up straighter. "Hello… May I please speak to Mikkel Courtenay?" Though Kai's voice has calmed, there's a sharp, furious edge to it. I loathe that I'm the reason for the boiling terror and rage emanating from him. "Yeah, uh, hi. It's Malakai. We got your letter and—" Whatever Mikkel says perplexes him enough that his bewilderment momentarily eats everything else. "Oh, wow. Okay, well, um, we're here." Even though his chuckle is awkward, it's still soothing to hear. "Yeah, but Adriel's hurt really bad, and I was just recognized at a store." Someone knows we're here? That's not good. He sighs in relief, telling Mikkel the name of the convenience store. His stance loosens, making him appear lighter. "Thank you. I know this is crazy." Kai's relief is comforting even from across the room. After giving Mikkel the address, he thanks him again and hangs up. Dropping his head, he loses himself in thought before finally looking up at me.

I have oodles of questions about what he said and what happened at the store. More importantly though, I'm worried about why he's bleeding. He didn't even mention it to Mikkel.

"What did you do to your leg?"

The expression I get from him is one I don't understand. It's as if not even he knows what he's feeling. "I got shot."

"What?!" I sit up straight, the movement sending currents of heat pinching between my thighs.

Crawling on the bed next to me, he leans against the headboard. "Luckily it just grazed me. I'm fine."

I watch my hands shaking in my lap. He could have been killed. Caressing his fingers, I hold his hand. "What happened?" He shows no indication that he heard me or plans on responding. "Malakai?"

"How long have you known?" His eyes dart to mine, the fury burning in them darkens his ashy eyes.

"I didn't. Princess Sparkle reminded me how late I was."

"So, you did this based on a possibility? Why didn't you take a fucking pregnancy test before impaling yourself?"

I look at Princess Sparkle, but she hasn't been alive since Malakai got back. "I…I was scared you would be mad at me because it's my fault. I made you come inside me in the mausoleum. Princess Sparkle told me how to stop it. My creations are usually right."

His arm wrapping around me is the safe warmth I've been craving. He rests his head against mine, so I can hear his shallow breathing. "Mikkel's on his way."

"What did he say?"

"It's actually kind of creepy. He's apparently been keeping tabs on us ever since he found out that Mom and Dad died. Surprisingly, he knows all about the video and that the cops are looking for us. He didn't sound like he was bothered by it either. He just didn't know how to find us." With a kiss on my head, he gets up and goes to my bag. Pulling out a blue sleeveless dress he says, "Here. Let's get some clothes on you before he gets here."

I raise my arms so he can slip it over my head. "Is he a doctor? I think I need one."

"I don't think so. He just said he would bring 'help.'"

"Are you still mad at me?"

His dark eyebrows narrow as his lips press together. "I'm pissed as hell that you would do this to yourself. There's definitely some shit we need to have a talk about when you're better. Right now, though, all I care about is that you're okay." Careful to be gentle, he lies next to me and pulls my head to his chest. His fingers comb through my hair while he sings, "*You are my sunshine. My only sunshine…*"

Little Killer

Malakai
18 years old

Knock. Knock. Knock.

Adriel jolts next to me, gasping from the pain she put herself in. As enraged as I am, for several reasons, her surviving this is all I can focus on right now.

I'm across the trailer in three strides. Swinging open the door steals the oxygen from my lungs as I take in the appear- ance of the man on the trailer steps. For a split second, I think my father is standing in front of me. When I take in that he's much younger and dressed way nicer than my dad ever was, I'm able to move my feet.

"H-hi…um, thanks for coming. She's over here."

Another man is with him and follows us to the bed. Mikkel stands at the footboard, looking down at Adriel with his familiar blue eyes. From her expression, she sees the re- semblance as well.

"I've been eager to meet you both. Though this isn't how I had hoped it would come to pass." He gestures to the older man. "This is Dr. Black. Can you tell us what happened?"

Another sob rises in my throat when she answers, "I think I cut myself inside..." she points between her thighs, "here. With a hanger." Not a single reaction crosses Mikkel's face.

"Lie down on your back for me," Dr. Black instructs.

I know Mikkel is helping us, but I still don't know him. I'm uncomfortable with the idea of him seeing her body, mutilated or not. "Maybe we should leave the room while he does this."

Adriel grasps my hand, looking up at me while she begs, "Please stay."

Glancing at our cousin, his face tells me nothing. Nodding, I agree, so she will relax. Dr. Black spreads her legs far apart, shining a light to see.

Even though he's given no indication that he is anything other than concerned with her wellbeing, it still makes my skin burn to watch Mikkel's eyes graze over Adriel. I open my mouth to ask him to look away when he does so on his own.

The doctor's gloved fingers prod inside her body. When he touches somewhere painful, she gasps, tightening her hold on my hand. I press my lips together to keep myself from yelling at the doctor to be more fucking careful.

"How many times did you do it?" he asks.

"Twice."

Mikkel's eyes shift between me and my sister, making me wonder what he thinks about all this. Dr. Black switches off his light before removing his gloves and turning to Mikkel.

"I want to take her to my clinic to inspect her better. From what I can tell, she didn't get anywhere near the cervix, though there are two cuts inside her vaginal canal that I want to treat for possible infection."

Energy surges from my stomach to my head, making me jump to my feet. "So, she'll be okay?"

Dr. Black nods. "I need to do a more thorough examination, but yes, she should make a full recovery. However..." Just as my pulse begins to slow, it speeds right back up. 'Howevers' are rarely good. "If she was pregnant before this, she still is. Assuming that it isn't wanted, we'll need to take further steps to terminate."

I feel Adriel's gaze seeping through my flesh, my chest rising and falling quickly. She could still be pregnant. A baby... What the hell are we going to do with a baby? The room spins around me. I really haven't spent much time thinking about being a dad, and never with my sister. How would we explain our situation to a child? I hate to admit that she might have had the right idea; she just went about it in the worst way imaginable.

"Which is something we can deal with at a future date," Mikkel interjects. "For now, we need to get Adriel taken care of. You'll both be staying with me from now on, so gather your things."

His urgency snaps me from my thoughts. I kiss her on my way to get our bags. Dr. Black passes by me as I watch Mikkel lean down, sliding his arms under Adriel's back and legs to carry her outside. I can't get a feel on him, and it's bugging me. Seeing her in someone else's arms sets my nerves on fire, especially with the way she's leaning in to him.

It only takes a couple of minutes to collect all of our stuff. After one last run through the trailer, I meet them outside where a large, black SUV sits out front.

A tall man, a little older than me and dressed almost as nice as Mikkel, greets me with a small smile. Where the hell did he come from?

"Hello. I'm Thomas Kregg. I'm Mr. Courtenay's personal assistant." He reaches out, taking our bags to load them in the back. "If you need anything, I can fulfill most requests."

I'm starting to get the impression that our cousin has a

much cushier life than we're used to. "Uh, okay, I just have to drop off the key at the front desk."

His palm opens in front of me. "Give it to me, I'll do it. Go be with your sister."

Dropping the key in his hand, I open the door to sit next to Adriel. Mikkel turns from the front seat to face us.

"We have a lot to discuss, you and I." I can't decide if his smile is menacing or comforting. His bright blue eyes shift to Adriel. "But first we need to get you to the clinic. How are you feeling?"

"I think I'm okay." Even as she says it, she shifts uncomfortably in her seat as she hugs her doll that I illogically hate. I know her mind distorts things, and the toy isn't real, but that doesn't make me want to rip it's head off any less.

He nods before straightening back in his seat to look forward. When he speaks again, I can't see his face. "The most important thing I need you both to understand is that there isn't anything you can say or do that will shock me. You are truly safe in the presence of myself and my associates. Your relationship is a non-issue in my home, and soon it won't be a problem at all." I look at Adriel who appears just as confused as I am. What is that supposed to mean? "However, I do need to know, are there any other bodies besides your uncle's?"

Despite him just telling us he's trustworthy, it's still a hard thing to discuss with a stranger, and who knows if he's being completely honest or not.

"Yes. Uncle Bennett was an accident. The others weren't though," Adriel says, wincing as she puts that stupid fucking doll in the seat next to her.

The skin around my eyes stretches knowing she's about to spill all of our secrets. He grins over his shoulder, arching a brow.

"The others? How many are there?"

Just as I open my mouth to stop her she says, "Do you mean since Uncle Bennett or before?" She seems tense, slowly releasing a heavy breath. "Because it will take me a while to count all those."

I caress her hand, attempting to distract her from the pain. Mikkel's laugh is loud and seems uncharacteristic based on the little bit I know of him. "You're definitely family, little killer." Shaking his head, he quiets down to a chuckle. "My list of questions is growing longer by the minute."

While his response might be unsettling under different circumstances, right now it allows air to expand my chest. At the same time though, I wonder what kind of person could take all of this so lightly.

Thomas returns from taking back the key. "Straight to the clinic?"

Mikkel nods as we pull away from the rental trailer. "While Adriel is getting looked over, Malakai and I will go back to the house to get their room situated." It makes me nervous to think about leaving her alone with someone we only just met. I want to object, but he's saving our asses and possibly Adriel's life. Making him angry is something I'm pretty sure I want to avoid. As if hearing my thoughts Mikkel adds, "She'll be fine. I trust all my associates to respect and protect those I hold dear."

Adriel kisses my cheek and whispers, "It's okay."

In the trailer, she'd begged me to stay. It's strange that she's comfortable with being separated now.

Mikkel looks to his assistant as we drive down the LA-1. "Is our convenience store problem resolved?"

Thomas nods. "Being taken care of as we speak."

'Convenience store problem'? They must be talking about

the guy that shot me. I can't help but assume that 'taken care of' means exactly what it implies.

"Perfect." Peeking around his seat, Mikkel nods to me. "I noticed your leg was bleeding. Do you need Dr. Black to take a look?"

Honestly, with my adrenaline, I can barely feel it. "It's fine."

The 'clinic' looks more like a huge garage than a medical facility. A large loading door opens, the bright light from inside illuminating the night. As the SUV pulls inside, I look through the tinted windows. Half of the building space is bare, with the other half set up like the infirmary at summer camp. Cabinets are set against the wall behind the three beds lined up next to testing equipment and shelves filled with different sized bottles. Portable surgical lights are beside each bed and a man wearing a lab coat filling up pill bottles at a table.

I climb out of the car to walk around and pick up Adriel. My stomach drops at the blood spot left on the white towel she was sitting on. Her arm hugs my neck while she holds her evil toy to her chest.

"I promise I'll be okay," she whispers. "I trust him."

Following Dr. Black as he weaves through tables and equipment, I lie her down on the stark white sheets of the bed.

Considering the odd location, I'm surprised by how impeccably clean everything looks. Daunting implements stare up at me from the metal table, and I wonder if any of them will be used on my sister. Dr. Black is having a hushed discussion with the man in the lab coat when Mikkel's fingers brush over Adriel's hair. "We'll see you soon, little killer."

My gaze burns as I watch his hand on her. What's worse is she turns toward his touch, making my heart freefall between my ribs into my stomach.

She tries to get into a comfortable position as Mikkel's

palm rests on my back. "Come on. Thomas will have her home before you know it."

With a sigh, I press my lips to her temple. "I love you."

Her smiles have always had an effect on me, and this one is no different. "I love you too, Kai."

Mikkel and Thomas lead me back to the SUV. I don't even get my seatbelt buckled when my cousin says, "Is something wrong? Besides the obvious of course."

Jesus, he's intense. "I'm just not used to seeing other people touch her."

The dark swallows the car as we pull onto the street. "While I will freely admit I immediately felt a connection when I first saw her, you can rest assured, I have no desire to fuck her. The pull I have to you is very similar. There's a likeness between the three of us. I just want to protect and care for you."

"But you barely know us. Why are you risking so much for us?"

Bending over, he opens the middle console and pulls out a flask. "Telling you the whole story is a conversation that I want both you and your sister present for. Just know that I've been curious about you your entire life. And I'm risking nothing. Family has always been important, which is why Micah disconnecting from us was such a blow." He takes a long drink before handing it to me. "It'll take the edge off."

Eager to numb my senses, I swallow as much as I can. "What happened between you and my dad?" I ask between coughs.

"I'm sure there are many things you want to know, as do I, though, I prefer to have a single conversation with the both of you simultaneously."

We pass the flask back and forth a few more times before

Thomas asks, "Are you hungry? Our cook could make you something. Like me, Eugéne Pierre can fulfill most requests."

"If you like Cajun, you'll have to try his jambalaya," Mikkel adds.

The mention of food has my stomach growling with emptiness. I chuckle to cover my embarrassment. "Never had it."

Every street we've driven on has been scattered with stilted homes. This one, however, only contains a single residence. Fences are another thing I haven't seen much of either, yet as if needing to be different from everyone else, there's a stone wall curving away from a wrought iron gate outside Mikkel's home. The detailed designs in the black metal are haunting yet beautiful. Thomas enters a code into the screen on his dashboard, granting us entrance. The property is much larger than anything I've seen so far.

The house itself is white, trimmed in an earthy green tint. The entire house is covered in windows, and the lower half is made of a wood material with four olive garage doors lined up in a row. The third one opens up, revealing at least twenty gorgeous cars, a boat, and a jet ski.

"Holy shit."

Mikkel laughs. "You'll get your chance to play with them, don't worry."

Thomas carries our bags, refusing my help when I offer. We climb up a staircase leading from the enormous garage to an elaborate sitting room.

This all has a bit of a Twilight Zone feel. I'm not sure what to say, and I already miss Adriel. She never has a problem saying what she's thinking.

Mikkel leads me into a large living room that I have to step down into. The gray carpet looks soft against the two white, crescent shaped couches. An actual black bear skin rug lies in front of a stone fireplace. The black and white paintings on the wall are—I guess I would say tasteful—depictions of mutilated bodies.

Mikkel walks to the bar in the corner of the room, taking out two glasses as Thomas moves behind me to climb a wide spiral staircase. The black iron railings are scrolled in the same swirled designs on the front gate. There are hallways leading from this room to at least three different destinations.

"This place is insane."

Handing me my drink, he swallows down his own. "The family business is a lucrative one."

"What is that exactly?"

"Be patient. As I said, I will answer all of your questions once Adriel has returned." He wraps his arm around my shoulder, leading me toward the stairs. "Let me show you where you'll be staying."

The top of the staircase splits off into opposite directions. We take the one on the left which brings us to a wide hallway. Once we get to the third wooden door on the right, he opens it.

"Whoa," I whisper.

Our bags are sitting on a black lounge at the foot of a giant four poster bed. A sheer black canopy surrounds it. The furnishings and the décor are all in a black, gray, and white color scheme. What really has me stunned, though, is the curved wall in front of me, made entirely of glass. Security lights show the palm trees swaying. I can only imagine the view in the daylight.

The room is pristine, and I smile at the fact that it won't stay like that for long. Soon it will be covered in Adriel's creations, stickers, and whatever else she adds along the way.

I really hope she gets back soon.

Pointing to a white door, Mikkel finishes off his drink. "The bathroom is in there. It's fully stocked with toiletries and towels. If you need anything else just let me know."

It makes me uncomfortable asking him for more. I also can't take a shower just to put on dirty clothes. "Can I use your washing machine? We're out of clean clothes."

"Certainly. And I may have a few things that you can wear until we can get you more." He walks to an odd little cabinet above the baseboard of the wall. "Gather your soiled items and place them in here." A laundry chute is revealed when he pulls open the little door.

He leaves while I empty our bags on the floor and do as he says. Even though I took a shower just a few hours ago, I need another one badly. Sweat and blood coat my skin, plus, I need to clean my wounded leg.

Lathering up my skin, my thoughts flip through images of Adriel pregnant. How would she look swollen with the life we created? Although I know it can't happen, I fantasize about her holding a child made from the perfect concoction of us both. It's unrealistic to think a baby would even be possible in our predicament. We already have a family history of hallucinations to deal with on top of the possibility that our incest might cause even worse issues. And that's if we somehow get out of the mess we're currently in.

The mirrors are fogged with steam as I dry myself with an epically soft towel. A stack of clothes and a first aid kit sit on the lounge. There's a black, spaghetti strap maxi dress and a pair of pink flip flops for Adriel that I set aside. Murmuring my gratefulness at the package of underwear, I tug on the black pants and gray, short-sleeved linen sweater before lacing up a pair of black oxford shoes. These are the nicest clothes I've ever seen, let alone worn.

Leaving our room, I have no idea where I'm going in this ginormous place. I somehow manage to find Mikkel back in the living room.

"Perfect timing. Eugéne is just finishing up."

As I follow him down the hall, I can't help but imagine living here. This place is a labyrinth, I'd constantly be getting lost. The dining room isn't any less breathtaking than the rest of the house. Three of the four walls are windows showing the reflection of the Gulf in the distance. There are three place settings at the end of a long table. Mikkel pulls out the seat at the head of the table, gesturing for me to take the one next to him.

"I have many connections, Malakai. However, to do the best damage control possible, I need you to tell me everything that happened following the night that you were filmed. Can you do that?"

Every second that passes with him eases my trepidation. I nod. "Yes."

"All right then." He fills our glasses before holding his up. "To family reunions."

Body Parts

Adriel

17 years old

The pills rattle in my hand as Thomas pushes the wheelchair through this super big house. I already told him back at the clinic that I could walk, but he said Mikkel insisted, so I didn't complain. The stuff Dr. Black gave me through the IV is definitely making me feel better. I'm barely in any pain at all. He told me to take the pills every day for two weeks in case I get an infection.

Princess Sparkle still hasn't come alive again which stinks because Dr. Black and the other guy in the white coat were really boring. Thomas pushes me down a hallway, and the moment I see Kai, I hug her to my chest. I don't care if Mikkel gets mad, I leap from the wheelchair and run to hug him. He's out of his seat before I reach him.

"Adriel," Mikkel chides. "Try to take it easy. I want you to heal as quickly as possible."

There's something about our cousin. From the second he stood in front of me at the trailer, I knew he would protect us. I love how much he looks like Daddy and how safe he makes me feel. There's an ominous force about him that excites something deep inside me.

My smile is instantly returned when I say, "Sorry."

"Are you hungry?" Kai asks as he takes my hand.

It's weird that I'm not hungry at all since I was starving earlier. As I shake my head in response, Mikkel stands. "Both of you, come with me." He gestures to Thomas, "Bring a chocolate milkshake to the study for Adriel."

Thomas smiles. "Of course."

Kai keeps giving me little kisses on the way down the hall, refusing to let go of me. I never realized before now that I'm glad Bridgett posted that video. Malakai might think this trip has been terrible, but aside from the man in Oklahoma and the last few hours, I've enjoyed it. He touches me without restraint or guilt. Being in his arms, even while on the run, is better than it ever was when he was fighting his feelings for me.

Mikkel leads us into a sleek room with the same high ceiling as the rest of the house. A long, fuzzy, black couch sits opposite a big mahogany desk. The photographs on the walls are what truly catch my attention though. Onyx frames hold portraits of mutilated men and women, their flesh ripped apart. The details in each of them are stunning. In black and white, the visual beauty of the images overshadows the actual content.

The one I'm staring at now has a very pretty lady in it. She's wearing a dark gown that's bunched up at her waist, exposing her pussy. Her long, light hair is curled, spread out around her head like a halo, bordering her tortured expression highlighted in make-up—A stolen scream frozen in time. I lightly trace my fingers over her legs that have been completely skinned, leaving only bone from thigh to ankle. Dark high heels adorn her still intact feet.

I don't realize I'm holding my breath until Mikkel places his hand on my back. "Exquisite, aren't they? The photographer is a client of mine."

Malakai sits on the weirdest chair I've ever seen. It's white and shaped like a half sphere, hiding his face when he asks, "What is it you do exactly?"

Walking to the bar in the corner, Mikkel asks, "Are you familiar with what System D means?"

I've never heard of it. Kai's head peeks out from behind the strange chair. "Like the black market?"

"Exactly. The shadow economy has many names. In short, I supply people with items that are either difficult to come by or too expensive in the mainstream market."

Malakai scoffs, "So what? You sell livers to people doing back alley surgeries?"

"Sometimes."

He was obviously just kidding, so Mikkel's response makes his jaw drop. I can almost feel my ears perk up with interest. I run my fingers over Princess Sparkles horns as I ask, "What about the other times?"

I'm starting to really like when he smiles at me. "While I have my fingers in a few pies, my biggest source of income is the buying and selling of human bodies, both dead and alive. For example, one of my wealthiest clients has developed a taste for...meat. The kind that can't be bought at a butcher shop, so he pays me a heavy sum to acquire it for him. There's of course the obvious run of the mill organ trade. Some of my more special clients, however, are...unique."

Kai's hollow expression tethers me to him. I take Princess Sparkle to sit on his lap in the odd chair, cuddling up to his chest. His apprehension gushes out of him in pulses.

I, on the other hand, am eager to hear more. "Did my daddy know you did this? Is that why he lied to us about you?"

He leans against his desk, watching us in amusement as Kai's hand rubs down my leg. "Yes, he was well aware of what our family does and he vehemently disapproved, apparently. I'll admit, most of my knowledge has been obtained through hearsay. I was only three or four when he left for some kind of student ministry. He was sent to Iowa of all places. Once he met Azalea, I think he decided to never come back." Listening to him talk about my daddy when he was my age is a puzzling feeling. Daddy never spoke of his life before divinity school. It makes me feel selfish that I never thought to ask. "My father used to joke that Micah was the 'white sheep' of our family. We Courtenays aren't exactly religious, yet in spite of that, he was drawn to the church at a very young age. Back then, we were as deep into the drug trade as we were the flesh trade. According to our grandparents, Micah never hid the fact that he despised what our family did." He throws back the rest of his drink before sitting on the fluffy couch. "The last time any of us saw him was at your parents' wedding. When I was fifteen, he told us Azalea was pregnant."

Thomas taps on the door, walking over to hand me my milkshake. I take a big sip of the delicious drink. It cools my throat and makes my taste buds happy. Mikkel yanks Thomas onto his lap, stroking his hand across his leg.

Kai and I look at each other. Daddy never preached against same sex relationships, however, they weren't something we were really exposed to in Lettleton. I've never seen two men together in person. It gives me a warm, funny feeling in my tummy...at least I think it's in my tummy.

"Both my father and grandfather made many attempts to

speak to Micah until he sent a letter demanding they never contact him or Azalea again. I was raised to believe that family is the most important thing. I'll never forget the impact that letter had on my father and our grandparents."

It makes me a little angry that Daddy kept them from us. Why didn't we get to choose? "Are both of our grandparents still alive?" Me and Malakai never had grandparents before.

Mikkel nods as he trails his hand higher up Thomas' leg, obviously arousing him with the erection straining his slacks. Watching them together is bewitching to me. I can't tell how Malakai feels about it. His stare is blank, holding no emotion.

"Now, tell me," Mikkel says, "I've been curious since you mentioned it…how many people have you killed? In your lifetime, I mean?"

Kai tenses under me, his hand squeezing my hip. I don't understand what his uncertainty is about. We were just told our cousin is like us. Though he may not eliminate sinners, he provides a service to them that protects people. It may seem like a gray area, but if you really look at it, Mikkel keeps sinners off the streets and away from attacking innocent people by giving them what they need to pacify their desires. While I don't necessarily believe they deserve it, at least he's still saving people.

I spread my fingers out and say, "Oodles of people. They were all evil though…like your clients." Mikkel chuckles when I add, "Mommy had a special gift that helped us find them."

"Oh, really?" His eyes raise as he rubs the bulge in Thomas' pants. My breath catches before I find myself touching Kai's chest the same way. "Do either of you have that…gift?"

Kai's eyes widen with a slight shake of his head, so I try to comfort him with my smile. "Kind of. It's just different. I don't talk to corpses like she did. I talk to my creations."

Arching his eyebrow, Mikkel stops moving his hand to grip Thomas' crotch. "Your creations?"

My lips form an O before I lift up Princess Sparkle. "That's what I call my toys. And sometimes I hear voices in my head. I also see strange things."

The zipper of Thomas' jeans is loud in the silence of the office before Mikkel slowly reaches inside his pants to reveal his erection. "That's intriguing. Did you enjoy it? Taking their lives?" His hand moves slowly up and down as Thomas rocks into his fist.

In any other situation, this might make me feel uncomfortable. Right now, though, I'm mesmerized watching them. It makes my body feel hot in the nice way.

Without thinking, I scoot back to press my bottom against Kai's stomach. "Yes, very much." Mikkel must have liked that answer because his eyes blaze before whispering something in Thomas' ear.

I reach between my legs to brush my fingers over Kai's zipper, making him jump beneath me. Looking over my shoulder causes me to rip my hand away at the panic darkening his eyes.

"What about you?" Mikkel asks Malakai.

Thomas lowers to the floor, unfastening Mikkel's trousers. His cock jumps out to meet Thomas' mouth sliding over it. I grip tight onto Princess Sparkle as I feel myself getting wet watching his head bob down to the base. Mikkel pulls his hair, groaning with each thrust.

"When they deserve it..." Malakai responds in a flat tone. I can't rip my eyes away from my cousin fucking Thomas' mouth when Kai pushes at my hips to get me off of his lap, so he can stand. "What the hell is this, Mikkel?" His hand gestures to Thomas, still giving it his all.

"I told you in the car," he moans, "I don't want to fuck Adriel." My skin tightens, and I freeze. I had no idea that was ever a discussion. Kai will always be the only one I want. His nervousness is making more sense now. "I don't want to fuck you either."

Kai's shoulders fall in frustration. "Then why are we watching you get your dick sucked?"

"The video of you two…I've seen it many times. It's gotten me so fucking hard, fantasizing about watching you together these past few days."

Mikkel's thrusts get faster making Thomas gag. It's really difficult not to touch myself over my panties. I just don't want to upset Malakai who, at the moment, looks more confused than angry. He looks down at me as I stand to hold his hand.

Kai tilts his head, narrowing his eyes. "Just watch? Nobody will touch either of us?"

"You have my word. That isn't what I want." Mikkel squeezes Thomas' skull as tears stream down his face, and still, he shoves harder into his mouth.

Kai shakes his head as if a thought got stuck while processing. "We can't have sex though." He gestures to me. "She just got stitched up."

"You can still use your mouths."

Every sentence he says is coated in arousal. It's a contagious feeling. While the thought of this is exhilarating, I only want to do what he's suggesting if Malakai does too.

Kai's hand wraps around my wrist, yanking me against his chest to press our foreheads together. "Are you okay with this?" he whispers.

I hold his face tight as my lips brush over his. "Yes, but only if you are."

The smirk that stretches his mouth sends tickles across my whole body. We look to our cousin who pats the seat next to him. Thomas pulls his head off, gasping for breath before Mikkel shoves it back down.

"Did I tell you to stop sucking?" He grins.

I giggle when Kai picks me up, carrying me to the couch. My legs spread automatically the moment he lifts my dress. Being openly watched by someone who sees our true beauty is so erotic. As soon as the air hits my exposed pussy, I thrust my hips.

Gentle fingers slide up my thighs as he kisses the inside of my knees. "Tell me if it hurts, okay?"

"Uh-huh," I gasp, holding tight to Princess Sparkle.

Mikkel's gaze is on my cunt as my brother lowers to his knees. His husky voice grows deeper by the minute. "Fuck, your so wet you're shimmering."

My eyes shift to Kai to gauge his reaction. While he looks at our cousin, the comment doesn't stop his tongue from softly licking around my entrance. Without his fingers inside me, it's almost agonizing. I rock against his mouth, trying to make him go faster.

Mikkel's fusion of aggression and passion with Thomas is intoxicating. He yanks his head away by his hair before slamming their mouths together. "I want that sexy, tight ass."

Thomas' eyes are captivated by Mikkel removing his slacks, moaning when he sucks his erection between his lips. The moment Kai licks at my clitty, the hand not holding Princess Sparkle flies to the top of his head. Pain from me clenching takes my breath away, though the wet warmth of his mouth soothes me. The drugs I'm on help a lot, but coming is still going to hurt. His tongue flicks at my most sensitive spot over and over. Suddenly, I don't care how painful it will be. Right now, this feels incredible. Pleasure and exhilaration consume every cell in my body.

"Kai…yes," I murmur, "lick it faster. I want Mikkel to watch you make me come."

The melody of his moans mixed with the vibration of his lips has me gasping. His fingers dig into my thighs as he feasts on me. The wet sounds of his tongue lapping at me is beyond erotic, and I rock against him faster. His head moving while he devours me is the sexiest thing on the planet.

"Fuck," Mikkel growls. He shoots to his feet, his hand squeezing the back of Thomas' neck to bend him over the couch next to me. "You're going to give me a run for my money, aren't you, little killer?"

I've never met anyone like Mikkel before. He kind of makes me feel like Daddy did, except I would have never wanted Daddy to see me and Kai this way. I want to make Mikkel proud. I want him to love me.

The pressure of Kai's tongue pushes my body into the tingling numbness that always consumes me right before I'm about to burst apart. I am so close when a quick, stabbing pain shoots between my legs, ripping me from the edge. Thomas holds himself up by his arms as Mikkel spreads his bottom cheeks apart, sticking his finger in the hole that looks like a crinkled star before spitting on it and violently ramming into him. Malakai hasn't slowed down, bringing my orgasm back within reach. He keeps a steady pace, taking me back to the brink. The second before I break into a million pieces, Mikkel holds my chin in his grip.

"Look at me when he makes you come."

I obey without thinking, Kai's mouth giving me an ecstasy I can't control. It hurts so badly, yet I refuse to tear my gaze from Mikkel's. When Kai's tongue licks me over the cliff to my excruciating orgasm, I cry out my release. Mikkel continues to assault Thomas' body when Malakai looks up to him.

"Do you think it would hurt her if I fucked her ass?"

He's never done that before. I'm not sure if I'm excited or scared. Maybe both. "You won't know unless you try," Mikkel responds.

The soft pad of his finger massages my secret place while he asks, "Is that okay?"

I realize, everything with him is okay. He would never hurt me. "Yes."

That ornery smirk has me rocking against his touch. He stays on his knees, unfastening his jeans and lifting my legs higher. The pressure of his cock pushing against the spot that's never been touched gives me goosebumps, until he tries to shove in deeper. Instinctively, I pull away from the unfamiliar pain. How the heck is Thomas taking it like that? And enjoying it?

"Lick her ass. She needs lubrication." Mikkel pulls out of Thomas, his tongue lapping at the puckered hole to teach Malakai how.

He watches our cousin with eagerness. After a few moments, he drops down, lifting my butt higher. Mikkel is a good teacher, and Kai is a quick learner because the way his tongue moves against my bottom is making stars light up across my vision.

"Like this?"

"Ask your sister," Mikkel answers.

Kai's eyes meet mine when he asks, "Does this feel good?"

"Y-yes…keep doing that."

Mikkel is making Thomas moan so loud. The harder he fucks him, the faster Thomas strokes his own cock. "Mikkel, I'm gonna…"

A stream of thick, white semen sprays against the fuzzy, black fabric. "That's my good boy." Mikkel kisses down his back, whispering words of praise.

Malakai sits back up, gently pushing against my now

slippery bottom hole. It doesn't hurt as bad as before, but once the head is all the way in, I squeeze Princess Sparkle, tensing as I dig my nails into his arms.

"You need to relax, Adriel. Keep your muscles loose, and don't tense up. It'll help him slide in easier, I promise." Thomas moans out his instructions.

"Don't forget the clit, keep giving her attention there too."

Kai obeys Mikkel, rubbing his thumb in circles. With a deep breath, I try to do as Thomas says, my body slacking against the couch. The uncomfortable sensation of him pushing inside me suddenly shifts, and I realize it actually feels really nice.

Really, really nice.

"Oh, oh God."

"Does it feel good? Because it sure as fuck does to me," Kai grins.

His words, his body above mine, this entire situation, has me pushing farther onto his shaft as I nod. He slowly increases his speed, and before long he's pounding into me as hard as he would my pussy.

"This feels so different." he gasps.

"Fucking beautiful," Mikkel growls. "You two are going to make me come."

My fingers dig into Kai's hips as they buck into me. He moans, "Fuck, me too."

They both groan with pleasure, emptying themselves into me and Thomas, their muscles flexing with their last few strokes.

Mikkel laughs as he looks at us both, taking in the scene a final time. He's still inside Thomas when his hand cups the back of Kai's neck. "Welcome home."

Stab

Four Months Later…

Malakai

18 years old

We're dead now.

Our bodies were pulled from the Columbia River, water logged and bound. The photos attached to the article are gruesome. The search for us picked up pace a few weeks ago when there had been multiple 'sightings' of us in and around Washington. They were all bogus of course. The closer they thought they were getting to us, the higher they raised the ransom. I'd be lying if I said I hadn't gotten a kick out of reading about the wild goose chase Mikkel had led the police on these last few weeks. They never found the couple that Adriel mutilated, but they did find the man in Oklahoma, though we were never officially charged for that one.

Until now, we've had to be careful in public, even with our changes in appearance, but since we're technically dead, we finally get the freedom we've been promised.

I've learned that while Mikkel makes it a priority to be personally involved in every one of his business dealings, he also has a large employee roster. He loves to say, *It requires many gears in order to make a clock work.*

With all the people it took to fake our deaths, I see what he means. He used one of his suppliers to purchase the bodies that were used and had a stylist come in to do their hair like ours before having them transported to Vancouver. At the same time he had people tipping off the police, he had others dumping the bodies in the river. Lastly, he used his law enforcement contacts to forge the coroner's report to say that the bodies were, in fact, ours.

Drinking my coffee, I watch Adriel inhaling her waffles. I chuckle at her, and she looks up at me, grinning with a mouth full of food. It's still weird to see her with blonde hair. Even her eyebrows are bleached light. I need to stop calling her Adriel. As of last week, she officially became Adeline Monroe. Mikkel wasn't lying when he said he had his hands in many pots. For him, obtaining new identities seemed to be as easy as ordering shoes online.

In my mind, she'll always be Adriel. When we're at the house, I still call her that, though Mikkel chides me every time, saying I need to get used to calling her Adeline. I still struggle answering to Matias Boudreaux. Not having the same last name as her bugs me more than I expected. I'm going to have to change that with a ring like normal couples do. I can certainly afford one now.

I recently found out how much work goes into hiding copious amounts of money earned illegally. According to legal documents, our family owns mineral mines, which Mikkel jokingly calls laundromats because that's how the money is 'cleaned.'

Sometimes I wonder how my dad could have chosen to leave this life behind. Other times, I know exactly why he did. There's a lot of shady shit going on that I'm sure gnawed on his conscience. Maybe that's how he rationalized ridding the world of the evil he believed he came from?

To me, there's no difference. Whether it's sinners or Mikkel's clients—it's all the same.

Adriel and I now have access to more money than I've ever seen in my life. We could easily get our own place, but Mikkel isn't too keen on us moving out yet. While he would never forbid us from doing anything, he doesn't hide his clear opinion on the matter either. He likes having us here. Honestly, I like us being here too.

Last night, as he sat in the chair by our bed, Thomas sucking his cock to the sight of us fucking, he told us he had a new job for us. Him watching us was not something I expected to be so hot, but it gets me stone hard to hear the things he says about us in the heat of arousal.

I can't help thinking that everything happened exactly how it was supposed to. Family nights with Mom and Dad prepared me for the things I now have to do. Sometimes, it's cutting up and storing body parts. Other times, it's packaging organs. There are days we deliver product and days we pick it up. Our more gruesome jobs are Adriel's favorite. I can't believe the stupid decisions people make based on greed. If they cross Mikkel, or even think about hurting me or Adriel, they are not only taken out of this world, they are taken out slowly. Just like my sister, my cousin likes to play with his kills.

Adriel and I do most of our jobs together, though sometimes we'll go with either Mikkel, Thomas, or one of his other associates. In the past few months, Thomas and I have become close. He's my very first real friend. He tries desperately to pretend as if he's not madly in love with Mikkel, but when he looks at him like his every movement is a work of art, it gives him away. I really hope my cousin realizes what he has someday.

Adriel's dark eyelashes flutter. "Matias, can we go to the beach today before we go to work?"

I love seeing her in a bathing suit. Her little tummy has the smallest pooch from the baby. After meeting Mikkel, the idea of keeping it wasn't so daunting. Not to mention the fact that she tried to end the pregnancy and it didn't work, tells me we were meant to be this child's parents. Mikkel definitely encouraged us to keep it. Now that some time has passed, I can honestly say we're all excited. Part of me is heartbroken that Mom and Dad won't ever get to meet or hold the baby.

I've really been working on forgiving my mother. Mikkel says she can't feel my rage. The hate only affects me. Talks with him have really helped. He told me that no matter how much I hate her, seeing as she felt death was her only option, she likely despised herself even more.

I look at Mikkel who nods his permission. "Sure. As long as you're at the address I gave you before seven tonight."

Adriel claps her hands in excitement. Our job doesn't require us to actually kill as much as she'd like. In my opinion, it requires it plenty, and I'm so proud of her for not shedding a drop of blood from anyone she wasn't supposed to since we got here.

Well, besides one, but that was shortly after we first arrived. It was only the third job Mikkel had given us and the night we learned that we don't possess the pacing or finesse required to torture someone for information.

Tonight, though, is a free for all. One of Mikkel's clients, Jeff Kneed, hadn't placed his regular heart, eye, and kidney orders in a while. Then three weeks ago, he requested more than he ever had before. Mikkel felt off about it, so he refused to fill the order. Through some investigation and light stalking, it was confirmed that Jeff had gotten in trouble with the authorities, talking where he shouldn't have. So, tonight we'll be cutting off that problematic loose end.

In my deepest thoughts, I still question if what we're doing is wrong. In reality, though, I don't really feel like it's any different than family nights were. Besides, the effect it has on Adriel is incredible. She's always smiling, free to be who she is without judgment or fear.

Mikkel offered to get her medication for her hallucinations, but none of us really want that for her. I love her exactly how she is. I don't want to change a single part of her, and she doesn't want her creations to stop talking to her.

Once her waffles are gone, leaving nothing besides excess syrup on her plate, she jumps up in excitement to go change.

Mikkel grins after her, placing his coffee cup on the table. "Do you have everything you need for tonight?"

"We're getting low on duct tape, and Ad…eline has almost used all the concertina wire. She loves that shit."

He laughs, shaking his head as he stands. "My little killer." His hand pats my back as he walks toward his study. "You'll have both in your cases this afternoon."

I climb the massive staircase to our room where Adriel is talking with Beddy. "I want to know too. We only have to wait a few more weeks. Then we can pick a name."

Coming up behind her, I slide my arms around her waist, resting my head on her shoulder. "What are you guys talking about?"

"If it's going to be a boy or a girl. It's driving us bonkers to not know yet."

Sometimes I love her so fucking much my chest feels sore. I can't wait to see who we created together. Kissing her neck I ask, "Are you ready?"

"Beddy wants to know if she can come too."

She's asking, yet she's already picking up the toy, so I'm pretty sure my response is irrelevant. "Of course." My shorts fall to the floor before I step into my trunks. "Who's coming with us tonight?" I make sure I have my camera and everything we need inside the mermaid beach bag.

Her sunglasses cover her sparkling eyes. "I promised Sluma she could come." Skipping out of the room she sings, *"I'm gonna stab, stab, stab the man, disembowel his guts, scoop out both his eyeballs, and cut off both his nuts!"*

Jesus. "Did you just make that up?" I laugh. She can be so fucked up sometimes.

"Yes. Do you like it?"

With a grin, I nod. "It's adorably morbid. Just like you."

She jumps down to the landing, telling me over her shoulder, "I'm going to say goodbye to Mikkel. I'll be right back."

"Sing him your song."

Even living in this beautiful place, her smile is the most exquisite sight I see each day.

Pulling out my keys still gives me such a rush. Mikkel got me an Audi A8 a couple months ago. I've never driven anything like it.

I slide onto the sleek, black seat, sighing at the sound of the engine purring. As I pull out of the garage, Adriel runs from the front door of our huge house with her hand on her stomach, smiling at me when she jumps inside.

One night, four months ago, my life went from perilous to paradise. I was terrified our lives were over when they were really just beginning. Lacing my fingers between hers, I pick up my sunglasses from the console.

"Let's go to the beach."

The site is already set up when we arrive. I was surprised the first time we did this at how similar things were compared to family night. Plastic covers every surface in the room. Our cases contain everything we could possibly need to kill this man and to take our time doing it.

Mikkel has us wear white uniforms. Adriel loves it because she likes to see how much blood gets on her. When she told him that, he laughed and said that he felt the same way.

A *ping* sounds in my white pants pocket. I take out my phone to see a text from Mikkel.

My evening has freed up. Thomas and I will be joining you shortly.

I text back a quick response as Adriel unpacks our cases. "Thomas and Mikkel are coming."

She claps her hands with a squeal. "Yay! It's been so long since it was just the four of us!"

I've learned over the past several weeks that Mikkel and Adriel are very similar. Blood and violence turn them on. They both see things through a different filter than everyone else. Somehow, they balance kindness and malevolence with precision. When they get the chance to kill together, their grim collaboration can be truly awe-inspiring.

As I watch her dance around in her white dress with Sluma, only hearing half of their conversation, Thomas and Mikkel come in through the back door.

"Mikkel!" She barely lets him walk in the room before she presses her palms together about to ask for something. "Can we please set up a booby trap? I've always wanted to."

He and Thomas are both dressed like I am. We, along with everything else, are clean and clinical, but in less than an hour, this place will be a mess. The fact that he has his own personal clean-up crew is very convenient.

Holding her chin in his hand he asks, "What did you have in mind, my little killer?"

For a moment, she's silent in contemplation, then her head suddenly jerks to Sluma, eyes widening with a smile. "That's a great idea! Sluma thinks we should turn all the lights off and fasten concertina wire at the base of the door, so when he walks in, he'll cut his legs and trip over it." Nodding her understanding to her doll, she runs to her unpacked case and picks up a box of caltrops. "Then we can put these on the floor. He'll land on them when he falls."

Mikkel tilts his head, clearly conflicted about the idea. Eventually, his desire to make her happy wins out, just like it always does. "Go on, set it up. We'll try it."

Using a hammer, she nails the wire at the entrance, testing its tautness. I cross my arms and stand next to Mikkel. "How did you talk Jeff into coming here, anyway?"

"He thinks he's meeting McKenna. He likes his woman to have a little something extra."

"Like what?"

"A dick." He takes a flask from Thomas' hand, throwing back a long swig before handing it to me. "All it took was one look under her skirt, and he was begging her for a time and place." He watches Adriel strategically placing the caltrops on the floor. "You've met McKenna, right?"

I nod. She's one of his employees. Last month, Adriel and I went with her to South Carolina to deliver vials of adrenaline to a creepy, mute guy in a suit.

Once Adriel's trap is prepared, she runs over to ask

Mikkel, "Can someone bring him to my creation station when we're finished?"

His finger bops her nose. "Of course, that's what I gave it to you for."

She gives him a tight hug before coming to stand next to me. Thomas turns off the light, leaving us to wait in the dark. Adriel's singing is the only sound for the next fifteen minutes.

The door opens, sending orange streaks of the evening sun across the room. I hold my breath when I hear a man's voice. "What is—" His holler is cut short by a *thud* before he really starts screaming.

Mikkel switches on the light, revealing Jeff, a middle-aged man desperately trying to get away from the metal spikes. Adriel jumps up and down. "It worked!"

"Help me get him up, Matias." Mikkel crouches next to him.

Careful to not step on the sharp metal, I assist in lifting him to his feet as he blubbers worthless pleas and apologies through cut up lips. We toss him in a tall, wooden chair against the wall when Adriel steps next to me holding a mallet and four large railroad spikes. Blood drips from the holes on Jeff's face as he shakes his head. "No, no, no. Please, Mikkel, there must be some sort of misunderstanding."

"Well, we don't want you to move, silly," Adriel answers.

I push down on Jeff's arm as Mikkel and Thomas keep the rest of him still. She lines the pointed spike up with the space right above his wrist. With a grunt, she brings the mallet down as hard as she can, successfully attaching him to the armrest. One more hit gets it all the way through. Blood and sweat makes Jeff's skin slick as his yells bellow in my ear.

"Hold on, I want to take a couple shots of this." My new Nikon Z6 is easily the most badass camera I've ever had.

Through the viewfinder, exquisite viciousness flutters across her features when Adriel slams the mallet down on the second spike. I hold the shutter release button, not wanting to miss a second.

"You found out about the investigation?" Jeff sobs between screams after Adriel finishes doing the same to his ankles. "I haven't mentioned your name, I swear!"

Ignoring his statement, Mikkel wraps an arm around me and one around Adriel. "You haven't had the pleasure of meeting my cousins. This is Adeline and Matias."

Jeff's face goes white beneath the streaks of crimson. "Mikkel, you have to believe me."

"You're not even going to tell us how nice it is to meet us?" Adriel asks. She looks to our cousin. "He doesn't have very good manners."

Mikkel chuckles. "No, he doesn't."

I walk to the table as Thomas leans against it, his erection already prominent in his pants. He knows where this is going to go. After setting down my camera, I open my soldering kit to remove the butane soldering iron and a roll of rosin core solder. Adriel has her favorite things.

This is mine.

Removing the neck brace from my bag, I carry it over to Jeff where I fasten it securely enough that he can't move his head.

"What are you going to do to me?!" he wails.

I smile at him. "It's a surprise." Adriel squeals and claps her hands as I return to the table.

Once I take off the protective lid from the pen shaped soldering iron, I adjust the temperature to around six hundred degrees.

"I've made it clear what would happen if you ever betrayed

me, haven't I? This shouldn't come as a shock." Mikkel says behind me.

Jeff's response consists of words indecipherable through the sobs and gasps. I remember when sounds of torment would make me distraught. Now, they're just excess noise.

The mallet falls from Adriel's grip to the floor when I walk back to her. She bites her lip, her hand lifting her skirt to rub over her panties. "Where are you gonna do it?" she whispers.

I enjoy watching her fingers for a moment before answering. "Where do you want me to do it?"

She's examining Jeff to decide when Mikkel says, "Just remember, losing one sense intensifies all the others." He stalks toward Thomas, kissing him deeply the moment he reaches him. They aren't really the type to waste time. Before I turn back to my sister, they're unzipping each other's pants.

Adriel's smile widens, "I can't decide between his eyes or his nose. He won't be able to scream if you do his mouth."

Blocking out Jeff's pleas, I shrug. "We can always do all three."

Mikkel groans from behind me, stroking his and Thomas' cocks together. "You two are going to kill me."

The way I feel when he praises me is addictive. I don't have to be in competition with Adriel for his affection because he doles it out evenly. He loves us the same.

I nod to the table, telling Adriel, "I'll need your help. Go get the plyers."

She obeys, but before she returns Mikkel says, "Leave your panties here."

The white cotton falls to the floor so quickly, I'd swear she knew the words he was going to say before they even left his mouth. Climbing on top of a blubbering Jeff, whose face is now shiny with snot, she straddles him, using the plyers to lift the skin of his right eyelid away from his eyeball. I unravel the thin, wiry rosin core solder, placing it between his eyelashes. She makes sure the top and bottom lids are pressed together evenly over the metal.

It's necessary to be very precise while doing this. Adriel grips his hair to hold his head back, using all of her weight to keep his body as still as possible. The moment the heated tip of the soldering iron touches the rosin core, smoke rises, the melted metal bonding the seam of his closed eyelid. He screams louder than he did when Adriel nailed him to the chair. He's thrashing around beneath her so violently, it's difficult to spread the silver solder across the line where his eyelashes meet with the pointed tip of the soldering iron.

The nice thing about rosin core solder is that it not only melts rapidly, it also cools very quickly. With his right eye fused closed, we shift over to his left. The horrific noises flying from his throat are grating on my nerves, distorting my concentration. If I were doing this on my own, his mouth would have been the first thing I closed.

Jeff bucks beneath Adriel in agony, making her nipples lift the white fabric of her dress. Her breathing picks up pace as she rocks on his lap ever so slightly, being careful to pay attention so she doesn't get burned. My erection tents my white trousers, making it more difficult to focus on the task at hand.

Mikkel's eyes blaze watching us as he leans against the table, pushing down on Thomas' head. It's not the violence that turns me on, it's what it does to Adriel and Mikkel that gets my cock hard. I love when he orders us around sexually, telling us what he wants to watch us do to each other.

I nod my head for her to follow me. "We'll solder his nostrils in a minute, come here."

Hopping off the howling man, she meets me at the table

where I clean off the iron tip and return it to its case. She lifts her skirt to give me a clear view of her bare pussy. Her fingers rub her clit as her eyes dance between the three of us.

Glancing over her shoulder, I look to Jeff who appears to have finally passed out. Part of me kind of regrets soldering his eyes closed first. I've learned I enjoy it when I fuck Adriel with an audience.

My gaze shifts down to Thomas on his knees with a mouth full of cock and drool dripping down his chin. Lowering my zipper, I lick my hand before stroking myself. "I think they have the right idea."

She bites her smiling lip, sending more blood between my legs. Over half of my erection disappears in blissful warmth the moment she drops to her knees. My fingers grip the table's edge as I groan. It's impossible to not thrust between her soft lips.

Her tongue slides down my shaft and she grins before looking at Thomas. "Betcha three hundred dollars I'll make Matias come before you make Mikkel."

My head jolts in surprise as I chuckle, "What?"

Mikkel's laugh booms at the same time Thomas says, "Awe. That's adorable. I've been sucking dick for a decade. But sure."

She grips my base, stroking and swallowing as much of me as she can. Oh, holy shit…When there's a bet on the line she really fucking goes for it. My hands grip at her skull. "Jesus Christ, Adriel."

Once I say her real name, I look at Mikkel's raised brow. "If you want to call her that during sex, I understand, but you must get used to calling her Adeline without thinking about it."

Her tongue glides around my shaft while she looks up at us. "I know," I moan.

If I were to look into my future a few years ago and see this scene, I would have been horrified. Unless, I was able to feel the things I feel in this moment.

Is this unusual, dark and a little depraved? Yes. But with my soul on her knees in front of me with our child in her belly, it's more than I ever could have fantasized. We're finally back in a safe, loving home, and I've found my nirvana. I haven't cut myself once since leaving Lettleton.

For the first time in six years, there's no pain to get rid of.

Ashes

Adriel

21 years old

"Come on, Mommy! I want to paint a picture!" Ashes stomps her little feet as she crosses her arms.

"I told you, we're having dinner with Mikkel's friend tonight. I don't want you to get dirty."

Her little face scrunches up with her frustration. "Fine. But your mean!"

She's so stubborn. I sigh because I hate her being upset with me. "Go play in the backyard. Your daddy will be home soon. After dinner, if your good, we can play with the paints."

She throws her stuffed panda bear across the living room as she stomps to the back door holding her blank piece of paper.

There are plenty of people on this property to keep an eye on her, so I turn toward the stairs to finish getting ready. Vines with sharp thorns crawl their way up the iron banister next to me as I climb up the staircase. Shiny, lapdog-sized black bugs scurry across the walls of mine and Malakai's bedroom. The older I get, the more I see stuff. Most of the things, like the pink lights and my creations, I enjoy, but the bugs terrified me at first. Then when one looked up at me and smiled, I gave it a chance. Now I know none of the things I see will hurt me, including the dog-bugs. I pick up one of them, it's six legs resting against my chest as if hugging me. Sluma has suggested that we name them, and I wish we could, there's just too many, and they all look exactly alike.

I sit next to the window with the bug in my lap as I tie a bow in my hair and watch Ashes out the window chasing a nutria rat. I roll my eyes. There's no way her dress will stay clean until tonight. When she stomps on the critter with her sparkly, buckle shoes, I gasp with my giggle. I see so much of myself in her. The absence of life has intrigued her ever since her pet kitten was hit by a car. She slept with the feline corpse for two days before Malakai finally got rid of it. I obviously understand the attraction. Death can be a hauntingly confusing thing, especially at her age.

Using its tail, she slams the rat against the ground. I drop my head back with a groan. She's going to need another bath. Since the animal is clearly dead, I don't understand why she picks up a rock to hit it over and over until she uses the blood to finger paint on her paper.

I set the bug on the floor, laughing to myself as the vines follow me to her room, stretching across the hall walls. I can't really get mad. I would have done the same thing.

While I pick out a new dress for her to wear to dinner, I glance out her window, smiling to see Kai and Mikkel walking across the yard to Ashes. Malakai is gorgeous in anything he puts on, but I have to admit, I really like that Mikkel makes him wear suits for business meetings. While I can't hear, I can see Ashes' face light up and the movement of her mouth suggests she's screaming, *Daddy*! He picks her up and

Mikkel's head drops back with his laugh. Presumably at her art supplies.

They've been gone since this morning. I miss them so much when they're away. Dropping her dress on the bed, I run down the stairs faster than the vines can grow. The melody of their laughing and voices always gives me a sensation that I don't understand. I don't need to, though, because it's the best thing I've ever felt.

"There's your pretty mommy." Malakai flashes me a smile that speeds up my heartbeat. "She was…painting."

Mikkel chuckles as he takes her from Kai. "And it's the best painting I have ever seen,"

The moment his arms are free, I run into them. He holds my waist tight, pulling me close for a kiss.

"I missed you," I say.

Mikkel puts Ashes on his shoulders, pressing a kiss at my temple on his way back outside. "Make sure Eugéne has everything for Jack's dietary needs. I'm going to take Ashes to play in the yard some more."

"Yes, yes!" She hugs his neck so hard she has got to be choking him. He won't ever complain about it though. He spoils her more than Malakai does. "I want to go super high on the swing again! Will you push me?"

Even though he closes the door, I don't need to hear his response to know what he says. My body lifts off the ground when Kai picks me up, touching our foreheads together. "I missed you too, Adriel," he whispers.

Hearing my real name fall from his lips always gives me a thrill. In my heart, he will always be Malakai, and I know he feels the same way about me. He says it every time we're alone.

We don't separate hands as we go to the garage. My

creation station is on the way to the freezer, so I tug him inside. Everything I could ever want is in here. Doll parts and torn stuffies fill the bins. Ribbons, buttons, stickers, and glitter sit in jars along the work table. I have more tools to help me make perfect creations than I've ever had before. Photos of past human creations line the walls, and right now, they are each moving in their own photographs, dancing, laughing and singing.

My newest one is still here, but Mikkel says he has to take him away tonight. His name is Larryufflegus. His torso is from the giant bear Kai bought me last month. He still has the man's head and lower body, though, I replaced his penis with an elephant trunk and gave him antlers.

"Have you developed the pictures of him yet?"

Kai tugs my hand, guiding me through the connecting door that leads to his dark room. "I was running late, or I would have shown you this morning."

He's always taken unbelievable photos. However, lately, his style has truly transformed into an untouchable brilliance. He has a few private buyers that will buy anything he's willing to sell.

Even these pictures of Larryufflegus are breathtaking. I grin as I run my fingers over the slick photograph. "I love it."

His lips press against my temple. "Come on, Eugéne is waiting on us."

The large walk in freezer sits at the opposite end of the expansive garage. Chills run through my body as we make our way to the back, stopping at two large crates labeled, *J. Crowner.*

Jack Crowner is one of Mikkel's three cannibal clients. He purchases an entire body once a month, paying per pound, so bigger people are better for everyone. It also means we see a lot of him. He's actually somewhat charming for someone who would eat you. I try to be extra nice because I know he is one of Mikkel's favorite clients.

All the meat is packaged, organized by part. Kai reaches into the crate labeled 'Lower Body.'

"What's his favorite?" I ask.

He picks up a piece of flesh wrapped in butcher paper with the word *thigh* written on the front. "I have no idea. I guess the meatier pieces."

With the partial leg under his arm, he clasps my hand and leads me to the kitchen. Eugéne is lining up ingredients and cooking utensils when Malakai hands him the package.

"Perfect, thank you." He unwraps the thigh and places it in a bag full of marinade. His finger points to a large purple serving dish. "Mr. Crowner's food will be brought out on that plate. I don't want you to accidentally eat the wrong thing. Just remember: purple means people."

Malakai snorts. "Thanks for the heads up." His hand slides under my skirt and into my panties, fingering me in front of our chef. "Will you tell Mikkel I'll be in his study later? I want to spend some time with my wife before our dinner guest arrives."

Eugéne is immune to this kind of thing. Mikkel and Thomas used to have sex literally everywhere in this house. Now, they have to be more discreet with Ashes running around.

"If you catch me, you can fuck my ass," I say softly in his ear.

His grin has me running out of the kitchen. I sprint down the hall to go to our room, the people in the mutilated photographs screaming at me the whole way.

Just before I run up the stairs, the sight of Ashes' blood

painting stops me. It's sitting on the small, decorative table by the backdoor right beneath the last family portrait Kai and I took with Mommy and Daddy. She's painted five stick people. Three tall, one medium, and one small.

Her family.

Prickles poke at my heart, and I gasp. Something crawls down my cheek and when I swipe at it, my hand comes away wet. Kai wraps his arms around my waist.

"Caught ya." He looks at the picture and grins. "She's quite an artist. We just need to work on her medium." When he lifts my chin, his smile is erased by a frown. Reaching up, he puts his finger under my eye. "Is this a tear?"

I softly laugh with my nod. I've never felt anything strong enough for it to leak out of me this way.

Until now.

R.I.P. Playlist

1. *Six Feet Under* Billie Eilish
2. *You Are My Sunshine* The Phantoms
3. *Dead Man's Arms* Bishop Briggs
4. *Broken* Lund
5. *The Secrets In The Telling* Dashboard Confessionals
6. *Death Of Me* PVRIS
7. *Cry Little Sister* Marilyn Manson
8. *Put It On Me* Matt Maeson
9. *Bloody Creature Poster Girl* In This Moment
10. *Deathbeds* Bring Me The Horizon
11. *Die A Little* YUNGBLUD
12. *They Know My Name* Big Little Lions
13. *Dance In The Graveyards* Delta Rae
14. *Two Coffins* Against Me!
15. *Flowers Grow Out Of My Grave* Dead Man's Bones
16. *Voices* Motionless In White
17. *I Just Want You* Ozzy Osbourne

Acknowledgments

The more books I publish, the more I realize how much others make such an impact on me and my stories, and I couldn't do this without any of them. There are really so many people I wish I could thank individually. I appreciate everyone who has believed in me and helped me along the way.

Kim BookJunkie. Oh man where do I start? You not only help make my words beautiful, but you have been a personal cheerleader for me and a fabulous friend. I am so grateful to have you in my life professionally and personally.

My Betas. I couldn't have published this without you! T.L. Martin, Kathi Goldwyn, Gizel Alvarez., Tania Rentaria, and Maureen Goodwin. Your honesty and feedback are invaluable, and it truly means the world that you take the time to help me so much to make pretty stories.

The ARC-adians. You guys have been there for me sharing and spreading the word for me, all out of the kindness of your hearts, and it truly touches me. You guys are the VIBs (Very Important Babydolls)! Thank you for all that you do!

The Babydolls. Where would I be without my Dollies? I don't want to know! You guys are my tribe, my support system, and have given me a place to truly be myself. I love how kind and loving you all are. You are what makes the Dollhouse the incredible place that it is! Love you guys!

Jay Aheer. Your work never ceases to amaze me. You have such incredible talent, and it's such an honor to have you design my covers. Thank you for giving a stunning face to this story.

Champagne Formats. I am so blown away with how beautiful you make every single book look in its finality. Thank you for all the care and beauty you put into your work!

Bloggers. I would love to name every single one of you, but I'm bound to leave someone out. You know who you are. Thank you for sharing my stories with your fan base. You are such an important part of this industry, and we couldn't do it without you! Thank you for your love of books!

Readers. Of course, the readers. None of any of this would be possible without you. Thank you for taking the time to read my words. I can't tell you what it means to me to know someone chose my book to read, so thank you for helping my dreams come true.

There are so many more people that should be listed, but for fear of hurting someone by forgetting, I'll just say, I know who believes in me and supports me and my dreams. You guys helped me get here. You guys gave me the courage when I didn't have it in myself. You never told me it was dumb or unrealistic. You believed in me enough to tell me to go for it and have continued to support me. I love you all. I'm here because of you.

Books by
CHARITY B.

Standalones

Anointed

Series

Candy Coated Chaos (Sweet Treats #1)

Sweetened Suffering (Sweet Treats #2)

Cupcakes and Crooked Spoons (Sweet Treats #3)

Rest In Peace (R.I.P. #1)

Rot In Pieces (R.I.P. #2)

Anthologies

Thou Shall Not: A Dark Ten Commandments Anthology

About the Author

Charity B. lives in Wichita Kansas with her husband and ornery little boy. She released her debut series, the Sweet Treats Trilogy, in 2018 and is constantly working on her next release. She has always loved to read and write, but began her love affair with dark romance when she read C.J. Robert's The Dark Duet. She has a passion for the disturbing and sexy and wants nothing more than to give her readers the ultimate book hangover. In her spare time, when she's not chasing her son, she enjoys reading, the occasional T.V. show binge, and is deeply inspired by music.

For more on Charity B. and her books visit her website at
charitybauthor.com

Printed in Dunstable, United Kingdom

81366206R00184